Ink My Heart

Jean Haus

SKYSCAPE

SKYSCAPE

Text copyright © 2013 Jean Haus
All rights reserved.

Printed in the United States of America.

Published by Skyscape, New York

www.apub.com

ISBN-13: 9781477847084
ISBN-10: 1477847081

Ink My Heart

TO AWESOME READERS EVERYWHERE

Chapter 1
Justin

I need a beer, a shot, and a woman. Or several of each. And not necessarily in that order. After five hours of singing, my voice is hoarse, my throat is sore, and I want to get away from the three other twits in my band. I've been playing *and* arguing with them all day. The van has been tranquil since we left the recording studio. The echoing bump of the highway is the only sound other than snores as we travel north from Detroit to mid-Michigan, where we go to the local university as juniors—well, except for Gabe. The loser goes to community college.

We'd still be in the recording session if Gabe, Sam, and I hadn't forced Romeo to call it quits. Romeo the perfectionist, our lead guitar player and my annoying roommate. His fingers should be bleeding after playing the guitar so long, but no, the bastard is one big callus. He could have put in another five hours, but instead, he's had a pissy look on his face the entire drive home while I've been in the passenger seat ignoring him and trying to doze. Snores are coming from behind us. Sam is sleeping on the first-row bench seat. Gabe is passed out next to his drum set on the floor in the back.

It was Romeo's asinine idea to make an album of his originals. He hopes it will make us a few bucks on the indie scene. He may be right, but after the hell of a day we had at the studio, we'd better make more than a few bucks.

A beep from my phone wakes me up fully. I dig it out of my pocket. A picture of Mara, one of my regular girls, appears on my screen, and the text: *You coming out tonight?* I don't text back but keep Mara as a reserve while hoping for the possibility of meeting someone else. A sexy new adventure.

Romeo takes the exit ramp into town, and I drop my feet from the dashboard. "Just take me to Rats."

He gives me an irritated glance. "I'm going over to Riley's. Not coming back into town to pick you up later."

I shrug. Though the main strip of bars downtown isn't as busy in the winter, I can usually find a girl to take me home. If no one else, there's always Mara. "I'll find a ride."

Waking up, Sam stretches and yawns. He runs a hand over the fuzz of his buzz cut, then punches the back of my chair. "Shit, Justin, you're a machine. How can you go to a bar after partying last night and working all day?"

"It's Saturday," I say with a tone of obviousness. Sam likes the attention we get from women too. He just likes partying a lot more and, as usual, went overboard last night. His bright blue eyes, which the girls gush over, are bloodshot today.

"Thought you would have got enough ass last night," Gabe says from the back.

"Never," I say.

"Well, that was one seriously *big* ass you went home with."

I recall Emily—or was it Emma?—with a slow smile. Gabe's girlfriend is stick skinny, with huge tits. Nothing wrong with *that*, but I like all women. I like the way they smell. I like the soft sighs they make. I like how they ease my loneliness, if just for a night. I like them in all shapes and sizes. Toned and angular or round and soft. Lingering on that last thought, I say, "Oh, she was big in all the right places."

"Dude, there's nothing you won't sleep with," Gabe says sarcastically.

"I have standards." I raise one finger. "They have to be hot." I raise another finger. "They can't be wasted." I don't take advantage of the incoherent. "And they can't be a bitch," I say with the flick of a third finger. Because Gabe is always such a prick about everything, I add, "Which is why I turned down your cousin."

"Stay away from Rachel," he snaps. "But what is that supposed to mean?"

"Well, the girl is hot and she didn't drink too much last night. Figure it out."

"Mother fucker!" Gabe yells, and dives toward the front of the van as instrument cases clank and roll around the back.

While I laugh, Romeo throws up his arm in a clothesline move and Gabe's lanky body bounces backward.

He crashes into Sam, who immediately sits up on the first-row bench seat and says, "Shit, Gabe! I was sleeping!"

"I'm kicking his ass," Gabe shouts, his longish brown hair falling into his face. "In this van. Now."

Sam hauls Gabe back by the sweatshirt, but he kicks at my seat. I keep laughing. I have several inches on Gabe and almost twenty more pounds of muscle. "More like get your little bitch ass kicked."

"Fuck, Justin. When are you going to grow up?" Romeo says, clutching the steering wheel. My laughter instantly dies. I'm sick of Romeo telling me I need to grow up. I'm busy staring him down when a fist connects with and then slides from my jaw. "Asshole," I gasp, letting my seat belt loose and turning.

"Stop it, Gabe!" Sam yells. "And Justin, shut the hell up!"

I'm ready to pounce when the sight of Gabe struggling like a hyperactive kid in Sam's grip makes me pause. I want to punch Gabe back, but I'm not like him. I don't throw blows when a guy is being held down or not looking.

Gabe starts repeating, "I'm going to kill him."

Sam is becoming red in the face from holding Gabe. Though Sam is the most muscular of us all, Gabe is wiry, pissed-off strength.

Trying to control my urge to sucker punch him, I glance out the window. I want to relieve Sam. "We're almost downtown. Just let me out."

"Good idea," Romeo says under his breath, hitting the brakes. I brace myself on the dashboard with a spread hand.

Sam and Gabe bounce off the back of my seat, then thud to the floor as I jump out of the van.

Before slamming the door, I say, "Tell Riley I said hi."

Ignoring me Romeo takes off with tires squealing. He's in a rush to drop Gabe off at his hovel across town and dump Sam at his apartment so he can race to his girlfriend's house. Romeo's pussy whipped in addition to being a band dictator.

The brisk air stings my arms. The cement under my feet is crusted with dirty bits of remaining winter snow. Shit. I forgot my coat in the van. Cars whiz by as I take in my surroundings while rubbing my sore jaw. I'm in a part of town I don't know well, but I can't be too far from Rats. Fucktard Gabe. Ever since he joined the band more than three months ago, he's been a prick because I didn't pick him to be our drummer when he'd first auditioned. Instead, I'd picked Riley—a girl—and the dude was never going to get over it. The little bitch wasn't pissed at Sam, who also wanted Riley, just me. Now I'm walking because of his stupid ass, and freezing.

After trudging through the cold, I get my bearings and realize it should be less than ten blocks to my favorite bar. Two blocks later, a bright neon sign across the street catches my eye—DRAGONFLY INK. I stop rubbing my jaw and stare. Either the tattoo parlor is new or I've just never noticed it. In seconds, after waiting for a car to pass, I'm crossing the street.

My motivation isn't just to get out of the cold—I'm addicted to ink and body piercings. My body art started as a silent *fuck you* to my parents, but even though it didn't get their attention, I continued doing it because I liked it. The sting of the needle and the bold statement of the ink on my skin has become addicting. Adding a bit of tarnish to my pretty boy looks is a bonus.

I warm up in seconds inside the shop, but it takes my eyes a minute to adjust after leaving behind the cold dusk outside. Track lighting illuminates the framed art on the walls, and the space is filled with glass display cases of jewelry.

A girl comes out from behind a counter in the back. She's smoking hot in her slinky half shirt, which shows off the circular tattoo around her pierced belly button.

"Can I help you?" she asks. Her gaze slides over the tattoos on my arms and pauses at the ring in my eyebrow while she flips her long brown hair behind a shoulder.

"Maybe." I give her a slow smile. "I want to check out some of your art."

Her hips sway and her heels click on the floor as she steps closer, pointing to framed pictures on the walls. "Those are our most popular basics." She then points to a rack of laminated images. "These are more intricate." She taps her nails on the cover of a binder on the counter. "And in here we have the works of art." She leans with both hands behind her on the counter and sticks her chest out. "Have anything in mind?"

With her tits beneath my nose, there's not much in my mind besides what's right in front of me. "Not sure. Just checking things out."

Her frosted lips curve into a knowing smile, and I grin back.

"Mandy," a male voice says from the far end of the shop. "You need to schedule Jack's next appointment."

"Give me a sec," she tells him, still staring at me. She pulls her hands from behind her on the counter. "Take your time—I'll check on you in a bit."

Mandy can check on me anytime. Smirking, I nod and watch her saunter away toward the guys waiting near the counter. I reach for a binder of designs, but really, I'm waiting on Mandy. Appears I may have found my "sexy new adventure."

After glancing at the barbells, earrings, and gauges in the glass case, I page through pictures of skulls, stars, crosses, and tribal art designs. Nothing's really grabbing me, so I open a binder labeled *Custom Designs*. Inside are a bunch of photos with people showing off their awesome tats. There's a sexy '50s pinup girl, a flaming sun setting into its reflection on rippling water, a rose that looks like it's growing out of a woman's hip, an arm sleeve of Japanese art . . . The intricate ink is blowing me away, but I'm brought back to the shop when someone says, "Show me your other side, Paul. Let me see how Todd did on the last one."

Though the words are commonplace for a tattoo parlor, the feminine voice grabs my attention—it's dripping with sex. Low and husky, the voice wraps around me like a lush naked body might, taking me to dark, sweet places.

Pretending to examine another book, I glance at the owner of the voice.

She is bending over and staring at the guy's ribs. Dark auburn curls spill across her profile. I can't see her clearly, other than her lowered thick black lashes and the pout of her red lips.

"Very, very nice, Todd," the voice purrs to the other guy, who I'm assuming is the artist—but fuck, I wish she were talking to me.

Hell. My hands grip the edge of the glass countertop. If she keeps that purring up, I'm going to get hard just listening to her.

The guy drops his shirt over his tattooed ribs. "You should design my next one."

Nodding, she turns toward the counter and away from me. "Anytime, Paul, just set up an appointment with Mandy."

The guy beams at her as I flip through the book of photos absently. I'm guessing the owner of that voice designed the ink in the pictures—and all I can think about is how to get an introduction to her. I haven't been this fascinated by a girl since . . . Damn. I don't remember when. And I haven't even seen her face yet.

I'm staring at art that I'm not really seeing when a finger drumming on the counter pulls my attention from the binder. Expecting Mandy, my mouth falls open at the sound of that voice.

"Finding anything interesting? Anything giving your skin an itch?"

Her sensual tone shoots lust down my spine and right to my dick. I gradually flip a page, getting control of myself, then at last look up and take in the face that owns that voice.

Holy shit. She's better looking than I could have imagined. Two tiny silver stars dangle from the barbells at the end of one eyebrow. A lip ring I instantly want to suck pierces the corner of her lower lip. Her gray eyes fringed in black stare back at me. Those eyes are as erotic as her voice. She's all contrasts. Pretty, yet edgy with her piercings. Her pale skin and light eyes paired with rich auburn hair and dark, slashing winged brows make another contrast. She's sexy as all hell. *Get a grip, Justin. Do not drool,* I think. I tap on the book. "These are really good," I say.

She stares at me wide eyed for a moment before coolly saying, "Thanks. I take pride in my work."

Standing up straight, I feign stupidity. "These are yours?"

Her black lashes lower as she glances at the book. "Every one."

My eyes wander over her, taking in the loose sweatshirt with the store's logo and the leaf tattoo that wraps around her wrist. She's not like Mandy, who is in-your-face hot. Instead, she radiates a half-buried sensuality that has me wanting to peel back her cool demeanor and get a glimpse inside. I want to find out what's beyond those slate-gray eyes watching me warily. They remind me of mournful lyrics, the way they hint at deeper emotions and pull at your soul.

"Well, judging from these photos you have to be the most talented tattoo artist I've ever met. And I've met a lot," I say smugly.

Her smoky eyes narrow a bit before her gaze travels the length of my arm. "Looks like you're ready for some real ink."

As long as you keep looking and talking, you can do anything you want to me, baby. "Yeah, I'm ready for something a little more . . . in depth."

"Any ideas rolling through your head?"

About tattoos? Not fucking one. Considering what a tattoo artist might suggest, I blurt, "Something more personal?"

She lets out a low chuckle and leans forward. "So you have no clue?"

I glance at her short silver nails while I rack my lust-ridden brain. "I'm thinking something relating to music?"

She cocks one eyebrow, and a silver star jingles. "You're a musician?"

"Kind of," I say, reluctant to admit I'm in a band. I instinctively know that bragging won't get me anywhere with this girl. I look her over slowly, so there's no confusion that I'm checking her out. I slide my hand across the counter and flick a finger toward her wrist, nearly brushing the skin. "That your only tattoo?"

She stands and folds her arms across her chest. "Oh, I have others."

"Really?" I gaze at her intently.

She leans against the wall behind the glass case. My body wants to get closer to hers, and I fight the urge to jump the counter. "They're not available for stranger perusal," she says.

I run my eyes over her body and imagine where the ink might be. When I look again into her gray eyes, they have a sparkling defiance—but I hold out my hand anyway. "Nice to meet you," I say. "Name's Justin."

Her lips twist into a smirk, but still leaning against the wall, she shakes my hand. Her palm is soft and warm, but I can feel the rough, callused skin along her index and middle fingers, right where a pencil would lie. She must sketch a lot. The contrast makes her even more interesting.

"Al," she says in that smoky voice, then she releases my hand. "And the tattoos are still under wraps."

"Al?" I say, forgetting about the tattoos for a moment. "That can't be your real name."

"Short for Allie."

"Allie," I say softly, lowering my chin, "is far prettier than Al. But I'm still interested in those tattoos . . . or maybe in the idea of what inspires you."

She lowers her eyelashes. "Since *you're* not inking me, let's stick with what inspires *you*."

Her tone has me changing tactics. Obviously, the traditional smolder that I pull out to make most girls melt isn't going to work on this one. "Do you only design?" I ask.

She shakes her head slightly. "No. I ink too."

"How . . . fascinating," I say. And hot. Propping my elbows on the counter, I lean toward her. "We should go out for a drink and talk about what inspires both of us."

She blinks at me with those eyes the color of gunmetal. "Ah, I don't date potential inkees."

Shit. Still trying to move too fast here. "I'm not a customer . . . yet, but a drink doesn't mean a date. People do go out to converse— don't they?"

"Maybe I don't drink."

"Coffee then?"

Her chin drops. "Caffeine is the world's most addicting drug."

I'm getting desperate here. "Milk shakes?"

A deep, sexy laugh escapes her. "If you're really interested in me designing for you, Mandy"—she nods toward the back counter— "can set up an appointment. But I have to get back to work."

Damn. She's leaving me high and dry, and all I want is to hear more of that voice. "Oh, I'm *interested*." Those eyes. That lip ring. I force a smile. I can't keep my tone from conveying that I'm interested in more than her talent.

Her chin lifts slightly. "Okay then, I'll see you soon, Justin."

"Very soon, Allie."

She gives me a slow nod, then walks away.

I watch her—a figure dressed in a shapeless sweatshirt and tight jeans—until she disappears into a hallway beyond the counter.

After taking in a deep breath and snatching a hooded sweatshirt from the shelf at the end of the glass case, I move toward the counter.

"What did you decide on?" Mandy asks, giving me hot eyes.

She hasn't gotten any less sexy since I walked in the door, but—with Allie now in the mix—my lust-o-meter isn't registering even a one for her. "This," I say, dropping the hooded sweatshirt on the counter. "And I'd like to set up a design appointment with Allie for Monday, if possible." I'm already haunted by her smoky voice and those stormy gray eyes.

Fuck. I've fallen in lust. Big time.

Chapter 2
Justin

When I signed up for a communication class called Persuasion and Attitude Change, it sounded like it would be a breeze—and maybe somewhat interesting. But the class blows. And I have to deal with it every single Monday afternoon. How can it be called a communication class when the professor lectures at us for three hours?

I doodle possible tattoos in my notebook for my appointment with Allie as the professor drones on. I couldn't concentrate on the art of communication even if I wanted to because I'm trying to come up with ideas to inspire her art. And I'm going to look like an idiot because all I can think of are musical notes or instruments. Or even worse, the traditional skull or dragon shit.

I'm not too deep. I don't like deep. I sing. I party. I fuck. Occasionally, I study. In general, emotions pretty much suck. I try to stay away from them. I shouldn't be surprised that creating a meaningful graphic illustration is beyond my skill set and emotional range.

The guy next to me takes pages of notes while I sketch a shitty snake wrapped around a musical note, like middle school kids draw all over their notebooks. As if I'd show this crap to a tattoo artist. Much less one who has been on my mind sexually for the past three days. I went home alone Saturday night, that's how infatuated I am with Allie. Caught a ride with another dorm student. None of the girls who'd hit on me at Rats had that voice or those eyes or a lip ring. Until I have her, no girl will be able to compare.

Finally, the professor who never shuts up releases us.

With my notebook clutched against my hip, I race across campus. Several people, mostly girls, try to stop me to chat and others yell out hellos, but I just nod. I'm on a mission.

In our dorm room, Romeo sits at his desk in front of a laptop. He glances at me over his shoulder as I throw my notebook on my dresser, then turns back to his work. "You need to apologize to Gabe before practice tomorrow," he says while typing.

"I'm not apologizing to that dick after he hit me. As far as I'm concerned, we're even," I say, searching my closet for a clean shirt. Something dark that will bring out the green in my eyes.

"If shit blows up during practice, then I'll dock both of you on the next gig for wasting time."

Shrugging—our pay is like chump change to me—I spray on some cologne and grab my keys.

At the rattling of keys, Romeo's head snaps around. "Where are you going?"

I almost snicker at his confusion. I rarely drive, and not just because my car has only two seats. The main reason is that if I'm not on campus, I'm usually out partying. And since I don't really date, whatever girl I end up with usually does the driving. If we have band practice, I catch a ride with Romeo.

"Dragonfly Ink," I say.

He raises an eyebrow.

"Tattoo shop."

His eyes roll and he turns back to the computer. "You're not lifting tonight?" he asks absently, referring to our usual workout.

Since he trains people—mostly kids in an after-school program—in boxing, he has access to the weight rooms on campus. And since the weight room is the one place where we get along, we've been spotting each other since freshman year.

"I'll be there. Just going for a consultation today. Might be getting a custom tat this time around."

He shakes his head.

Grabbing my coat from the bed, I almost snort. Romeo is such an uptight fuck. If they hadn't stuck us together freshman year, the two of us would have never agreed to room together. Though my parents won't spring for an apartment, I could afford one on their ridiculously generous allowance, but living in the dorm makes life easier. I'm all about the easy life.

Done with my stupid ass roommate, I head out the door.

It's almost a hike to my car in the back corner of the dorm parking lot. I've had the car since I turned sixteen, when my father bought a new car and gave me his old one. He only drives BMWs, so I do too. Not a big deal. Not like he was giving me a Lamborghini or some other car from his collection, which sits 99 percent of the time in his monstrous garage. But I have no problem with my Z4, and I'm lucky my father went on a sports car buying spree in his early fifties. Otherwise, I would have ended up with a sedan.

I get into the car, push on my sunglasses, and start the engine purring with a turn of the key.

A glance at the clock tells me I'm going to be early. I drive slower than usual. People pass me on the highway, but I keep my speed around fifty. Damn. I'm nervous. Music usually blasts while I drive, but I'm hoping the quiet will help calm my nerves. I can't remember the last time a girl made me nervous. I'm not sure if I want to date her—shit, I haven't dated anyone since high school, and that was just a few times—or what. Though there is one thing I know I'd like to do with her.

After a twenty-five-minute ride that should have taken fifteen, I park across the street from Dragonfly Ink. I do some breathing techniques I regularly use prior to going onstage, then force myself out of the car. Time to turn on the charm. Just like onstage—time to shine.

The girl behind the counter isn't Mandy or Allie. "Hello," she says with a smile. "May I help you?"

With her bronze skin and a mane of light brown curls, this girl is hotter than Mandy. She could be a model. Like runway in Paris shit. But like Mandy, she doesn't move me. She doesn't have that voice or those eyes. Or that talent.

Out of habit, I smile back. "I have an appointment with Allie," I say, walking to the counter.

She reaches for a leather appointment book with a hesitant look. "Um, let me take a peek."

"Is there a problem?" Somehow I keep the tension I'm feeling from my tone.

"I'm not sure." She quickly turns pages. "But Al usually doesn't come in today." She turns some more pages and her finger scans. Tapping her finger on a page, she looks up. "Justin Noel?"

I nod.

She glances at the skull clock above the shelves filled with logoed T-shirts. "You're a little early. Al's not here yet, but she's never late." She gestures to a row of chairs along the wall. "You can sit and wait."

Damn. After driving slow and breathing like a moron, I'm still almost ten minutes early. "I'll take a look around."

"Okay. Can I get you anything? Bottled water? Coffee?"

"I'm good."

"Okay. Name's Shaya, if you need anything," she says politely.

I wander over to the counter with the photo albums containing custom work, hoping for some inspiration. I flick through the stuff again. Although it's great work, nothing grabs me.

My phone vibrates as I shut the book. Since I'm expecting it to be one of the many girls who constantly blow up my in-box, I'm slightly annoyed to see it's a bank update. My monthly allowance just went into my account. Gotta love my parents, coming through with the only form of love they know how to deliver.

With nothing else to do, I hit my father's number on speed dial. He doesn't answer and I don't leave a message. My mother doesn't answer either, but her recorded voice says, "Leave a message, but we're in Barbados until the end of March." I smack the phone on my leg. They could have told me they were taking a month-long trip out of the states, but no. They don't tell me shit. Don't even answer my calls.

Pissed off, I move over to the row of chairs and plop onto the middle one.

My parents have always been the distant kind. I had a nanny until I was ten, and though they were hardly around, they seemed to at least like me. But once my full-time babysitter left, my attention-getting antics brought nothing but perpetual sour glares. When they weren't too busy. And ever since my father retired two years ago from being a surgeon, it's felt like we live on opposite sides of the US instead of opposite sides of Michigan.

My elbows dig into the hard metal arms of the chair as I wearily rub my hands across my face. Even though I'm twenty years old, thinking about my parents still makes me feel like that lost ten-year-old boy, which has me peeved. I don't need anyone. Much less their lame asses.

Chapter 3
Allie

I race—if nine miles over the speed limit can be considered racing—to work. I'd been so wrapped up in finishing my paper for Business 302 that I'd forgotten about the appointment Mandy had scheduled for me on my day off. Or maybe I wanted to forget. I'm not looking forward to working with Mr. Hottie, whose bedroom eyes will be striving to strip away my casual indifference along with my clothes. His bad boy aura bugged me—I'm beyond done with bad boys—but his gaze bothered me most. The last thing I want to do is design for him. Then there's the fact he hit on Mandy, which she was *very* vocal about, prior to hitting on me. Nasty as that is, though, I don't really have much choice since I'm trying to build my business. I'd be an idiot to turn away a new client, especially a musician. Word of mouth is the best marketing tool out there. And musicians are some of my best customers.

After parking in the lot behind the shop, I rush through the back door.

Shaya bursts into the hallway. "You're late. You're never late."

"Got distracted working on a paper."

"Well, he's been waiting for almost a half hour."

"I'm not *that* late."

"He came early."

I cock my head to the side, thinking. Either he's the punctual type or he thought Mandy would be working. That wouldn't surprise me—I hired Mandy because she's attractive. She may not be the brightest bulb in the box, but I'm not above using whatever tactics are necessary to keep people, males to be exact, in the shop. Her looks along with her flirting help distract them from me. Many guys who are into tattoos are attracted to girls who can ink. Like artistic talent means that a girl will be a kinky, sexual gymnast in bed.

"Huh," I say, opening the door to my office and pulling off my jacket. I yank my iPad out of my bag and toss my coat on the desk. "Don't get all worked up. I'll take care of it."

Out in the shop, I'm greeted by the sight of Justin's long body curled in one of the chairs along the wall. His hands cover his face while his fingers dig into his temples. I walk over to him, but he doesn't look up, so I clear my throat. His green eyes, as deeply shaded as a painting of an English garden, are filled with a pain that makes me step back. The flirty guy from the other night has been replaced, at least for the moment. Somehow I find my voice. "Hello, Justin, I, um, want to apologize for my lateness."

The tortured expression on his face dissipates as he stares at me. Though I'm wearing a tank top with the shop logo, skinny jeans, and calf-hugging brown boots, I feel naked under his gradually warming gaze. "No problem. Can't say I minded waiting for you to come," he says, smiling like he holds some secret knowledge.

It's easy to ignore what is probably innuendo with his deep dimples distracting me. Dang, dimples get me every time. But I *will* stay immune. "Why don't we get started?" I gesture to the corner where my art table sits.

He stands gracefully while I try to ignore those dimples.

"All right," he says. "But I have to warn you, I'm counting on your abilities as an artist to bring me some inspiration."

Tall and lean, he towers over me. The hint of a five-o'clock shadow on his sharp jaw contrasts with the dark blond rumpled hair falling over his forehead, and the white of his teeth contrasts with his coppery skin. In his distressed jeans and a faded, fitted T-shirt with sunglasses resting in the V neckline, he looks like he stepped out of a magazine ad for something ridiculously priced and European. Or maybe for an exotic men's cologne. Because he smells fantastic. Words like *clean*, *woodsy*, and *dusky* come to mind as I breathe in the dark scent.

I pull out the chair in front of my drafting table, putting on my best professional face. "Have a seat," I say. "I should be able to come up with something."

I hold in a sigh as I set my iPad on the surface and then drag out the stool from under the table. Sometimes part of my job is pulling inspiration from my clients. But for some reason, I don't want to know more about this man. Those dimples are enough already.

"So you're a musician, right?" I say, sitting down and plucking a pencil from the cup on my table.

"Singer actually," he says.

I try to ignore the image of him on a dark stage that flashes through my mind, intent on staying on task. Dang. This would be much easier if he played an instrument. "For a band?" He nods. "What kind of music?"

"Mostly alternative rock."

The image in my head of him onstage becomes clearer. His lashes lowered. Hips cocked. Strong hands wrapped around a microphone. I ignore it. "Is that your favorite type?"

"I like all types of music. What about you?"

"Not preferential either. You want a tattoo related to singing?" I want to stay off the topic of my own likes and dislikes, especially under his intrusive gaze. He nods while I tap my pencil in frustration. I don't know how I'm going to survive an hour or more of him staring at me with those hot, shaded green eyes. He flashes another smile at me. When he brings out those dimples, he really is something. "Any ideas?"

"Music notes? A microphone? Art is a bit out of my realm of knowledge."

I give him a pointed look. "Music's considered a form of art."

He leans back to stretch, his legs spread and his muscular shoulders strain against his thin T-shirt as he reaches behind the chair. "Then graphic art's not my thing."

Trying hard not to gawk at the picture of masculinity across from me, I force myself to focus on artistic possibilities and reach for my iPad. "Where were you thinking of getting the ink?" I ask, absently biting my lip ring.

He stares at my mouth and my face heats, and for a brief moment I feel like the shy, insecure girl I used to be.

"My back would probably be the best idea," he says. His tone has me guessing there's more than the matter of tattoo placement behind the statement, but I can't imagine why. Glancing at his arm of ink, I release the ring from under my teeth, then somehow say without dread, "Could I see your other tattoos?"

"Sure," he says, reaching a hand back and yanking off his shirt in one smooth move. He stands, with both arms at his sides and his shirt bunched in one hand.

Um . . . I push the profanity from my brain and settle on *Holy crap, Batman, shut the front* and *back door!* The sight before me sizzles onto my retinas and will forever be scorched on them.

Justin's body is an ancient Greek statue come to life. Though lean, he's all ripped muscle. And unlike the cold surface of marble statues, his skin is warm and golden. I do a full inspection, trying to keep my expression neutral as my eyes roam over his rippled abs, the sexy hoop through his nipple, and the designs inked on his body. He has tribal art on one arm that swirls and loops across a rib to touch the corner of his pectoral. Japanese letters run between the tight skin under his belly button and the waistband of his boxers, which rides above his low-slung jeans. Though I've tattooed Japanese calligraphy, I know only the most popular sayings by heart, and this isn't one of them.

"Any on your back?" I ask, my mouth dry. Wow, this guy is hot.

"Just one," he says, turning.

His back is as ripped as his front. Now that he's turned around, I allow myself to swallow. I'm not sure what my problem is. It's not like I haven't tattooed lots of hot bodies, but staring at his, I have to resist the urge to fan myself.

He glances over his shoulder.

It's the way he looks at me. Like he's trying to see into me and learn my secrets. Secrets that aren't all that mysterious, just rather sad. *Stay on task, Al.* I again force myself to concentrate on his ink. A sharp, pointed tribal design rolls across his shoulder blades. The lines are clean and the ink dark. In fact, all of his tats are well done. He either knows how to choose his artists or has been lucky enough not to run into a hacker.

"Were you thinking lower back? Or middle?" I ask casually.

He runs a finger down the center of his spine, and his lats ripple as he turns to me again. Ugh, I'm staring like a fan girl. "More like in between," he says.

I breathe heavily through my nose. I'm bordering on ridiculous, but I just might hyperventilate if his skin doesn't get some cotton over it soon. "Okay, you can put your shirt back on."

While he pulls on his T-shirt, I scroll through images on the iPad and avoid looking across the table so I can concentrate. After several searches, an idea forms in my mind. I've always believed one of my greatest talents is how quickly I can create art. "Give me a few minutes and I'll make a quick sketch," I say. "If you like it, I can draw a more in-depth design."

Sitting down again in the chair across from me, he gives me a flirtatious grin. Very sexy but light. I must have been imagining the pained look earlier—not to mention the searching one. He's just another guy looking for a hookup. I reach for my pencil and start to sketch. Except for the scratch of the pencil and the music that always plays in the shop, it's painfully quiet until he asks, "What's between the blue on your arm?"

He's referring to the sleeve of flowers and branches wrapped around my upper arm, curling around my elbow, and ending at my wrist. On my upper arm, between the branches sprouting pale pink, almost white flowers are various shades of blue. Though it appears to be filler, at closer inspection the blue is full of dragons, stars, skulls, butterflies . . . the various art I've spent years creating on people's skin.

Without looking at him, I answer, "Branches. Not exact but van Gogh. Inspired by his almond branch painting."

Justin sits up a bit. "The guy who cut off his ear?"

My teeth grind. "Why is that what everyone remembers? Like it's the one defining moment of his life and art?"

I sense more than see him shrug as I shade in an edge. "Guess self-mutilation is hard to forget."

The pounding song coming from the speaker behind the counter changes to something low and jazzy. I let Todd pick the music, and his taste goes beyond eclectic. The variety of playlists he has is endless. I rarely hear the same song twice.

"So you're into classical art?"

"I'm into all art."

"But your favorite is the ear-slicing van Gogh?"

I nod and keep sketching. I'm hoping my silence will give him a clue that talking about me isn't an option.

"You busy Saturday night?"

My pencil pauses. "Now, Justin, I already told you I don't date customers." I rarely date at all, but he doesn't need to know that.

He leans forward, resting his chin on his steepled hands. "You did, and I wasn't asking, but I have some extra tickets for our show this Saturday."

"Oh," I say, thinking of a way to dig myself out of this hole. "I usually work on Saturday nights, but if you have an extra two or three, I'd love to give them to my employees."

He raises an eyebrow. "Employees?"

I match his brow raise. "The ones who work here."

"You're the owner?" he asks with an incredulous tone, glancing around the shop.

Though he can't see it, I smash my eraser into the tabletop. "Why is it so hard to believe? Because I'm female?"

His long dark lashes flicker. "Ah . . . no. You seem kind of young to be owning a business."

My irritation fades along with the pressure on the pencil. "Well, to be honest, I'm part owner."

He gives me the look again. Like he's trying to glimpse inside me. I didn't imagine that searching look after all.

"That's still impressive. You're what?" He studies me. "Twenty-four?"

"Twenty-two. Just turned."

A dimple appears. "Now that is impressive."

"Thanks," I say, becoming intent on finishing the sketch. I want both him *and* his dimples gone. I shade in some shadows, add a bit of red around the edges with a colored pencil, and hold out the sketch. "See if something like this will work."

He reaches for it slowly, raises the paper, and stares at the drawing. His lips curve. "Damn. This is perfect. Awesome really."

I shake my head at his amazement. "It's hardly perfect. Just a rough sketch, but if you like it, I can resketch it in more detail, then we can set up some appointments." I nearly squirm in my seat at the thought of tattooing him. Being in a room alone with him for hours is going to be putting my hormones in a state of salivation for far too long.

"Also," I say, holding out a sheet that explains payment and hourly prices, "here are my rates. You're looking at about five to six hours." I'm almost hoping the eight-hundred-dollar bill will dissuade him.

He gives the price sheet a quick glance. "We can set it up now. I trust your work. But *appointments*, as in plural?"

I nod, recognizing he must have had all his work done by separate artists, even though, except for the Japanese lettering, the tribal designs all coordinate. Again, the man has ink luck. "You indicated almost a foot of your spine. I'd first do the outline, then the interior tribal work, shading, and coloring. Two separate appointments. At least a week apart."

"A week apart?"

"Or more. Your skin needs to heal in between each session."

"Two sessions," he says in an almost ardent tone. "Okay, let's set it up."

With a feeling of dread, I push up off the stool.

"Well," Shay says from the counter, holding my appointment book in one hand. We both turn to her with startled expressions. It's obvious that neither of us was aware she was in the room, and I'm slightly off-balance at how much Justin commands my attention. I never get this way around guys, hot or not. "Today's your lucky day. Al has an opening on Friday afternoon. Usually people have to wait a couple weeks or more for Al unless they do Saturday nights."

Justin nods. "Friday will work."

Friday feels too soon. "Friday's probably not a good idea if you have a show on Saturday." He gives me a questioning look. "You'll be in pain."

He shrugs. "Let me worry about that. I'm not exactly a novice. Friday's fine. Perfect in fact . I'm class free on Fridays. We can do the next one the Friday after that if you're open."

Against my better judgment, I nod, and Shay pencils him in for the next two Fridays. I'm about to step back behind the counter and put space between Mr. Hottie and me when the front door bursts open.

At the sight of the person standing there, I freeze, overwhelmed as a messy kaleidoscope of emotion bursts within me. Bright yellow hope tangles with soft pink longing. Never forgotten black humiliation drips beneath dark blue streaks of despair while red-hot anger splatters over everything. I push down the strong desire to run as those familiar eyes meet my own. He takes a step farther into the shop. *He* is less than twenty feet away from me.

I need a buffer.

In desperation, I stupidly choose the one next to me.

My arm wraps around Justin's waist while my eyes beg his. Though his expression is confused, he doesn't step away.

"Hello, Allie."

I force calmness and look into the face that haunts my dreams and nightmares. Except for the new tattoo along his neck and the nearly shaved dark head, he appears the same. A harsh, angled face with contrasting soft, blue eyes. The thin line of his lips is unforgiving. He's as magnetic as ever and completely off-limits.

I force myself to appear composed, but inside I'm a shocked mess. "Trevor. What are you doing here? Why didn't you tell me you were coming home?" *Why didn't you warn me? Let me freak out before coming face-to-face?*

Perhaps sensing my distress, Justin wraps an arm around my shoulders. I place my other hand on his stomach, the muscles tight under my palm.

Trevor shrugs the wide shoulders I know so well. "It was a spur-of-the-moment decision." He scowls at the man I'm holding on to like a life preserver. "Who's this?"

Justin puts a hand out. "Justin Noel."

They shake hands stiffly while I chew on my lip ring. Though I'm trying to appear comfortable in Justin's embrace, this whole thing is so whacked, it almost feels like an out-of-body experience.

Trevor lifts his chin and glares down at me. "You said you weren't dating the last time we talked."

Of course he'd come out and say it. I refuse to contemplate why he sounds angry. "I . . . well," I mumble, searching desperately for a plausible explanation. Recalling the last time we talked, I say, "I didn't want to say anything with Ben there."

Trevor's eyes narrow, and he crosses his arms against his chest and glances around the shop. His dark eyebrows rise as he takes in the vast changes. As soon as he left, I repainted the walls, changed the art on them, and rearranged the furniture. I didn't want to be reminded of him one bit. His tightened gaze comes back to me. "Since I'm in town, I thought I'd take a look at the books."

"Okay, yeah, sure," I say, trying to sound casual. "Let me walk Justin out and I'll meet you in the office." I don't wait for an answer, just grab Justin's hand and tug him toward the exit. He follows but stops to grab his jacket off a chair and says, "Catch you later," to Trevor, whose upper lip curls slightly.

As shock continues to roll through me, my breathing turns shallow. I tug Justin's hand harder. On the sidewalk outside, I drag him past the shop's window, let go of his hand, and bend over, dragging air into my lungs.

Justin's boots come into my vision. "Allie? You okay?"

With one hand on one knee and the other in the air, signaling for him to wait, I shake my head, hoping I can avoid a face-plant onto the ice-speckled cement. Though suffering a concussion might be better than explaining the situation to Justin or facing Trevor in the office. After sucking in air for a few minutes and trying to exhale as slowly as possible, my breathing slows down to normal. I stand up and meet Justin's worried gaze.

"I'm sorry." I lean my head back and let out a groan at my idiocy. "I'm so embarrassed I did that to you."

"Hey, it's no big deal." He holds the jacket in his hand out to me. "You have to be freezing."

I wave the jacket away. I'm still shaken, and the cold isn't registering. Though my behavior doesn't seem to be bothering him, I can't stop my apologetic explanation. "Shock just got the better of me. He's my business partner and my ex."

Justin nods. "I kind of guessed the last part."

"I haven't seen him in almost two years. He lives in California. Owns a shop there too." I rub my forehead. "Why isn't he in California? Ugh, I really can't believe I did that to you."

Justin grins deep enough for his dimples to show. "I don't care that you let him think we're together. It's not like I didn't already ask you out."

I slap my jean-clad thigh hard enough for it to sting. "Well, *I* do. Wow. I feel like a complete idiot."

"No worries. You're not an idiot."

A self-deprecating snort escapes me. "Oh, I most definitely acted like an idiot, but thanks. And thanks for going along with my ridiculous act." He watches me as I take in a deep breath. "All right, I've got to get in there."

"You going to be okay?" He puts on his jacket in one smooth motion.

I nod. "I'll be fine. Just super shocked there for a minute, but I'm good." I take a step toward the shop. "See you Friday, and thanks again for not blowing my cover."

"Anytime, Allie," he says, slipping on his sunglasses as I walk past him.

Still mortified by my behavior, I don't reply or look back. The shop appears to be empty when I walk back in. Not caring where Shay is, I go to my drawing table and lean over it. The sketch of a treble clef decorated inside with tribal designs and wrapped around a microphone lies in the middle of the table, reminding me of the man I just left on the sidewalk.

"What the fuck is wrong with me?" I mutter under my breath.

"I heard that!" Shay yells from behind me, and in seconds a jar half filled with ones is under my nose. "Hand it over, sister."

Sighing, I dig into my pocket, count off five ones, and drop them in the jar. Ever since I instituted the swear jar, Shay and Mandy have enforced it like bulldog cops.

Shay smiles sweetly. "Maybe Mandy's right. You need to get laid."

My eyes cuss at her.

She shrugs. "Seems like there's ample opportunity around here today, but hey, I don't mind you paying for pizza night."

Chapter 4
Justin

Thursday morning, I race across campus. Freezing rain pelts my face as my untied shoelaces slap against the wet cement. It's not a surprise that I forgot to set my alarm, since I almost never use one. If a class starts before noon, it's not on my schedule. But I can't miss meeting Lila this morning in the library. She's been my go-to girl for papers all year, and she could only meet me today at nine. She's going to be totally pissy if I'm late.

Outside the library doors, I shake the water from my head and tuck the wet laces into the front of my boots, then head into the hushed main room. The low murmur within the library is overlaid with the noise of rain pelting on the roof. After a quick walk around the perimeter of the lower level, I find Lila in a secluded seating area near a window.

When I stand over her, she looks up from a textbook. Her lips thin, and she says flatly, "You're late."

"Sorry," I say, bending to give her a quick hug. I make sure to slide my cheek against hers, slow and sexy.

"Ugh, you're all wet and freezing," she somehow wails within a library whisper.

I plop into the chair next to hers and gesture toward the floor-to-ceiling windows. "Rushed through the rain to get to you."

"Rushed? Really?" She rolls her eyes. "One would think that since I'm doing this for *you, you* could at least be on time."

I give her an imploring look and make up an excuse. "I forgot to switch my phone from vibrate."

She sighs and holds out an open hand. "The assignment?"

A chuckle stays locked behind my lips. Freshman girls are the most gullible creatures in the world. Leaning forward, I dig the handout from my back pocket.

She snatches it from my grip, then reads over the requirements. Partway through, her mouth falls open. "Ten pages?"

My expression turns contrite.

Hers turns livid. "You're going to the Spring Fling with me for this."

It isn't a question. It's a statement. I weigh my options. Sorority and fraternity mixers aren't my thing. Ten-page papers are *really* not my thing. And Lila, with her long hair and pouty lips, *has* been my thing—more than once. I smile lazily. "I'd love to. As long as we don't have a gig that night." Her lip curls, and I'm hoping we're booked.

Her lids lower. "If so, then the end-of-the-semester bash."

Writing a research paper or partying with douche bags? I nod my consent, and she goes back to reading the paper requirements.

Obviously, showing up with me at a party is enough of a reward to do hours of boring research and writing. Since I joined the band, getting girls has become far too easy. More than me, they're after my persona. And I'm okay with that. I think. Getting deep isn't my style. The real me is off-limits anyway. But fuck—where's the challenge? I search through memories from several encounters, trying to remember what Lila was like in bed. Fast. And there wasn't a bed.

Rather, the back of a door. Maybe the party won't be too bad. Or more specifically, the after-party.

I tap my fingers on the circular armrest while she finishes reading the lengthy assignment description. In the sitting area next to us, a group of students compare notes. Beyond the study group is the checkout desk, where a short line of students wait. My fingers stop their tapping at the sight of the last person in line. I'm out of my chair in seconds and moving across the library. Though Lila hisses my name, I snag a book from a shelf and then keep walking to the end of the line.

I stare at the waves in each of her dark auburn ponytails—she looks hot with her hair up. I wait for her to turn my way, then say, "Hey, Allie, didn't know you went here."

The large bag on her shoulder almost hits me in the stomach as she turns around. Her charcoal eyes slightly widen. "Well hello, Justin."

"You'd think that since we're dating, I'd know we go to the same college," I say with a smirk. I wonder about her ex, then wonder why I give a shit. It's not like I'm after anything more than a fling. An extremely sexy fling, given that husky voice and the many hidden tattoos to discover. But my pursuit has been slow. Her rule about not dating customers is a total cock block.

Her lashes flutter at me. "I forgot to tell you over our romantic dinner date. With all that lobster and your cute dimples, sharing my educational pursuits escaped my mind." Her sarcasm brings a grin, and probably dimples, to my face. Her smile drops, and the usual restraint returns to her expression. "But then, I only take two classes a semester. You?"

"Full-time." Studying her face, I wonder why I've never seen her on campus. With those eyes and that lip ring, I would have noticed this girl in a hallway packed with people or the bookstore or on a sidewalk or . . . anywhere. Next to her, I'm alive with lust. In a fucking library. "You must take morning classes."

She nods. "Tuesday and Thursday mornings."

I drag my gaze from her mouth and notice *The Fundamentals of Business Law* title wrapped in her arms and pressed against her chest. "Business? I would have thought art."

"Couldn't get away from it totally. Art is my minor," she says, studying the spine of the book in my hand. "And you?"

I glance at the book in my hand: *Taking Charge of Your Fertility*. An internal groan rolls through me. Leave it to me to lift something that makes no sense. "Communication." I tap the book. "Family communication. Big paper. Fertility's more of an issue in marriage than most people imagine."

As Allie's expression turns skeptical, Lila is suddenly next to me, shoving the handout I gave her into my chest. "You forgot your papers, Justin," she says, sneering at me and then giving Allie a dirty look.

I don't reach for the handout. "You can have it," I reply. "I have another."

She pushes harder and snaps, "I don't want it. *Take* it."

People are starting to watch us. The last thing I need is for Lila to go apeshit on me in front of Allie. I reluctantly take the handout.

Lila huffs under her breath, "Asshole," then stomps off, her blonde hair flying and big ol' bag swinging.

Besides being gullible, freshman girls can be overly dramatic. I shove the handout into the fertility book. "My paper partner," I say. Allie's face changes from skeptical to cynical as she watches Lila exit through the double doors. When her gaze comes back to me, I shrug.

"She's not a morning person, but she's excellent with words. A truly amazing lyricist." Allie's expression doesn't get friendlier.

Wanting to change the subject fast, I ask, "Things go okay the other day with your ex?"

Her lips tighten. "Things went fine. I sort of freaked out over nothing." She steps forward with others in the line, and I'm staring at her back. When she readjusts her bag and her sweater shifts, I catch half of the sunflower tattoo on the base of her neck. The colors are vibrant. Her skin looks soft. I'd like to kiss the yellow and brown ink. Slide my lips around the dark outline of the flower.

I lean close to her ear and ask in a whisper, "Also inspired by the ear slicer's work?"

She slowly turns to me with a pensive expression. "Are you guessing or do you truly recognize it?"

As if I'm not trying to impress her, I shrug. "I've seen the painting."

Her gray eyes widen for real this time. "Get out. Where?"

"London? Paris? New York? Those museums all seem the same inside."

She blinks at me with an amazed expression. "London and New York, yes, but the paintings at each are actually a bit different. But you've been to Paris too?"

I was trying to impress her with my knowledge of art, not my travels, which weren't impressive but lonely. They were never family trips. My parents did their thing. I did mine. How else would I have wandered into an art museum? My parents certainly weren't interested. But if she's impressed, I'll roll with it.

"And Rome. I'll never forget Rome."

I'd been sixteen, and the dark-eyed girls had liked my height and light hair. A handful of them had been older than girls, and I still remember what they'd taught me. But even after all that lush flesh, I refused to go to Barcelona the next summer. The moments of pleasure didn't compensate for the loneliness of being in a foreign country while my mother shopped ten hours a day and my father relaxed into becoming a zombie. The one month of summer vacation was when he relaxed. The *only* time he relaxed.

Allie stares up at me with interest while clutching her book to her chest. "So you're into art?"

Honesty should have me admitting art is intriguing—I've always welcomed the way it brings feeling to my usual emotionless state for at least a few moments—but it's not my style to be deep. Opening up to people feels as foreign as the countries I visited across the ocean were. I remind myself what I'm here in this line for, and grin. I lower my voice and say, "I like lots of things."

She raises a brow, but the request of "May I help you?" has her moving to the counter.

After she checks out her book and starts for the exit, I can't help calling out, "See you Friday, Allie."

She nods over her shoulder before slipping out the doors.

The librarian behind the counter looks at me expectantly. I'm clueless for a second, but stuck with a line of people behind me, I check out the book on fertility. At the entrance, I jerk out the research paper directions and drop the book into the return bin. Time to find Lila. While freshman girls can be overly dramatic, they are also extraordinarily forgiving.

Chapter 5
Allie

Though usually soothing, the small space of my tattooing room feels confining as I prepare for Justin's appointment. I'm so nervous it's hard to stay focused, but luckily I could fill ink caps in my sleep. I've done it for years. I haven't been this attracted to anyone since . . . well, Trevor. And in many ways, the insane attraction I have for Justin reminds me of how it was with Trevor in the beginning. I still find Trevor attractive, but it's tainted now by all the heartbreak he put me through. Trevor has made me wary of all men. The pain he caused is enough to last a lifetime. I'd rather let my idle lady parts dry up to dust than deal with another rampage on my heart.

My apprehension about Justin might be for nothing. After meeting him three times, I'm quite sure that he's a relentless flirt. His intense gaze, which always throws me off, is most likely part of his calculated bad boy act. But I'm very, very tempted to use his act to my advantage. He could be the perfect buffer to help me deal with Trevor's return. Justin seems shallow enough to agree to play the part. When it comes to Trevor, my emotions are so warped I don't trust myself.

Todd strolls into the room and lifts the thermal paper with Justin's design on it from the tray stand. His lip curls. "More tribal shit?"

"Todd," I say in a warning tone. He is forever complaining about people who come in and pick "cool" or "cute" ink. Tribal designs and fairies top his whine list. I don't care what people pick. I'm always honored they let me permanently mark their skin. But Todd is the textbook image of a tattoo artist. Attitude. Shaved head. Two arm sleeves. Ear gauges. Pierced everything, which is why Todd *is* the shop's piercer.

"Hey, I quit saying *shit* in front of customers."

"Quit saying sh—stuff, period."

"Oh." He leans back and points a finger at me. "I almost got you."

I give him a low-lidded stare, then nod toward the stencil. "Take a better look, beep face. That one is custom. The guy is a singer."

"Beep face?"

Letting out an exasperated sigh, I say, "Figure it out. Fill in the blank." I point at the design. "Just take a look."

He peers closely at the stencil. "This thing would rock without the lame tribal shit."

Irritated, I point to the door. "Go find something to do. Clean the bathroom if you can't figure out anything else."

He wrinkles his nose until the end of the septum ring practically points at me. "I'll find something."

Once he's gone, I set up the tattoo chair so Justin will face away from me, leaning over the arm chair, which makes it easy for me to pull up my stool and work on his lower back. I'm rechecking everything on my tray when Mandy brings him into the room. He's dressed casually swanky again—dark jeans, a white button-up shirt with a gray tank underneath, and black boots. With the wave of blond hair tousled over his forehead and the slightest hint of a five-o'clock shadow, he is picture perfect just like last time. The small room, with its plain white walls and bright light—I like to work within a clear canvas—was finally feeling calm and, somehow, quiet even with the thrashing music blaring from the overhead speakers. But Justin's entrance brings a crackling energy that ruins the tranquility.

Ugh. The sooner this is over the better.

"His paperwork and payment are finished," Mandy says to me, then smiles at Justin. Her eyes travel the length of him. "See you in a couple of hours."

He grins at her, reaffirming my sense that his flirting is habitual.

I hand him the final sketch I'd made two nights ago. "Make sure this is exactly what you want."

He studies it for several seconds. He shakes his head slightly. "You are unbelievably talented. It's perfect, Allie."

"Thanks," I say, suddenly shy as a blush warms my cheeks. What am I, twelve? I stuff down my embarrassment and put on a professional face. "Um, if you take off your shirt, we can make sure I'm putting it exactly where you want."

"Trying to undress me?" he asks with a grin.

I shoot him a level, emotionless glare. I'm not Mandy. I'm not into playing flirtatious games. Not sure if I'd even remember how. If I ever knew how.

His response to my look is to slowly—it's too slow to me—unbutton his shirt, then reach for the bottom of his tank and lift it off in a sensual motion. Shirt gone, his eyes connect with mine—and I'm once again telling myself his gaze is just part of his flirty nature. But it's still very hot. And regrettably I'm not immune.

Ignoring the reawakening of my stupid hormones, I gesture to the long mirrors in the corner. "Show me again where you want the tattoo."

He stalks over to the corner, glances over his shoulder, and runs a finger along his spine. The movement is as sexy as the last time he did it. "I'm thinking here. Or do you think lower would be better?"

His muscular chest is facing me. His defined back is in the mirrors. Um . . . Damn. Though a flush travels over my skin, I force myself to consider his question and not devour him with my eyes, but the picture he makes is stunning. Something I'd like to re-create with harsh brush strokes in black-and-white. I clear my throat. "I think a few inches lower would spatially work better."

Still glancing over his shoulder, he cocks his head in thought, then runs a finger lower. Near the band of his boxers. "Here?"

"Ah-huh," I say, getting more flushed, which is ridiculous. I never get like this anymore. He needs to get away from the mirrors. Now. I lift the thermal paper. "You can check the transfer once I apply it."

He turns to me. "No need. I trust your judgment."

Wanting to get this over as soon as possible, I motion to the chair. "All right, then let's get started."

Like a graceful panther, he folds himself onto the chair and leans over the armrest, pressing his flat stomach against it.

The stretched muscles and the skin of his back stare at me. Shoulders sleek with strength rest below the line of his dark blond hair. As I step closer, that same dark, sexy fragrance I remember from before makes me pause. Gah. This stuff is ridiculous. It has to be called something like Drive the Ladies Wild. The way it gets my hormones going, it should be illegal.

"Comfortable?" I ask, sinking on my stool and reaching for a pair of disposable gloves.

"As comfortable as I'm going to get."

I can hear the smirk in his words. "Anytime you need a break to stretch tell me. The ink will take better if you're relaxed." I start prepping his skin to shave.

"This is always the weird part," he says after the first swipe of the razor. "Never thought I had a hairy back."

"You don't," I say, and unfortunately my tone is slightly wistful. Stupid hormones escaping again, but he has a gorgeous, ripped back that has me wishing like an idiot I weren't wearing gloves. "Has to be done. Even the smallest hairs can cause problems."

Finished shaving the area, I push my nervous fingers to his back and press on the transfer. Done, I ask him to check the placement in the mirror again. He doesn't get up. "You're the artist."

At this point, I'm not going to argue. Reaching for the tattoo machine, I force myself to relax. *Get yourself together, Al. Forget about the gorgeous male and flawless skin inches away from you and do your job.* "I'm sure you're aware it hurts the most at first, but I want to warn you."

He laughs. "Well, let's get the first part over so the endorphins can kick in."

"No more laughing," I warn, pressing a vinyl-clad hand on his back.

"Gotcha, Boss."

With a slight shake of my head, I push the needle to his skin along the bottom of the outline. He doesn't even flinch. The first half hour is quiet, and he's still as I concentrate and enjoy filling in the outline until he says nonchalantly, "This is a great song."

Used to tuning out the music, I pause and listen. I can't place the loud banging melody.

With the needle paused and me quiet, he asks, "It okay to talk?"

I'm not usually a chatterbox, but I'm all about the client. If they want to gab, then I'll listen. The talkers are better than the cadavers who don't say one word during the entire process. "Sure. Sometimes I'm focusing, so I don't always reply right away. Or I may ask you to repeat something." I press the needle back to his skin.

"Understandable." He lets out a soft breath, I'm guessing from the pain. "How long have you been inking?"

I wipe at a dot of blood. "For almost six years. Obviously, I wasn't licensed the first couple." Through years of tattooing, I've learned people like to talk about themselves. It has become habitual for me to steer the conversation toward them, since I'm a private person. "How long have you been singing?"

"Two years."

"Would I know anything you sing?"

"Yeah, I think so. We do a variety of covers from the Stones to Chemical Romance, but we have some originals too."

"What's the band?"

"Luminescent Juliet."

Deliberating over the name, I fill in a corner. "Huh. You guys play at the Creed a lot, right?"

"You've been?"

I shake my head before realizing he can't see me. "No. I don't get out much. Too busy."

"You should come to a show sometime."

"Maybe," I say, not wanting to commit. As wound up as he gets me here half naked, seeing him onstage could put me over the edge. My hormones might turn me into a raging groupie. The thought of me jumping onstage and dry humping his leg almost causes a snicker to burst from me.

"My singing's not too bad, but our guitarist and songwriter is really good. Even though he's a dick, he's like you. Extremely talented."

I'm not even going to comment on the talent thing. "Not too bad, huh?"

"Well, you'd think I was an egotistical prick if I said I was great."

The needle pauses over his skin and a laugh escapes me.

"You have an incredibly sexy laugh," he says in a soft tone.

My mouth draws into an O. Nobody has ever told me *that*. "Um . . . thanks?"

It's quiet except for the loud music in the background until he asks, "So I'm guessing you started tattooing when you were in high school?"

Still startled by his opinion of my laugh, I blurt, "Yeah, I'm lucky I never got in trouble. You'd think at least one parent would have had a fit. Maybe the ink stayed hidden before their parents could catch up to me."

"How did a teenage girl get into inking?"

"Major art geek with an older boyfriend who tattooed. Once I started, I became addicted to creating art on skin."

"Okay, I get the boyfriend connection, but I can't imagine you as a geek."

I shake my head. "Like I said, *major*." He's quiet for a moment and the buzz of the machine echoes with the music. Wanting to get off the topic of me, I ask, "So exactly how many art museums around the world have you been to?"

"Too many to count."

The zing of excitement that sizzles through me at the thought of his interest in art is almost as electrifying as the attraction he produces when he pulls off his shirt. "Huh, you must really be into art."

He shrugs. "I was stuck in a European city for a month every summer growing up, but art is . . . great."

Great? The word kills my excitement at his interest in art. My love of art goes beyond the staleness of cliché. No art lover says "great." But I keep the conversation going by asking him about different museums. While it's evident he's been to many of the greatest ones in the world, it's also clear he's nearly clueless about what he saw at any of them. He looked. He liked. He moved on. But I'm glad I've found a topic to pass the time and keep the conversation from getting too personal. And I'm glad his art obliviousness is a turnoff, because if he were into art as much as I am, I'd find him irresistible. Besides, talking to him about museums is comfortable because it prevents me from obsessing about the muscle and skin under my gloves.

Finally done, I lean back and eyeball the outline. Even I have to admit that it looks awesome. After letting him look in the mirror to check it out, and grinning at his grin, I clean the tattoo then apply cooling ointment and a bandage. Peeling off my gloves, I explain how to care for the tattoo, hiding the internal struggle I'm having over whether to follow through with my planned invitation. I take a deep breath and decide to go for it. His ignorance of art and his totally superficial, flirty personality have persuaded me I can handle the havoc he inflicts on my hormones.

"Speaking of art . . . I . . . ah . . . well, you seemed so cool with what I pulled when my ex showed up, I was hoping you'd go to an art show with me. I'm sure he'll be there." Justin watches me as he unhurriedly pulls his tank top back on. I bite on my lip ring like I always do when I'm nervous. "We can go as friends, but he doesn't need to know that."

A slight smile stretches across his face, and a gleam shining in his green eyes almost has me backing out.

"I would love to skip the entire thing," I continue. I can't seem to stop explaining. "It's just, my friend is extremely excited about having her own exhibition I feel like I have to go, but I—I don't want to go alone."

"When is it?"

"Next Tuesday night at seven."

He reaches for his sunglasses lying on the counter. "Tit for tat?"

Confused, I tilt my head in question.

"You come to my show; I'll go look at art while your ex hovers."

Ah, bribery. I consider his offer. Going to a show isn't a date and I could leave right after. Though I'm not sure why he wants me to go so bad. Maybe he's trying to get around my refusal to date customers. Not that I'm going to change my mind. "I can't make it tomorrow, but your next one?"

He nods. "It's a deal. I'll pick you up?"

Though I'm relieved he agreed to go, picking me up sounds way too date-ish. "Thanks, but I'll be coming from work. We could meet there."

"Or I could pick you up here."

His tone is persistent, and it's kind of unfair to make him barter to be my fake date. "Okay, seven forty-five?"

He nods and holds out two slim cards for me to take. My expression is confused as I reach out.

"Two tickets for tomorrow night," Justin explains.

"Oh yeah, I forgot. Great. I'm sure Todd or Mandy would love to go and bring a friend. Thanks."

"Anytime." He reaches for his coat. "See you Tuesday, love," he adds with a grin before strolling out the door.

His dark, earthy scent lingers in the air. I link my hands behind my head and stretch back, groaning. "What the fuck am I doing?"

"I heard that!" Shay yells from the hallway.

The girl has bionic ears or something. I let out a sigh and dig in my pocket for a five. At this rate, I'm going to be paying for pizza *and* sub night for the rest of the year.

Chapter 6
Justin

We're almost done with our second set. Though my lower back has been on fire all night from my new ink, the pain can't destroy the high of performing. Adrenaline pumps through my veins. Being the center of attention fills me up and leaves me high. It's my only real addiction. I could sing forever, with the crowd below me and the guys playing music next to me. Even sex comes after this high. Unfortunately, the rush is almost over since we're about to start the second to last song of the night.

The lights dim and I pluck a pair of sunglasses from the pocket of my open shirt, stepping back to Gabe's drum set so that Romeo and Sam can have the stage for the intro. One of our originals, the song is slower and more bluesy than most of the stuff we play. Romeo, who writes most of our music, has a thing for blues, folk, and combinations of the two.

The crowd sways and moves to the beat. Some hardcore fans, knowing the song, shout and whistle in excitement. As the opening bridges into the repeating chords of the chorus—Romeo also likes to start songs with the chorus—I walk to the microphone, grab it, and share it with Sam as all four of us sing the first words.

The volume of the guitars drops and the drums pump a slow beat behind me as I walk away from Sam, who's bouncing like normal to the edge of the stage, singing the first verse low like a whisper. The crowd crushes forward. Some chick's hands grab on to the edge of my boots, which hang over the edge of the stage, but I keep singing. Rabid fans don't bother me—they get me more pumped up. After another repeat of the chorus, I step back behind the drums again while Romeo plays the solo. Leaning on Romeo, we end the song with one more round of the chorus.

As the song fades, the crowd roars.

I slide the microphone back into the stand and lower my glasses. "You guys rock! With that response, I'd like to stay here all night!" Their response is deafening. "But we've left a classic for the end."

When I step back, Romeo breaks into a charging riff and the crowd goes wild, recognizing Lit's "My Own Worst Enemy." Sam, Romeo, and I jump together to the beat, and the crowd is soon copying us. I'm pumped with unquenchable energy as everyone sings with me and raises drinks at the refrain. It's the perfect hard-driving song to end the evening.

Tilting the microphone stand over the edge of the stage, I sing the last line as the whole room bounces with us. On the last note, the lights cut out. The masses below the stage go wild. The lights come back on. The four of us bow in a line at the front of the stage. The chant of "More! More! More!" rings out, but Romeo put a stop to giving in to the "more" chant after the first six months. If it were up to me, we'd always do more.

Backstage, Sam passes around the obligatory bottle. At my turn, Gabe shoves it at me. I snatch it from the immature little prick and take several swigs. My inked back hurts more now that the high of performing is wearing off.

After we load up Romeo's van, he's off to see Riley. He's one whipped asshole. The rest of us head toward the closed-off balcony—most of the places we play are old movie theaters turned into bars—but some guy stops me at the foot of the stairs.

"Hey, man!" he shouts over the recorded music playing. "I wanted to say thanks for the tickets. The show rocked."

I'm trying to figure out who the hell he is when I notice the *Dragonfly Ink* logo on his T-shirt. Then my stupid ass notices his piercings and tattooed arms. Damn. I'd been hoping Allie changed her mind. Obviously not. But I force the tightness from my face. "No problem . . ."

"Todd," he fills in, and gestures behind him. "This is Mac. The old man only inks part time."

With his gray beard, Mac looks like he's closing in on sixty. Compared to everyone else I saw working at the shop, he's an odd choice, but I'm guessing he's good because Allie appears to take her business seriously.

Noticing people slowly gathering around us, I take the first step and say over my shoulder, "Come on up and have a drink with the band."

Without hesitation, they follow me up. Sam, Gabe, and a bunch of girls already wait in the balcony area, standing at tall tables. Mara comes at me and throws herself into my arms. I give her a long hug, enjoying the way she's rubbing herself against me, then grab two beers from the tray on a table and give them to Todd and Mac. After grabbing my own beer, I introduce them to Mara, who's now glued to my side.

Standing around one of the tables, we talk music for a while until we switch to ink. Mara's mouth is quiet, but her body is as suggestive as hell each time she moves. Someone orders a round of tequila shots, and a minute later Mara and I are licking the salt from the same glass, feeding each other the shot, and sucking on the same lime. She wraps a leg around my waist as our lips touch during the suck. I'm liking it until I glance up and see Todd and Mac still holding their own shots and watching us enviously. That's when the situation I've put myself in hits me.

They work with Allie. In fact they work *for* her. And Mara's been hanging on me all night, practically fucking me with her clothes on. Definitely fucking me with her eyes. They might say something to Allie. Maybe even warn her away from me. Normally, I wouldn't care if a woman turned me down because I'm promiscuous. I sure as hell don't owe anyone anything. But Allie's different. She's a challenge. A challenge that now has a newly opened door for me—in the form of a fake date. Allie, hearing about Mara and me tonight, has the potential to shut that door. Business owner, talented tattooist, and college student, Allie is the whole package. The more I get to know her, the more I'm committed to the challenge she presents. Mara, on the other hand, is a way to pass the time.

A hot, wild way to pass the time.

Sam comes over and starts talking to Todd and Mac about ink while I weigh my options. Mara stays pasted to me. Damn, her tits look good. She must have one of those push-up bras on. The kind I like to leave on when we have sex. I mentally compare the two girls to each other. Sure, Mara's hot, but there's not much else there. Allie is also sexy but talented too and easy to talk to. Then there are her sad, guarded eyes. I want to rid her of the storm in her gaze, if even for a night. It's become part of the challenge.

It takes only one more second of thinking about Allie's eyes to realize that I want to get myself out of this predicament. I've never tried to get a woman to *quit* hitting on me. Oblivious to my thoughts, Mara leans close and whispers in my ear about leaving, then explores my neck with her lips.

I glance down at the amazing tits pushed against my arm. I conjure up Allie's sexy voice. Mara's teeth nip at my ear. I imagine Allie's lip ring. Mara squeezes my ass. I imagine Allie's rainstorm eyes.

I draw in a deep breath and shake my head no. "Can't. Got to get up early." That *is* true. Romeo has us booked tomorrow for another recording session. But Mara knows early mornings never stop me from staying out late.

She stays pushed up against me but starts to pout.

I shrug.

She glares.

I drain half my beer.

Finally, Mara jerks away from me, yanks her purse from a chair, and walks away without looking back. Both Todd and Mac watch her swaying ass disappear down the stairs. Good. They'll remember she left without me.

We drink some more. Todd and Mac try to talk Sam into checking out the shop. He just shakes his buzzed head and grins, showing them the lame tattoos on his arm. Though he's cut like a fucking bodybuilder, I swear the pussy is scared of needles. Girls are hanging around us, but none are as aggressive as Mara.

Sam switches to Sprite. He may be a heavy partier, but he never drinks and drives. I used to, back in my teenage years. Sideswiped a tree once. Totaled my motorcycle. Walked home. With a broken arm. It was the next morning by the time the cops showed up and tried to pin me with careless driving, but my parents threw a fit. At them and me. I didn't give a shit, but liked the attention. Was probably looking for it. But with one hotshot lawyer, the case was dropped within a month. And once again I was off my parents' radar. Yet after having several nightmares about not hitting a tree but a person, I never drank and drove again. Not even to get my parents' attention.

The bar announces last call. I decline. Sam wants to go. He is all about getting home and doing his best tomorrow. The ass has bought into Romeo's plans for our indie glory. Gabe already left with his stick-with-tits girlfriend. We give Todd and Mac some fist bumps and leave them at the table, which is still populated with girls.

We drive home, and my buzz dissipates at the thought of my lonely dorm room and my even lonelier bed.

Chapter 7
Justin

When I pull up in front of Dragonfly Ink, I'm nervous as shit. I went on a few real dates in high school, but they hadn't scared me. Now I'm about to go on a fake date and my balls are tied in knots. I'm not worried about going with the flow and acting the boyfriend. I'm freaked out because I want to make an impression. Something I never worry about. And I'm clueless about how to do it while on this sham of a date. My charm hasn't gotten me far with this girl.

Yet.

As soon as I open the shop door, Allie's coming at me. Hot damn. She's wearing a dress. Black. Short. Tight. It has only one sleeve, her tattoo acting as the other and her bare shoulder gleaming under the track lights. "Hey," I say as she lifts a coat. I reach for it, then hold it out for her. "You look beautiful."

"Thanks," she responds hastily, sliding into the coat and flying past me out the door.

Opening the car door for her, I notice the reason for her quick flight. Mandy, Shaya, and Todd peer at us from the shop's window. Todd gives me a thumbs-up. I give them all a quick wave and hurry around the car, wanting to get away from our audience as quickly as Allie clearly does.

"Where to?" I ask, starting the car. She gives me directions as I try not to stare at the sleek length of her legs ending in sexy heels. She finishes the directions with, "By the way, you look pretty good too."

"Thanks," I say. I don't share that it took me for-fucking-ever to pick out my clothes. I finally ended with a black Armani button-up shirt, frayed jeans, and low black boots. Not exactly the outfit of the year, but with my nerves in overdrive, I couldn't fathom what to wear to an art show.

The silence in the car is awkward for the first few minutes, until I ask, "So should I know anything about your ex? Will he be breathing down my neck all night?"

She waves a hand. "He'll be fine. I just don't want anything to do with that revolving door."

The revolving door comment hits my conscience. Though I've never slept with more than one girl a night, the *next* night could always mean someone new. At that thought, I decide to stay off the topic of her ex. "Is this a good friend who's showing at the gallery or an art friend?"

"Both. We've known each other since high school. I haven't had much time to see her lately, which is another reason I didn't want to miss the show."

"Another art geek?"

"Yes. She was never as geeky as me, and obviously way more driven, considering she's doing the whole gallery thing."

"I'm going to be honest, I didn't know there was an art gallery in the area."

"You from around here?"

"Been here three years, but I grew up in Grand Rapids."

"Actually, there are two art studios around here. One is more a mix of photography and art, and the one we're going to is mainly paintings and sculpture but also offers classes. But yeah, art galleries exist outside of New York or London or Grand Rapids. Smaller scale, with less commas on the price tags."

I can smell her perfume, something clean and flowery scented. It fits her perfectly. "Your friend . . ."

"Hannah."

"She paints?"

"No. She does constructed sculpture."

"Constructed sculpture?"

She nods. "Instead of molding the piece or chiseling it from stone, it's built."

"You like her work?"

She glances at me. "Well, yeah."

I give her a look that says, *Tell me the truth*.

Allie laughs and the low, husky sound fills the interior of the car. Damn. She could giggle and it would be sexy. She pushes auburn waves behind a shoulder. "I do like her art. I would love to own a piece, if I had the extra money. She has major talent."

I slow as we near the address she gave me. It's in an older, renovated part of town filled with boutiques and little restaurants. Since the gallery parking lot is full, I pull a U-turn and park on the opposite side of the street. "If the amount of cars out here is any indication, she must do well."

Allie nods. "Hannah eventually wants to make it to New York."

I kill the engine and shoot her a look. "Any last words before we become a public couple?"

Her hands pause on the seat belt as she glances at me. "Thanks for coming. Hopefully, it will be tame and we'll just have fun checking out art and sipping cheap wine."

"You. Me. Art. Fun. Cheap wine. Sounds good," I say as she reaches for the door handle. "Hey, let your date get that."

She rolls her eyes but lets out a soft, nervous giggle. I was right. Her giggle is sexy too.

After opening the door, I take her hand and we walk across the street. She doesn't pull away, and the way our hands fit together feels perfect. We hang our coats on a rack in the entrance, and as soon as we enter the studio, a waitress dressed in a top hat offers up a tray of drinks. I almost laugh at the ridiculous display. Gummy worms lie at the bottom of a plastic flute of sparkling wine and red wine fills a plastic glass with a flashing pink stem. Keeping my inner wine snob in check, I reach for the red wine. Allie goes for the flute of sparkling wine. Hand in hand we start roaming the huge gallery space, which is split down the middle by sleek white panels. Soft Spanish guitar music plays in the background.

Our first stop is a metal bird with long wings extended, perched on a motorcycle about half its true size. It's kind of cool.

"Can you tell what it's made of?" Allie asks before sipping her wine.

I look over the piece more closely, enjoying the feel of her hand in mine. Never thought I'd enjoy something so innocent. "A thin, shiny metal?"

"Close. Large paper clips. Cool, huh?"

I'm examining the piece again when a loud "Hey, girl!" sounds behind us.

As Allie turns and breaks our hand connection, she's enveloped in fuzzy, bright green arms. The words "You made it!" come out of the fuzz. Allie laughs, returns the hug, and the owner of the fuzzy arms finally materializes. I'm looking at a girl who's wearing a funnel-collar coat that's impossibly fuzzy and green. The funnel is higher than her spiked pink hair.

She grabs Allie's arm and leans close. "I'm sorry. I didn't know Jazz would bring Trevor." Allie's mouth tightens but the pink-haired woman doesn't notice. "And when did he get back? It's like he materialized out of thin air. I know you—"

"Hannah," Allie says, cutting her off and gesturing to me. "I'd like you to meet Justin."

"Oh." Hannah's bright blue eyes drift over me for several seconds. "Well hello, Justin." She gives Allie an approving look. "Didn't know you had it in you, Al, but he's delicious."

Allie gives a tight half smile.

I grin at Hannah. "I'm not sure if I should say thanks or if Allie should."

Hannah cocks her head. "Maybe both?"

A guy in a pink top hat clamps on Hannah's elbow and whispers in her ear. She listens intently, then lets him drag her away while waving in our direction.

"She'd fit in New York perfectly," I say, then take a sip of wine. It's horrid. Or maybe I'm just used to the really good stuff.

"Yeah, she was flamboyant even in high school." Allie motions forward with her wine glass. "Let's check out the rest of her collection and then find somewhere inconspicuous to hang."

I follow her to the next display and almost run into her when she suddenly stops.

A few people away, Trevor stands next to a woman in a dress much smaller and tighter than Allie's. The woman cackles loudly before Trevor leans down and says something in her ear. A slow smile spreads across her face.

Allie stands frozen, watching them. The look on *her* face has my gut clenching with the realization that maybe this girl *is* untouchable because she already belongs to *him*. She turns abruptly and wraps an arm around mine. Her nails dig into my arm as she drains the rest of her wine. The hand holding the empty glass trembles a bit.

"Hey, you okay?" I ask softly.

Her lips unclench from a grimace and she nods. As a waiter passes, she exchanges her glass for another gummy-worm sparkling wine. She drains half of it in seconds, then spins toward the closest display. "I'm good," she says stiffly. She gestures to the sculpture in front of us. "What do you think of this one?"

I glance at the piece, some sort of tower with crazy metal shit spilling down its sides. Like a cellular tower vomiting on itself. "It's all right," I say, though I couldn't give a fuck what it looks like. Not when Allie appears shell-shocked.

She tugs at my arm and robotically says, "Let's go check out the pieces on the other side."

Our fake date has suddenly turned sour. I'm definitely not anywhere near charming her. Not sure it's possible now.

We wander past people, some of whom Allie nods to vaguely, and check out art, but her mind is clearly far from this room. Far from me or fun or even art. Her hand stays clamped around mine. When she talks, her voice is a monotone. She's soon on her third glass of wine. As we browse without really seeing, a few people come over and talk with us. Each of them says something about Trevor being here. I'm getting the idea they must have been together for quite a while and that their breakup was big news when it happened.

After touring a bunch of pieces that I hardly pay attention to, we end up at the back of the studio next to a wall of paintings. Seconds later Trevor, without his scantily clad date, comes up to us.

Allie stiffens and her hand slides to my shoulder.

Trevor steps in front of her. "So tell me, Al, you're aware I wouldn't know sculpture from a pile of turds, what do you think of the exhibit?"

Allie blinks as if coming to life, then says steadily, "It's cohesive. The pieces build on one another and show her strengths. The three she picked as pivotal works do stand out the most. The exhibit is whimsical yet keeps her usual focus on the contrast between nature and technology."

Trevor takes a long drink of red wine. "Then it's good?"

She nods. "More than good. It's actually up there with amazing."

Twisting bleached hair over her shoulder, Trevor's date slides closer to him and wraps an arm around his waist. Her cool gaze settles on us. "Hello, Allie."

"Jazz," Allie says frostily.

"Good to see you without your claws out," she says, and Allie's eyes turn to slits. Ignoring the murderous glare across from her, Jazz glances at me. "You going to introduce him?"

Allie's hand glides slowly from my shoulder to wrap around the back of my neck. "This is Justin. Justin," she nods toward the woman dressed in two feet of fabric, "this is Jazz." Her fingers curl into the hair along my neck. "And of course, you've already met Trevor."

"You enjoying the exhibit?" Jazz asks me, ignoring Allie's rudeness.

Before I can answer, Allie presses to my side and winds her other arm across my waist. "He's enjoying being with me."

Trevor's expression tightens while Jazz gives me a flat smirk.

I glance down at the girl wrapped around me. "It is hard to notice the art next to Allie."

Trevor's about to say something that I'm betting will match his scowl when Hannah enters—more like crash-lands in—our little group. The conversation turns to art then the past, and it's obvious these four people went to school together. Hannah talks the most. Jazz watches Trevor. Trevor watches Allie. Allie's hands keep roaming over me.

Though her wandering hands are a turn-on, the whole thing pisses me off more with each passing second. Yes, I know this is a fake date. Yes, my intentions toward Allie aren't exactly noble. I simply want to get her in bed and move on to the next conquest. But after witnessing her obvious obsession with him, and noticing that he is a complete asshole, I can't help feeling used. I don't like the idea that she's hitting on me to make him jealous—it occurs to me I might even be her way of getting him back. This thought gets me truly pissed. Normally, I don't mind girls using me for my body but that's something entirely different. This is emotional warfare and I don't *do* emotions. And I don't get used unless I'm down with it. I'm not down with this.

Unable to take the situation a second longer, I murmur an "excuse us" and drag her into the hallway that leads to the bathrooms. She follows quietly but looks stunned when I push her body to the wall but don't shove mine against hers. Rather put my palms on each side of her head.

Her gray eyes grow wide. "Justin . . ."

A pant of anger escapes me. "You keep running those pretty hands all over me and I might take you up on your offer."

She blinks at me in shock until something catches her attention over my shoulder and her body visibly stiffens.

My temples pound with outrage. Aware that her prick of an ex is not only behind us but also extracting a response from her, I give in to my anger. My body crushes hers into the wall. With a swift bend of my head, I catch her lips and stop her gasp, loving the touch of her lip ring pressing against my mouth. Under me, she is as unyielding and still as the sculptures we viewed. Indignation has me not caring. My hips grind against hers as my tongue strokes into her mouth. Though this is about showing her she can't fuck with me, I can't help notice the taste of her mouth on my tongue is as sweet as the wine she drank.

I'm about to pull back and get some control when her lips and body soften. The ire of my kiss spirals into something else as she responds. Her fingers grip my shoulders. Her tongue slides with mine. Her response wipes out my anger. I forget about her ex and that we're in public, and deepen the kiss.

Cupping the sides of her face, I push into her and she moans ever so slightly into me. Ah hell. My outrage fizzles at her response. I want her *now*. I tear my mouth from hers and reach for her hand. "Come on. Let's go."

With heavily lidded eyes, she nods.

Lust pounding in my brain, I haul her past an open-mouthed Trevor, through the crush of bodies, grab our coats at the entrance, and cross the street before the gloss of lust dissipates from her gaze.

Still dazed—I'm hoping it's my kiss not the wine—she lets me help her into the passenger seat. Rounding the front of the car, I think of where we could go. My dorm room? Shit, I should have used my ridiculous allowance to get an apartment instead of being such a lazy ass. Her place? Does she have roommates? Does she live alone?

I slide into the driver's seat and ask, "Where to?"

Allie remains facing forward. Her bottom lip quivers. Her clasped hands tremble in her lap. She draws in a deep breath, then suddenly bursts into tears.

Her soft sobs echo in the car.

Ah shit. Her tears kill my lust. I have no idea how to deal with a crying woman.

"I'm such a fool. I'm so—s-sorry," she sputters.

"Hey," I say. I'm desperately trying to think of a way to calm her down when the face of her dickhead ex pops up outside her window.

"Oh no, please go," she wails.

He raps a knuckle on the glass.

What's with this fucking circus? I just want to have sex with that voice, those legs, that lip ring. All this other shit is getting ridiculous. I start the car. He pounds on the window. I'm out of the car in seconds, leaning across the roof. "Get your hands off the glass."

"I want to talk to Al," he sneers.

"She doesn't want to talk to you. So step away from the car and move on."

"Not till I talk with Al."

I'd like to pound this prick into the cement, but fighting with her ex while Allie cries in the car might put an even bigger damper on my chances than her tears. "Get it through your head. She doesn't want to talk," I say, gritting my teeth.

"Trevor!" Jazz wails from the other side of the street. "What the hell are you doing?"

His face twists in a scowl. "Tell Al I'll call her later." He whips around and stalks across the street.

Who is this asshole? I drop into the driver's seat.

"Thanks for getting rid of him," Allie whispers, wiping the wetness on her cheeks with shaky fingers.

With a sigh, I reach over, brushing my elbow on her thigh, and she flinches. Getting irritated again, I open the glove box and dig out some old napkins. "Here," I say, dropping them in her lap.

"Thanks." She reaches for the crumpled paper as I pull onto the street.

I drive. She wipes at her tears, then lets out a deep sigh. "I thought I could handle it. Obviously I was in la-la land. I didn't mean to use you that way. I really did think we could go out and have fun." The napkins are fisted in her lap. "Then I saw them together, freaked out, drank too much wine, and acted like an ass."

Turning a corner, I shrug but I'm still annoyed. I try to remember I agreed to a fake date but can't help snapping, "Your relationship must have been pretty serious. Two years and you're still affected by this asshole dumping you?"

She turns toward the side window. "He didn't dump me. I left him. And he wasn't just a boyfriend."

"What does that mean?"

She leans her forehead on the glass. "My husband."

Those two words have me feeling like the wind was just knocked out of me. "You were *married* to him?"

She doesn't lift her head. "For over a year."

Fucking married. My hands clench around the steering wheel. I want to punch it. That's why this guy is such a huge deal to her. I'm pretty sure he's the reason her eyes always churn with the depth of a stormy gray sky. And why she's so distant. "You must have been young," I somehow get out.

"Eighteen."

I guess a connection. "He cheated on you with Jazz."

She lets out another sigh. "And others but mostly her. He always goes back to Jazz. Childhood sweethearts."

"Sounds to me like you were his childhood sweetheart."

"After Jazz. Always after Jazz." Her voice is small and sad.

I pull up in front of her shop. "You should have warned me about the past between you two. Maybe I wouldn't have gotten so pissed off and attacked you."

Her laugh sounds miserable but it's still sexy. "I try to pretend the past doesn't matter. Explaining it makes it matter. Besides, I wasn't really complaining when you pushed me against the wall."

At this point, I'm not sure what to make of that. "Allie . . ."

She reaches for the door handle. "See you Friday. Good night, Justin."

With those final words, she's out of my car, leaving me as confused as shit.

Chapter 8
Allie

I've been dreading Justin's appointment since he dropped me off Tuesday night. Beyond being embarrassed by my meltdown, I'm having a hard time forgetting his kiss. I haven't been kissed like that in ages. Heck, I haven't been kissed at all in ages. But it doesn't matter. Justin is not the man for me. Not even close. If I were looking, it would be for someone mature. Definitely someone not on the one-night-stand merry-go-round. So when Shay brings him into the room for his appointment, I force myself to appear calm and professional. I don't want him to notice my jittery nerves.

Of course, Justin is his usual grinning, smooth self. "Hey, Allie," he says, dragging off his designer sunglasses and leaning a hip against the tattoo chair.

Shay gives his whole body a slow once-over, then looks at me pointedly as she leaves. I ignore her. The last thing I need to be reminded of is that he's hot. All I want at this point is to clear the air. I want the elephant out of the room before I stick a needle in him. Putting my twisting hands behind my back, I start, "I want to apologize again for Tuesday. Regardless of my reasons, my behavior was unacceptable—actually, ridiculous."

He gives me a slow smile. "Come to my show tomorrow and no apology needed."

Oh, crap. I forgot about our deal. I bite my lip ring. Why he'd want me to go after Tuesday's debacle is beyond me, but I can't back out after what he put up with at the art show. "If I don't have anything scheduled, I should be able to go. If not, when's your next show?"

He taps his sunglasses on his thigh. Though his face is relaxed, the motion suggests irritation. "In four weeks. We rarely play back-to-back Saturdays, usually once a month or so."

"If not tomorrow, then four weeks gives me enough time to work out my schedule." Ignoring the frown turning his full lips down, I reach for my stool. "You ready to get started?"

He answers by setting his glasses on the counter and reaching for the bottom of his T-shirt. He pulls his shirt off in the same efficient yet sensual way as usual, then straddles the chair. I ignore the "Holy crap, Batman!" comment ringing through my head again as I stare at his muscled back, then apply another transfer. After that I get to work filling in the tribal work inside the treble clef. I'm 99 percent artist and only one percent female, and am totally focused on the process. I keep the question of why he'd want me to go to his show so badly in the far recesses of my mind.

Everything's quiet, smooth, and lovely until the endorphins kick in and he starts talking. "I'm curious, did your ex call?"

Yes. He did. And had the audacity to warn me away from Justin. This was thanks to Jazz, who had heard that Justin was known for moving through his band's groupies like a fast-moving summer thunderstorm. I was not amused by a warning from cheating Trevor. "Yeah, but ugh. Let's talk about something else."

"Art?"

I pause and lean back, checking out my work. I'm almost half done with the interior. Unconsciously, I switch the topic to him. "How about music? What do you like to sing best?"

"Mmm . . . Never thought about it."

"You have some time now."

His fingers tap on the armrest he's leaning over. "Probably the songs that get the crowd wild. It's more about the energy between the crowd and me than the enjoyment of singing the song. Their energy gives me a natural high that no amount of alcohol or drug can beat. It's like their excitement, their enthusiasm flows into me. It puts me on top of the world, but it humbles me too."

I'd been trying to make small talk with the question about singing, but his explanation deepens the conversation and gives me a glimpse beyond his playboy persona. I find it intriguing that the crowd's enthusiasm humbles him. I can't help asking, "What songs get the crowd going the most?"

"Different songs produce different kinds of momentum. Something rocking and fast like 'Remedy' gets them excited and moving with the music. With that song, an almost tangible energy comes off the crowd."

"Remedy?"

"It's a heavier song, almost metal. By Seether. You've never heard it?" He glances over his shoulder.

I wipe at the blood and ink on his skin. "Probably. It's not ringing a bell though."

He shakes his head slightly and I imagine the expression of incredulity on his face. "While that song is loud and rocking other songs like 'Twenty-One Guns' by Green Day . . . You've heard of that, right?"

"Yes," I say wryly. "I'm not totally out of the music sphere."

"Well, dramatic songs like that bring a different energy, a sort of passion to the crowd. I've even seen tears. Those songs are like riding an emotional wave. It can be draining, a roller coaster of emotion worth the drain."

The needle hovers over his skin as I take in his words. "Why?"

He draws in a deep breath, and luckily I wasn't inking him because his muscles ripple from the acute rise of his shoulders. "Not sure if I can put it into words correctly. . . ." His fingers drum again on the vinyl armrest. "It's like we're connected for the length of the song. Their memories, their regrets, their hopes crash into me, and all of it becomes part of the song. For a few minutes we're on the same wavelength of emotion, connected by compassion, sometimes sadness. Though strangers, we understand each other in that moment."

His explanation astounds me. I'd like to rest my forehead on his skin and take in *this* moment—part of me can't believe he has opened up and let me see beyond his playboy persona. I'd never expect such depth from him. He's cocky and an obvious womanizer, yet his heartfelt explanation makes him more attractive because it's a perfect description of how I consider art. In its highest form, art ignites universal emotions that transcend the differences among people.

Instead of giving in to the urge and pressing my cheek on his back, I simply say, "I think you explained it rather well."

He shrugs but says, "I'm not sure I did but thanks." A soft rock song fills the silence. "So how long have you been into van Gogh?"

I wipe at a bead of ink on his skin. "Since I was about twelve."

"How does a twelve year old girl get into van Gogh?"

"We had to do a two-page paper in art. I picked his name out of a hat. The first time I saw *Starry Night* it was love at first sight. Then I read about him and read his letters to his brother, and I don't know . . . He seemed so lonely and sincere yet troubled. My little twelve-year-old heart went out to him."

"Huh. You must have been one mature girl. At that age, I was drooling over Beyoncé and Gwen Stefani. Sincerity didn't enter into the drool."

"There were *Tiger Beat* boys pinned to my wall too. Not just van Gogh prints. I wasn't a total nerd."

"You sound sweet not nerdy."

Me sweet? I'm not a raging beezy or anything, but sweet? There's only a small circle that gets sweetness from me. "Don't get any wrong ideas about me. Remember, I'm sticking a needle in you."

His laugh is rich and deep.

"You might want to stretch while I change needles," I say, wishing his laugh didn't make me want to open up to him.

He pushes out of the chair, and I adjust my rear post to modify the supply of ink and then attach a large mag needle for the shading and coloring. The changes to my machine keep me from watching him stalk around the room and in front of the mirrors.

Finally, he sits all that skin down and I get back to work. We talk about art and music as I shade the tattoo, then fill in the tiniest amount of red for some extra definition. Once again, he's easy to talk to. It's nice. But not as nice as his kiss, which shouldn't be in my thoughts while I'm working—or at all.

I let him look at the finished tat before I put the bandage on. While he checks it out in the mirror, deep dimples form as he smiles, just like the last time. He studies the defined treble clef filled with intricate tribal work wrapped around the detailed microphone.

"It's amazing." His eyes meet my reflection in the glass. "You're beyond talented."

My murmured thanks receive a quick hug. A moment later he slides away, brushing his slight five-o'clock shadow with my cheek and leaving me frozen as he plops into the chair. I stiffen from his embrace and try not to recall the sensation of his warm, lovely skin. I slowly reach for some goo, then apply it in a dreamlike state to his back. I haven't been to dreamland in years. Nor have I felt fuzzy and warm, which are the only words that describe how I feel from his hug.

Not good.

After applying the bandage, I shake my head to clear it. Head in the clouds leads to idiotic things. Like fake dates.

Once he's dressed—I peeked very little by keeping myself busy cleaning up—he hands me two tickets. "You need to come see your work. It'll be center stage tonight."

My fingers reach for the tickets, and warning bells ring in my head at the touch of his hand. I snatch the tickets and clasp them to my thigh. "That will be a first."

He snags his sunglasses off the counter, and gives me an uncompromising stare with those clear green eyes. "I'll be looking for you in the crowd." Then he and his inked body are gone, leaving only the scent of his dark, sexy cologne.

About two minutes later, I'm still standing next to my tray like an idiot and debating if I really should go to his show when Todd walks in. His pierced mouth curls into a smirk. "Knowing you tatted him, I get why Justin had the look." The look refers to the tell-all smile a customer has when seeing their finished tattoo. "But why do *you* have the look, Al?" he asks, then grins mischievously at me.

The smile I hadn't known I was wearing turns into a frown. "Oh fuck off, Todd."

"Shay! Bring the jar!" he yells, then hoots and points like a twelve-year-old.

I dig five ones out of my pocket before she even puts the dang jar under my nose.

Since Justin first came around, my swear jar idea has been biting me in the rear.

Chapter 9
Allie

Saturday nights at the shop are usually walk-ins. However, I did have one regular coming in for a scheduled appointment. The client happened to be Holly, who is also my roommate. The minute I suggested we reschedule our session and go see Justin's band instead, she was all over it. She's been trying to hook me up for the past two years. After pressuring me until I couldn't take it anymore, she has dragged me to house parties, college bars, and even fraternity mixers, including the one where she met her current boyfriend. But I never met anyone. Instead, while out I always felt out of place and lonelier than if I were sitting at home. She didn't give up but forced me into the blind date thing instead. Holly set up the two dates I've been on in the past two years. One was with her boss. Financially stable. Mature. And as boring as a visit to the dentist.

Holly goes to college part-time—like me—but she takes evening classes because she has an awesome job as a pharmacist assistant. Seeing her at work, you'd never guess she had a wild side. She's smiley and cheerful, and except for a star on her wrist, she appears tattoo free. When she goes out . . . Well, it's hard to keep track of her ink because her outfits reveal almost all of it. Not all tattoo fanatics are wild. I'm definitely not. Holly most definitely is, even with a boyfriend she plans to marry. She's impatiently waiting for a massive rock to put on her finger.

While we wait for the band to come on, the guy next to us at the bar is checking out the huge butterfly that looks like it's about to fly off her back. She likes backless clothes. There's not usually much to the front either. So when she turns around with a drink in each hand, the guy isn't checking out the pretty swirls circling her belly button. Or the ladybugs—the only tats I didn't do—along one side of her ribs. He's not even checking out the scrolling words across the top of her chest. Because his eyes are glued to her cleavage. She's had work on that too, and in her own words, "ain't too proud to admit it." Though we're both in jeans, she has heels on. I'm wearing my knee-high calf-hugging boots. And except for the dress I wore the other night, the sexiest top I have is a tight white tank with a bit of lace at the edges, which is what I'm rocking for the show.

Holly hands me a mojito. "It's about high time you had a good time, so I buy and you drink."

I take a sip. "Slow down, chica. About three of these and I'll be passed out."

She lifts her own mojito. "Lightweight excuses aren't going to fly tonight." She wiggles her ass on my thigh. "We gots to get our krunk on before the band comes on."

My eyes can't help a roll while the guy next to us drools at her rubbing against my leg.

While declining several offers from guys who want to buy us drinks, we split another mojito, then order two beers and head out into the crowd in front of the stage. Holly uses a combination of "excuse me" and her tits to get us about fifteen feet from the stage. To get us any closer, she'd have to show more than cleavage. I don't push the issue because she probably would. Holly is not exactly shy.

We sip our beers, bounce to the blaring music, and wait for the band to come on. If the crowd here is any indication, Luminescent Juliet is a lot more popular than Justin led me to believe. I haven't told Holly anything about Justin except that I've inked him. But somehow, perhaps because I asked her to come, she's already rooting for me to hook up with him. Or at least with one of the band members. Not sure what's with everyone trying to get me laid. Okay, it's possible I'm a bit uptight. But sex isn't going to fix that. I'm not even sure it's fixable. I'm planning to stick to my plan. Which is to watch the band, say hello to Justin, and get the heck home.

Holly has started flirting with the guys next to us when the lights dim and the dance music dies. The empty stage lights up, then darkens, causing the crowd to cheer. A smoky blue spotlight follows the guitar player as he walks to the edge of the stage, strumming softly. Another light shines behind Justin, standing in front of the microphone. The outline of his body hints at his masculine beauty and has me, and probably half the crowd, wishing another light would flick on to show him fully. He begins to sing softly, a few lines about keeping in the dark, then suddenly loud drums join in and the guitar escalates. Justin's voice grows loud and angry, matching the growing volume of the guitar.

"Oh, I love this song!" Holly shouts in my ear.

"What is it?" I shout back.

"Foo Fighters! 'Pretender'!" she yells, bouncing to the music.

Everyone's moving and bobbing their heads to the beat. We're crushed into the mass. I'm shoulder to shoulder with not only Holly but also the girl next to me.

I drain half my beer and let my buzz coax me into the crowd's enthusiasm. The band sounds good. I'm guessing Justin sounds good, but it's hard to tell. I've never understood shouting songs.

But holding the microphone and standing in a wide stance with a boot on the edge of the stage, Justin looks as rocker hot as his silhouette in shadow promised. He's in an unbuttoned white shirt with the sleeves rolled up, and his tattoos and muscular chest add to the display. I've never had as harsh of an opinion of tribal art as Todd, but I'm starting to like it.

During the guitar solo, Justin steps to the side and shuffles the microphone stand between his hands. Then he comes back, sets one boot on the edge of the stage, and goes back to shouting, coming across as commanding and sexy.

The song ends. Holly turns to me with a dazzled gaze. "They're freakin' good. And they're all hot." She takes a gulp of beer. "Which one do you like again?"

My gaze throws darts at her.

She chuckles.

"Everyone feeling good tonight?" Justin shouts into the microphone, and the crowd shouts back. "Then you must be ready for some Artic Monkeys!"

The crowd roars back again as the song starts with a rolling guitar riff, then the drums kick in, and Justin starts singing.

Once again, I don't know the song, but with this second one it's evident that Justin can sing, not just shout. Actually, he's quite good, his voice sounds low and sexy. Before I can ask, Holly shows me a picture of the original single on her iPhone while she dances. The title 'R U Mine?'sends a shiver down my spine, because when Justin sings it, it feels like he's asking me the question.

Obviously, the alcohol already has me stupid.

Holly and I dance next to each other while we watch. Well, I mostly watch Justin, but yeah, Holly is right. The guitar player is darkly hot in a button-up but open shirt. His dark hair has this way of falling over one eye that is sexy. The bassist is super cute as he keeps winking at girls in the front, nodding his dark buzzed head, and bouncing to the rhythm. He's dressed in a sleeveless T, and his muscular arms almost dwarf the bass guitar he plays. The drummer is lean, muscled, and graceful in a black tank top and long black shorts. His shoulder-length hair whips around him, but in between drumbeats, when his hair flies back, his lean angular face looks intense.

As we continue to watch, I'm super impressed not only with Justin's singing, but also by how at ease, how professional he appears onstage.

They play more songs. We watch and dance. Every minute, I fall more in lust with Justin. It's hard not to. He moves with the music flawlessly, changing his posture and his movements to match the tone of each song. I can't help imagining he's singing to me, even though most of the girls in the crowd probably feel the same way. I'm buzzed and my hormones are flying, so I'm going with it. Justin *is* singing to me. And with each gulp of beer, the idea of jumping onstage and leg humping him, the silly image that came to me while inking him, doesn't seem *that* farfetched.

About the sixth song in, Holly goes on a beer run and leaves me alone. The guys she was next to, and flirting with, scoot over and ask me my name. I murmur it without glancing at them. The closest one compliments my arm sleeve, but busy watching the band—Justin mostly—I mouth a thanks but then ignore them.

Holly comes back carrying two beers and a shot of tequila as the band takes a break. People shuffle around. Others leave—either to get drinks or wait in the bathroom line—and we're soon less than ten feet from the stage.

I force the shot down with a grimace, causing Holly to laugh. I stuff both my old beer cup and the little plastic shot cup in her huge purse as revenge. Then we wait while my head starts seriously buzzing. She's soon talking with the new guys next to us while I sway with the dance music playing over the speakers and watch stagehands rearrange the setup.

Finally, the lights lower and the recorded music fades out. The band comes back out along with two younger people following. One holds a violin, the other a small guitar.

The roar of the crowd grows deafening.

Clutching an acoustic guitar, Justin moves to the microphone. He views the mob of hooting fans. "As soon as you hear this tune, I'm sure you'll recognize it, but . . ." He pauses as his eyes meet mine. We stare at each other and neither of us moves. His lids lower before he lifts his gaze back to the crowd. I'm trying to figure out whether my inebriated imagination is in overdrive or if he really just paused onstage for a minute to stare at me.

"This is a first for us and we need a little help." He gestures to the side of the stage, where the girl and guy stand, looking nervous. "Not only will I be playing with Romeo but let me introduce Jane, who's playing the violin. And Robert, who plays a mean mandolin."

He steps away from the microphone and the crowd grows quiet. The others in the band watch him until he taps on the stem of his acoustic guitar. Robert and Justin start strumming. I recognize the melody, but I can't place it, especially since I'm buzzed up and completely enamored.

Justin leans closer to the microphone and starts singing.

Everyone else fades into a shadowy background. His voice and the music catch in my chest. I'm trapped in the moment. Caught in his intense gaze, I'm lost as his lush voice wraps around me. There's only the music and the sudden, fierce connection between us.

Holly nudges me with her elbow and yells in my ear, "It's like he's singing to you! Fucking 'Iris'! Unbelievable! These lyrics are hot! . . ."

I feel her jump up and down next to me. "It's like he really, really wants you to see past the rocker to the man inside!"

I don't comment. I don't look away from Justin's gaze either. But Holly is right. Though I can't concentrate on the words while he stares at me, I understand the soulful question in his voice—and his heartfelt plea hits me hard. I've seen glimpses behind his playboy persona, but as we stare at each other, I want to peel back the layers, reach in, and immerse myself in the real Justin, the one who I'm beginning to realize hides.

He sings and stares as I sway and melt.

Oh crap. He's the snake charmer and I'm the snake mesmerized by his melody.

And mesmerized I am.

Holly yells something else, but I can't pull my attention from Justin. The band plays, he sings, and I drown in the emotional waves that are flowing between us. A crashing sensation washes over me again and again. Each time he sings the song's soulful refrain, each time he glances down at his guitar for a second then back at me, I'm drenched with longing. It's not lust, exactly, though that is there in the surge. A fierce want I lost long ago—the sense that there is someone out there balancing me—fills me. Someone who understands me. Someone made for me.

And that someone right now feels like the man singing onstage.

With each passing note, he has me closer to believing it's true.

Want crashes into me as his voice rises in volume during the last refrain.

As the song's last notes ring out, the crowd goes wild.

"Holy shit!" Holly yells in my ear. "You two were so eye fucking each other!"

Pulling my gaze from his, I draw in a deep breath. It feels like I've come up from a deep dive. Air rushes out of me. I need to escape before I find myself drowning. "I need to use the restroom."

"What!"

I have to get out of here. I can sense stares from the crowd surrounding us, the interest in the girl Justin just sang to. "I have to pee." I grab her arm. "Now."

"All right. All right," Holly says, taking my hand and yanking me through the mass as a fast pounding song starts.

We join the end of the long line as I try to catch my breath.

"Girl, you've been holding out on me," Holly says, leaning next to me against the wall.

I shake my head.

She pokes my shoulder. "Then what was that?"

Closing my eyes, I try to figure that out. It's almost like I imagined what happened. It's hard to believe reality could involve that much intensity.

"Hey, you okay?"

I open my eyes and nod. "Just a little drunk."

Holly grins at me. "On alcohol or lust?"

A giggle escapes me. "Maybe both?" We shuffle along the wall with the rest of the herd. "He just likes to flirt, Hol."

"I call bullshit. What I just witnessed went beyond flirting. He sang 'Iris' to you. 'Iris' is some serious shit, Al."

I kind of recall her saying it before, but I want to make sure because I *will* be loading it on my phone. "That's the name of the song?"

"Yes, it's by the Goo Goo Dolls." When I give her a blank stare, she lets out an exasperated sigh. "It's famous. If it were a painting, you'd know it by sight, the artist, the year it was painted, and the story behind it too."

I shrug and scoot forward with the moving line.

After the bathroom stop, Holly orders me another shot. Knowing I'll be seeing Justin soon, I don't argue and swallow the tequila in one gulp. Liquid courage to the rescue. The thought of dealing with my emotions directly in front of him, without the crowd and the stage to provide a buffer, has me jittery. Each of us with a beer in hand, we wait at the edge of the crowd as Justin announces their next song as something new the guitar player wrote.

"Wow. This is good. Bluesy," Holly shouts, and takes a sip of beer. "They're tat worthy."

"You want me to ink their name above your ass crack?" I absently say.

She laughs. "Maybe along it?"

I can't help but snort. Leave it to Holly to get me out of the weird emotional place Justin has left me in. I take a gulp of beer and face the stage.

I keep reminding myself of the facts. I'm just watching a band with a gorgeous singer. I'm just out with a girlfriend on a rare night of partying.

That's all this is.

That's all I can allow.

Chapter 10
Justin

Water drips from my flushed face as I stare into the small, chipped mirror above the sink. Confused green eyes stare back at me. My hands grip the edges of the wet, cold porcelain sink. It feels like I sliced open my heart and gave a piece of it to Allie in the midst of hundreds of fans. Since the only pounding I'm usually aware of happens in my dick, I'd been pretty sure I didn't have a heart. I run a hand down my wet face.

So what the fuck was that?

I try blaming my behavior on the fact that she'd appeared out of nowhere. I was startled to see her below me after I'd been searching for her face in the crowd all night. Shit. It would have to be right before *that* song when I'd find her in the crowd.

Pounding rattles the door. "What the hell, Justin? You cuffing it after your little serenade?" Sam yells from the other side.

I grab a paper towel and wipe my face. "To a picture of your mom."

"Shut up, you sick bastard, and hurry up. Unless you want me pissing on the floor." After one last view of my troubled eyes, I open the door and Sam flies in toward the urinal. "I've had to go since we went back on, asshole."

"Why didn't you go out back?" I ask, reaching for my bag on the floor.

"Riley and April are out there, helping Gabe and Romeo load."

"And . . ."

"And I didn't want to hear Romeo's shit." He kicks the door shut, locks it, and plucks out a small ziplock baggie of white powder. "You up for a hit?"

I rub the sides of my face. After the shit I just pulled, I have to admit I'm in the mood. The invincible high of cocaine sounds appealing. But then I remember that Allie's out there. And I remember that cocaine makes me act like a prick—or, depending on the night, more of a prick. I cannot be *that guy* tonight. I shake my head, yank on a new shirt, and start rolling up the sleeves.

Sam wipes the sink edge clean with a paper towel. "Are you turning into some kind of Romeo pansy?"

I shrug. "Maybe. What are you, a pusher?"

Bobbing his head, he shakes some powder on the white porcelain and starts humming that old Curtis Mayfield song "Pusherman." It's from the 1970s. I'm not even sure how I recognize the tune—maybe because he's sung it before. He's into weird seventies shit. He sings the words to himself while he makes a line with a razor.

He bends with a chuckle and I grab my backpack, knowing I need to get the hell out before the sweet high of indestructible draws me over to the sink.

"Order me a shot and a beer," he says midsnort.

"Hit the lock," I say, jerking the door shut behind me as I leave.

I take a step into the room still littered with our shit, and pause. Romeo and his girlfriend, Riley, are against the far wall sucking face. They pull apart and a second later Romeo is staring at me over Riley's head, his eyes narrowed. "Why does he need to lock the door, Justin?"

I shrug.

Sam likes to party. He doesn't do drugs daily or anything, but when he parties he mixes it up. Two hours from now, he'll be out back smoking a joint and almost ready to call it a night. Yet Romeo acts like Sam is a hardcore druggie, and threatens to kick him out of the band every time he gets the slightest whiff that he's been into something illegal. Maybe I need to grow up, but Romeo needs to get some perspective. One, we're in college. Two, we live in mid-Michigan. We're not some drugged-out band on Sunset Strip in Hollywood. Sam isn't shooting shit into his veins or doing any crazy-ass shit. He's just letting loose a little.

Riley steps aside and Romeo takes a step toward me, pointing his finger. "Don't fucking shrug at me. Why did you tell him to lock the door?"

"Don't fucking point at me like I'm one of your little boxing bitches."

"Romeo . . . ," Riley says, reaching for his arm.

I shrug again, more dramatically. "Cause he was gonna take a shit."

Fists at his side, Romeo looks like he's going to explode.

I smirk at him. It won't be the first or, probably, last time we'll go at it. It's true he can box. But I've been kicking ass out of the ring since middle school. Fighting was another way I tried to get my parents' attention. It didn't work, but once my reputation was in place as a fighter, the line to kick my ass grew to the length of a city block.

"Stop it!" Riley says, stepping between us. She's done this a number of times. Either she doesn't like violence or she's worried about Romeo's pretty face. Probably both.

The door creaks open behind us.

"What the hell?" Sam says calmly. "Why don't you assholes just meet in the ring once a month?"

Romeo whips toward him. "What were you doing in there?"

Sam's brows rise. "Dude, can I use the toilet without you crawling up my ass?"

While Romeo's expression turns thunderous, I try to keep a straight face. I'm not sure if Sam overheard us or if he's that lucky, but his answer was spot-on.

Riley edges up next to Romeo. "Let's just finish packing up the van and go."

He looks cynically at Sam, then at me, but finally says, "Grab something."

To keep the peace, we follow orders, grabbing anything within reach, and head out into the alley. Back inside, done with Romeo and his shit, I toss my bag onto a chair in the narrow room behind the stage, take a deep breath, and charge into the crowd to find Allie.

The bar/club is still hopping. Instead of going straight to the bar, I walk the perimeter of the room, searching for that head of rich auburn hair. A minute in, some chicks stop me and ask for pictures. Two pose on either side of me while the third girl, a hot blonde, takes a photo with her phone. I decline the blonde's offer to buy me a drink, explaining I'm meeting someone. I only make it a few more feet before more fans stop me. They gush. I smile. They hang on me and it takes me almost ten minutes to detangle myself. This shit is getting ridiculous. We're a local college band, not fucking U2.

Usually I like all the attention.

Not tonight.

I'm starting to think Allie took off when I notice her, and her friend, standing at the far end of the bar. I'm hit with a wave of relief, then nervousness. Both are foreign emotions. I push up my sleeves and swagger over to them. Allie's looking simple yet smoking in tall boots, low-rise jeans, and a tight tank top.

Over a sip of beer, her gray eyes meet mine.

"Hi," I say stupidly, stopping a few feet from her.

She blinks and lowers the beer. "Hey."

I almost say "hey" back, like an idiot. We stare at each other, as though there's nobody else in the club. Her expression is a little dazed, but she doesn't look away.

"Well hello, Justin!" The shrill voice of Allie's friend pulls me back to reality as she wraps an arm around Allie's shoulders. She points a finger at her swelling cleavage. "I'm Allie's roommate, Holly."

Giving her a smile, I nod.

"The band was freakin' awesome. Betcha hear that all the time though."

"Enough." I glance at Allie, who's now studying her beer cup like it holds the answers to life's biggest questions.

"And your singing," Holly says, fanning herself. "Amazeballs. What was the one song you did with the violin?" she asks innocently, but there's a gleam in her eye. Allie tries to nudge her inconspicuously with an elbow in the ribs.

I glare at cleavage girl coolly. I'm fairly sure her tits are fake. "'Iris' by the Goo Dolls."

"Yes! That's the one! You sang it so beautifully. Emotion poured out of you." Allie isn't trying to keep her elbowing inconspicuous now. She's going crazy with it. Holly lets out a little gasp and squeezes closer to Allie until the attack elbow is locked between them.

"Dude, where's my shot? My beer?" Sam says, stepping next to me. Allie finally looks up from her cup at the newcomer.

"Well hello. . . ." Holly's lips curl into a seductive smile.

"Sam," I fill in. I hope these two hit it off so Miss Silicone Tits will back off. "This is Allie and Holly." I point to each girl.

His eyes do a double take on Allie, probably recognizing her as the girl I sang "Iris" to, and then do a double take on Holly's chest. He grins at her tits. "Hello back at ya."

Holly unwinds her arm from Allie's shoulders. "Did I hear shots?"

"Absolut?" Sam says.

"Lemon drops?" she replies.

They both laugh and stroll away to hit the bar.

Glancing past me at the roomful of people, Allie chews on her lip ring.

"So . . . ," I say, sidling up next to her and leaning on a stool. "I'm more interested in your opinion than your friend's. What's the verdict?"

The ring disappears into her mouth as she sucks on it. Damn that's hot. She watches the dance floor, where a few people sway drunkenly in pairs, their bodies tightly wrapped around each other's. "The band is really, really talented. And you're not too bad," she adds, her lips curving into a slight smirk.

I snort at her repeating my own words about my singing. "Guess I can live with 'not too bad.'"

She finally looks at me. "You're actually really, really talented."

An "excuse me" cracks into our bubble.

We break our locked gazes to find a group of women surrounding us.

"Could we get a picture, please?" the one at the front asks.

This is getting out of hand.

"Please?"

Allie gives me a look that says, *What is your problem? Just do it.*

What's my problem? I hate fucking cell phones with their fucking cameras at the fucking moment.

"Yeah," I say. "Sure. Of course."

They take turns grouping around me, pressing their tits against me, and "accidentally" brushing my ass, until I'm completely pissed off. Though this is ordinarily amusing, Allie waits to the side, watching the wannabe paparazzi with a guarded expression. Not a good sign.

Once they leave, Allie has her phone out.

I slide next to her. "You want a picture too?"

Her pierced brow rises. "It's getting late. I need to get home. Early morning."

After all the shit I went through to get her here, along with the plans forming in my head, not the words I want to hear.

She glances around. "You see Holly?"

I give a halfhearted glance around the bar. "No."

Allie takes a big swig of beer and sets the cup on the bar. "She's my ride."

My brows rise. "And she's doing shots?"

"She's been drinking less than me. I think." She waves a hand. "We can get a cab, but I really need to find her. Need to go."

I stare at her, wanting, wishing, and hoping.

"The band was really great though. You were great. Thanks for the tickets." She gazes around uncertainly.

Glad for the excuse to touch her at least, I grab her hand. "Come on, I'll help you find her."

Hand in hand, we wander around the huge club. The crowd is finally thinning out. Between her slightly glazed gaze, her slow gait, and the way she's absently leaning on me, I'm starting to realize Allie is a bit drunk. Sam and Holly are nowhere to be seen though we keep searching. I'm guessing they're out back smoking weed, which reaffirms the thought Allie should not be riding home with her friend. I'm pissed I didn't drive. Instead, I caught a ride with Romeo, and he took off with Riley as soon as we shut the back door of the van.

Allie is starting to get fidgety. Her hand grips mine with an edge of anxiety. We're taking a second turn around the bar when I spot Gabe sitting in the corner with his girlfriend. Just my luck that the bastard is the only one around whom I can ask for a favor.

"Hey, come here for a second." I lead her toward the corner, but when we're a few tables away, I say, "Wait here. I'm going to see if I can hook you up with a ride."

I tug at my hand so she'll release it, because there's no way I'm going to take her near toxic Gabe. She gives me a weak smile and finally lets go.

Of course, Gabe looks pissed when I step next to his table. His stick of a girlfriend gives me her usual sex eyes. She gives anyone in a band sex eyes. I ignore her like always. Never been adverse to trailer trash until her.

"Hey, I need to borrow your truck," I say, getting right to the point. Being nice to this asshole isn't going to help.

He reaches for his beer. "Screw that. My truck might be a piece of shit, but your drunk, high ass ain't driving it."

"Haven't had a drink."

The beer in his hand pauses midway to his mouth.

"Sober as your grandma."

"My grandma drinks a bottle of Wild Irish Rose a night." His chin lifts and he nods toward the rear exit. "You haven't gone out back with Sam?"

"Nope, and I need to take her home." I gesture at Allie behind me. His weasel eyes roam over her and I want to punch him.

"That the girl you were singing to?"

"Quit being a dick. Just give me your keys. I'll put some gas in."

He takes a swig of his beer slower than shit to piss me off. Setting it down, he says, "Full tank and I get front next time we go to Detroit."

What is this? Fucking grade school? "Fine."

He slides the keys across the table. "It's parked on the left side of the block."

I snatch the keys up without a good-bye.

Allie watches me cautiously as I step toward her. I lift and jingle the keys. "I can give you a ride home."

She frowns at the keys. "Um . . . could we look for Holly one more time?"

I'm not sure if she doesn't want a ride home from me or doesn't want to leave Holly without telling her. Damn, I'm hoping it's the second. "Sure," I say, grabbing her hand for another tour around the bar. I'm hoping Sam and Holly stay in the alley out back a little longer.

Luckily for me, Holly's nowhere in sight, and in minutes we're outside. Allie doesn't say anything about Gabe's rust bucket as I open the door for her. I can't help noticing the curve of her ass as she climbs in.

Slow down, Justin.

Inside, she gives me the directions to her apartment complex while looking straight ahead. I know where it is. I've been there. Two or three times. Different girls each time though.

As I drive, I try to make small talk by asking about school and the shop. She answers in a monotone, and her answers aren't more than one or two words. Her head's back and her eyes are almost closed. I'm racking my brain for how to save the moment. It feels like we're already at the end of something immense that never truly started. My tat is done. I could do another one, but I need to wait a few months unless I want to appear pathetic. My other choice would be to look like a stalker as I roam around campus on Tuesday and Thursday mornings, trying to act casual while I search for a glimpse of her auburn hair or olive branch–tatted arm or that purposeful gait I've come to recognize.

At the huge complex, she directs me to the building where her apartment is.

I'm strangely, stupidly torn up inside the closer we get. I find a parking spot near her building. She unclasps her seat belt.

"Which one is it?"

She points to the second floor.

"Let me walk you up," I say, unclasping my seat belt. I'm not looking for anything more than to prolong the time in her presence. I'm desperate for more.

I get around the car to find her staring up at a dark window. She wraps her arms around her waist. Sighing, she appears lost and disoriented.

"Allie?" She doesn't look away from the window. "You okay?"

"You don't have to walk me up."

My hand reaches for hers. "I do. I'd go crazy all night wondering if you'd made it."

With heavy-lidded eyes, she stares at me for a long moment. She takes in a deep breath. "All right then."

Hand in hand again, we move across the sidewalk and up the stairs. Her steps are wobbly. On the landing, she almost trips, but as I reach for her waist, she pushes me against the railing, shoves her hands into my hair, and covers my lips with hers, catching me in open-mouthed shock.

Her ring presses into my lip as her mouth moves over mine. Her attack has me against, then bending over, the rail until habit and lust take over. My hands find the small of her back and my tongue the taste of her mouth. She sucks my tongue deeper—holy hell—then pulls away with a little nervous giggle.

"Gah. I've always wanted to do that."

Inside a pant, I say in a low voice, "Kiss me or kiss someone on the stairs?"

Another nervous laugh escapes her. "Maybe both?" She grabs my hand and hauls me up the rest of the stairs.

Still astonished, I let her.

At her door, she surprises me again by falling forward and kissing me. Her mouth is hot and wet on mine. Her hands search under my shirt, caressing my stomach then ribs. She finds my nipple ring. Her thumb circles the metal as her tongue wraps around mine.

Holy double hell.

I grab her ass, jerk her up, and set her on my dick. Her legs wrap around me as we fall against the door. The kissing turns frantic. It sings of sex, sex, sex. Our mouths suck at each other until I pull her head back by her curls and slide my teeth along her neck. Letting out a groan, she sluggishly slides down my body, unlocks the door, and yanks on my shirt to drag me into the dark interior.

Without thinking, I put my hands on the doorframe and resist.

"You're not coming in?" she says, her grip slackening. In the shadows of light from outside her door, her gray eyes glitter with confusion.

I want to. I want her. Bad. But I'm frozen. What the hell is wrong with me? "I can't," I say in a rush of air. "Need to get the truck back."

Her fingers slowly release my shirt, and she steps back. "Oh."

Though the living room is dark, I can read the rejection on her face. I reach for her hand and tug her closer. "I want to badly," I say, brushing her cheek with mine and watching as her lids flutter closed. "I just . . . the truck," I repeat. What I'm really thinking is that this has one-night stand written all over it, with her all buzzed up and not acting like the Allie I'm starting to know. And suddenly, even though every single part of my body is pushing me to walk through the door with her, I know I can't. I'm not exactly sure what I want from her, but the emptiness of a one-night stand and the inevitable awkward morning isn't it.

To avoid temptation, I'm careful not to touch her when I lean down. "But I want to see you again," I whisper into her ear. "Soon." I give in to the urge and let my lips slide over the skin of her cheek. She leans into me. My tongue traces her lip ring. "Let me take you to dinner."

Her head wobbles slightly. "Huh? Dinner? No. Um . . . maybe coffee," she murmurs.

This girl is trying to drive me nuts. She'll drag me into her apartment for sex, but getting a date out of her is like pulling teeth. "Okay then, coffee."

I give her another quick kiss and then take off, rushing down the stairs we just stumbled up before I change my mind and push her inside to take her against the back of the door to her apartment. Getting into the truck, I glance up and see a shadow in her apartment window. By the time I raise my hand to wave, the silhouette is gone.

Chapter 11
Allie

My day has been sullied by a constant headache and a lingering mortification at how I behaved last night. Then there's the burning sting of rejection. I've never considered myself as an amazing babe or anything, but I believed myself to be somewhat attractive. Getting turned down by a known womanizer who has probably slept with more than half of his fans isn't doing much for my self-esteem.

Why, oh why, did I even attempt a one-night stand?

In between intervals of cleaning, going to my parents' for Sunday-afternoon dinner, attempting homework, and lying on the couch, I've found a number of things to blame my stupidity on. Maybe it was because I had the ridiculous notion I'd been serenaded. Maybe it was because everyone at work keeps telling me to get laid. I've also blamed it on the alcohol. But I can't fool myself. Deep down inside I'm aware that my behavior came from the fact I'm head over heels in lust with Justin. Seeing him onstage didn't help. His singing "Iris" to me *really* didn't help. Still, the simple truth is that I attacked him not only once but twice.

I grab a pillow from the couch and place it over my burning face.

Ugh. Superslut Allie turned down by Superslut Singer.

Not my finest moment.

"Mom?"

"What?" I ask from under the pillow.

"Someone's at the door."

I yank the pillow from my face and listen over the TV as Ben frowns at me from the other side of the coffee table. He's right. Someone is *pounding* on the door.

Standing, I step on a Lego. "Fu—" I stop myself from sounding out the *ck* and peel the plastic from the bottom of my foot. After one call from his kindergarten teacher about a few choice words that came out of his mouth on the playground, I'm trying very hard not to swear around him, or anywhere. Thus the swear jar at work that's depleting my extra cash.

"Ben, if you're done playing, please pick these up."

The knocking grows louder.

Ben lets out a big, dramatic sigh that lifts the dark curls off his forehead. "I'm still playing. You said you would play too," he whines as I walk around the coffee table.

"You're right. I did. I'm sorry. I will." Feeling like the worst mom in the world, I ruffle his curls. An adorable smile brightens the blue eyes behind the thick glasses that are held to his little head with a soft elastic strap. "Let's see who's out there first." I open the door to see Trevor standing there. Dressed in a beanie, T-shirt, and jeans, he looks exactly the same as when we were young and in love. Well. We're still young. And at least I was in love. Past tense. That part is very, very important.

Ben flies from behind me into Trevor's arms, yelling, "Daddy!"

"Whoa, trouper, slow down," Trevor says, lifting him and coming into the apartment.

The sight of them together twists my heart. Since Trevor moved to California, I haven't had to deal with this. Now in the past week, this is the second time I've had to watch father and son together. I glare at Trevor. "Why didn't you call first?"

He shrugs but we both know why. Because I would have taken Ben to him since I don't like Trevor in my home any longer than necessary. I'm not against them being together. In fact, time with his father makes Ben happy, and therefore it makes me happy. Real time with his father beats Skyping, which usually happens two times—if Trevor doesn't forget—a week. I just don't want to be included in their father-son bonding time. And ever since he showed up suddenly from California, Trevor has been especially interested in including me, which bothers me. I'm not some booty call because he's in town. I'm not Jazz.

I've refused to contemplate what his return home means because I cannot get sucked down the black hole that took me over a year to crawl out of. Ben helped me get over my depression, and I have no plans to let Trevor back into my life so he can toy with my emotions.

Walking past me, Trevor sets Ben on a dining room chair. "I thought we could go to a movie." He studies my tank and flannels. "Maybe your mom could get dressed and come too?" he adds with a rakish grin.

His smile brings back memories I wish I could forget. Picking me as a partner in art for the first time during high school. Standing by my locker and talking me into our first date while I blushed and stuttered. Teaching me how to ink with incredible patience. Kissing me right before we ran up the steps to the courthouse to get married. I shake my head in reply to his question about the movies, also hoping to shake out the memories. "No can do. I have a painting to finish and a hundred pages of reading to do."

"Aw, come on, Mom," Ben says, tugging at the bottom of my shirt.

"Yeah, Mom," Trevor repeats.

After giving Trevor a cold glance, I brush one of Ben's curls. "I really can't, but you and Dad will have fun together." He gives me a pout, but I say, "Go get your coat and shoes so you can get going."

His little hands reluctantly let go of my shirt, and he takes off down the hall toward his bedroom at the end. Since the apartment is just one big room with a galley kitchen, Holly and I gave him the biggest of the three bedrooms, so he'd have space to play.

As soon as Ben goes through the doorway, I say in a low voice, "Call first next time."

Trevor steps closer to me. "Quit being uptight and come with us."

He's close enough that I can feel the warmth coming off his body and smell his scent. A mixture of ink and spice. I try not to breathe in the familiar scent that brings sadness. Not like Justin's, which makes me a horny slut. "Don't. And I really can't."

He stares at me, then leans even closer. "You know why I didn't tell you I was coming home? Because I knew you'd be like this. I thought if I caught you by surprise maybe you wouldn't overthink it."

Trying to get away from the sudden lurch of my heart, I step back and lean on the dining room table, my hands clenching the edge. "Are you telling me you came back for me?" He nods gently and my stupid heart lurches again. No. No. No. "What about Ben?"

"Come on, Al, you know I care about him. Don't paint me to be the dick."

"If it's about me, why were you out with Jazz? Are you staying with her?"

He lets out a deep sigh. "You know Jazz is a good friend. We grew up together. How many times do I have to tell you if I wanted to be with her, I would've taken her to California?" He gives me an imploring, soft look I remember. In response, I harden my heart.

I cross my arms as my mouth twists into a scowl. "Maybe if you hadn't been sleeping with her through half of our marriage, I would believe you." My hands ball into fists at my sides. "Maybe if I hadn't walked in on you two in *our* bed, the memory wouldn't be tattooed on my retinas."

"Al—"

"Got my shoes on!" Ben says, rushing into the living room. "Tied them all by myself."

"Awesome," I say, letting go of my Trevor anger for the moment and holding up my hand for a high five, then reaching for the zipper of Ben's jacket. We've been working on the tying thing forever.

"We could bring back dinner," Trevor says casually.

I almost roll my eyes at his attempt to weasel his way into time with me. "That's okay. I have leftovers."

He rubs the dark scruff on his chin. "Your mom's Sunday dinner after church?"

"Yup," I say, moving toward the door, jerking it open, and ignoring his hint at an invitation. "He needs to be home by seven. Bed time is nine on school nights."

Walking by me, Trevor says, "It's just kindergarten."

"No later than seven," I repeat, and lean down for a kiss from my son. "Be good," I say after our quick peck.

"Then *we'll* see you at seven," Trevor says as I stand upright.

My reply is to close the door in his sly face.

Once they're gone, I lean against the back of the door. My semi-mended heart suddenly feels vulnerable. I draw in deep breaths, but my eyes still water. One tear escapes while I hold in a sob.

Sliding down the door, I sink, falling back into the emotional black hole Trevor left me in.

Though a constant lingering ache, the pain of the divorce lessened over time. I thought I was living with a tiny ache in my heart, but right now sorrow is tearing through me.

My hands in fists again, I pound on the floor underneath me. Damn Trevor and his bull crap about coming back for me. Though the sight of him brings back a fierce longing for us to be a family, I will never go down that road again. I might always have feelings for Trevor, but because he broke my heart twice, I will never trust him again.

With steely resolve, I unclench my hands, wipe the wetness from my cheek, and push myself up from the floor. I'm so pissed that after two years he can get a rise out of me. I march to the freezer and search for ice cream. Nothing but orange cream swirl, which is Ben's favorite. I'd prefer something with chocolate, caramel, and nuts, but the orange will have to do.

Standing at the kitchen island, I eat a third of the ice cream straight from the carton until my stomach starts to hurt. But it's a better hurt than the emotions my ex-hole induced. After putting the ice cream away, the blare of Nick Jr., Ben's favorite channel, has me searching for the remote. With the apartment now silent, I retreat to the corner by the living room window where my easel sits and begin mixing paints.

Though my Advanced Watercolors class has a grueling pace, with a painting due every other week, I don't mind all the deadlines. I've always found painting therapeutic. I like to make my watercolors unpredictable. Instead of flowers, lakes, and skies, I paint urban scenes of wet cement at night or derelict storefronts or an unfortunate bum sleeping in an alleyway.

My head clears as I focus on capturing the way neon light reflects onto cement and add the shadow of a streetlamp. After deepening other shadows, I clean my paint tray and brushes before picking up the toys strewn all over the living room. Then I sit at the dining room table and read about business fundamentals.

It's both boring and mind numbing, which is exactly what I need after Trevor's appearance.

Yet now that I'm not concentrating on painting, the apartment is quiet and lonely without Ben. The hum of the refrigerator and the sounds from the apartment next door echo in the empty space around me. I turn the page and the sound intensifies my sense of desolation.

When an incoming text beeps on my phone, the *ding* is a welcome distraction.

I go to the counter, between the main room and galley kitchen, where my phone is charging to read the text.

So when we having coffee?

Huh? I study the number. I've never seen it. I text back, *Sorry but I think you have the wrong number.*

Before I make it to the table, my phone is dinging again.

Oh, this is the right number. Holly wasn't that drunk.

I stare in dread at the text. I'm going to tattoo *bitch* on Holly's forehead. Memories from last night, most of which involve my tongue in Justin's mouth, flash through my brain. At last, I faintly recall suggesting coffee. I'd like to reach into the past and slap my shit-faced ass.

My phone dings.

You there?

Why does he want to have coffee with me but not sex? Maybe he really did need to get the truck back. But I wanted—past tense again important here—mindless sex. I don't want coffee. Coffee implies . . . something. Mindless sex implies nothing.

My phone beeps again.

You standing me up?

My fingers drum on the countertop. With a sigh, I type in a response.

11. Tuesday. Coffee shop next to campus bookstore.

After acting like an idiot twice with Justin, I don't have the heart to stand him up.

Though given the way I attacked him last night, I really, really should. I don't want to be Trevor's booty call. Justin shouldn't be mine. But *booty call* about sums up our possible future. There's no way either of us could ever be serious about the other.

Chapter 12
Justin

A few minutes before eleven, I walk into the coffee shop next to the bookstore. It's packed with students working on laptops. In Michigan, when it hits fifty degrees, the people come out in droves. Though I'm early—Romeo was shocked when I got out of bed before ten—I notice Allie already sitting in a corner. Her head is bent over a computer. Her auburn hair shines under the sunlight streaming through the window. My eyes narrow on the cup on her table. I'm kind of pissed she didn't let me buy her a coffee. Like she's stating this isn't a date. Because it's morning? Because it's coffee? As far as I'm concerned, it is a date. I've never met a chick for coffee. I don't even like coffee.

Suddenly, I'm annoyed. Not as bad as at the art show, but I'm definitely not happy. Allie and her mixed messages are fucking with my head. I don't get fucked with. Ever. I whip off my sunglasses and stalk past the girl waiting behind the counter, heading to where Allie's sitting. Another girl I don't recognize tries to get my attention on the way, but I ignore her. I slide onto the stool next to Allie, and her gaze rises from the screen of her laptop.

"Mornin'," I say, keeping my attitude somewhat in check.

"Hey." She offers a slight smile. But those gray eyes are guarded. Always so guarded.

"Thought I was buying," I say, pointing to her cup.

She shifts her legs and crosses a long jeans-clad leg over the other. One of the boots I've wanted to tear off her for a week now tucks behind her calf. She casually slides a curl behind an ear. "Thought we were just meeting for conversation."

Her offhanded attitude doesn't halt my rising anger. I lean toward her. Close enough to smell her familiar flowery scent. "That was before you shoved me against a rail and stuck your tongue down my throat."

The guarded expression in her gray eyes gives way to shock. Her lips part in surprise and I can see the sexy hoop curving around the inside of her lip.

I inch closer and say in a low tone, "Unless the kiss was as fake as our date?" I trace her lip ring with my index finger. "But then, I didn't see Trevor around."

Her eyes change again. Fury fills them. She jumps off her stool, snaps the laptop closed, and reaches for her bag. While I smirk at her, she jams the laptop in the bag. "Fu—screw you, Justin," she hisses, yanking the bag onto her shoulder, then rushing out of the coffee shop.

People around me stare. I don't give a shit.

My anger drops as I notice her lone coffee cup.

Releasing a sigh at my own stupidity, I grab the cup and race out the door too. It only takes me a moment to catch sight of her gracefully hurrying across campus. I'm almost to her as she rounds the corner of the science building.

"You forgot your coffee," I say, catching up with her.

She stops abruptly and snatches the drink out of my hand.

"Listen—"

She turns to go and I reach for her arm.

"Wait. I'm sorry. I was an asshole. You just seem to be jerking me around."

She wiggles my hand loose but turns to me. "Jerking you around?"

"Cold then hot then cold again."

She bites her lip ring and slowly adjusts the bag on her shoulder. "I . . . already apologized for the night at the studio twice. And you know I was a bit drunk on Saturday. I know that doesn't excuse my behavior. . . ."

"You don't need to excuse your behavior. I liked your behavior," I say, then grin lopsidedly, which most girls find irresistible for whatever reason. When the power of the grin brings only a raised barbell in her brow instead of the usual smitten response, I add, "I want to do something with you. No fake dates. No ex-husbands. No fan girls interrupting us. Just us."

She lets out a sigh. "Why?"

Funny how my grin didn't work but honesty did.

"Why?" I shove my hands into my jeans pockets. "I think it's obvious I'm extremely attracted to you."

"I've heard your attraction to the opposite sex is boundless. Besides, since when do you date?"

Fuck. I don't want to imagine what she's heard about me or if she's just making assumptions, but I'm not even going there. I rub my jaw and decide to be straightforward for once. "I usually don't." Her expression remains confused. "But maybe you're the exception," I say, startled by my own admission.

She blinks, then her head shakes slightly. "Justin . . ."

I lean down until our eyes are inches apart. "Come on, Allie. Go out with me. Saturday. I'm practically begging here."

Her hand tightens around the coffee cup between us. She holds it like a shield. "I work Saturday."

"Until . . ."

"Ten."

I step back. "Then I'll pick you up at the shop."

Her chin drops. "I didn't say I'd go."

"You were going to."

She takes a long sip of coffee as those guarded eyes study me. "I can't stay out late."

To say I'm relieved she has agreed to go would be an understatement. "I'll have you home before the Beemer turns back into a pumpkin."

She shakes her head. "You'll have to take me back to my car, so how about I meet you?"

Her reluctance sets me on edge again, but instead of acting pissy, I blurt, "You're *killing* my ego here."

She sighs. "All right, you can pick me up."

I rock back and forth in my Chucks. "Since I screwed that up," I gesture to the coffee shop with my chin, "let me walk you to your car?"

"Um . . . sure," she says slowly.

Her hesitance is the snap of a whip to my confidence, and it leaves a welt and a sharp sting.

As we walk together toward the parking lot, I consider whether her reluctance has to do with Trevor—or my reputation. I'm not sure which would be worse. Either I'm a prick or a jealous prick. And either I have to beat Trevor out or convince her my rep doesn't matter.

This is going to have to be one hell of a date. My brain flips through some ideas as we walk.

"So tell me," I say as we pass the circular fountain in the middle of campus. "You like wine?"

"It's okay."

"Red or white?"

"Ah . . . either."

"Sweet or dry."

"Sweet or dry what?"

"Wine."

"Oh." She glances at me. "Guess I should be honest. I don't know crap about wine. Rarely drink it."

I could bring up sparkling gummy worms, but except for our hot kiss, between her tears and my temper that night is best forgotten. "All right. How about chocolate? Milk or dark?"

"Chocolate?"

"You know the rich, smooth candy that sometimes comes in a bar."

Allie's lips curve into a soft smile. "Both."

A couple of girls walking toward us stare, then stop and whisper like schoolgirls. As we get closer, I realize I've slept with the taller one. Though I don't recall her name, I remember her long legs.

"Hey, Justin," she says. I nod. She gives Allie the once-over. "I'm still waiting for that call."

Fuck. Of course, this shit would come up now. I keep walking. "Sorry. Must have lost your number." Once we're past the girls and on the asphalt of the parking lot, Allie gives me a pointed look. Hands still in my pockets, I roll out a stiff shrug. "I can't help who gives me their number."

"Ah, girls throw their numbers at you?"

I shrug again. "Comes with being in a band."

"Sounds high schoolish."

Bitch slap to the ego. My confidence stinging from the snap of her whip. I let out a deep breath. Stay calm. "Yeah, sometimes it feels that way."

Allie stops behind a black midsize sedan. I'd expect something flashier, what with her owning a business, and a tattoo shop at that. She turns to me. "Well, I guess I'll see you Saturday."

I pluck my glasses from my shirt collar. "Pick you up out front?"

"No. There's a parking lot behind the shop."

"All right. Dress warm."

"Warm? What are we doing?"

I give her a slow smirk. "You'll find out Saturday," I say, turning back toward the dorms. Though I want to, I don't look back. A man has to have some pride. Pulling out my phone, I check the time. My walk turns faster. Jade and Bridget, a cute pair of freshman girls, are probably already outside my dorm room, anxiously waiting for my dirty clothes. I haven't done my own laundry in over two years—a bit of flirting and a few free tickets gets a girl every time. I start jogging. I'm not about to start doing laundry.

Chapter 13
Allie

Todd waits while I set the lock and timer. We walk together to the parking lot. As usual, he asks me about Holly, who I just spent two hours tattooing because she couldn't wait another Saturday to reschedule. He always asks me about Holly after she comes in. He knows she's very taken, but he still asks. I'm not sure if it's the boobs or the tattoos. Most likely both. I rarely take time out to chat with him about anything, much less my roommate. When it comes to the shop, I'm all work and no play.

"You know, Todd, she's never even home," I say. "She's always at Jake's. They pretty much live together." I don't mention that she refuses to officially move in with him until there's a rock on her finger. Of course, Holly would not shut up about Justin for the entire time I was inking her new palm tree—she wants Jake to propose somewhere tropical. I can't imagine what she would have been like if I'd told her I was going out with Justin after work tonight.

Todd pulls his beanie low over his forehead and shrugs. "She's out of my league anyway."

Smacking his arm, I say, "Holly's not like that. She probably would have gone out with you." I knock his shoulder with mine. "If you would have asked her *last* year."

He opens his mouth to say something, but the crunch of gravel interrupts as Justin's Beemer comes into view. Todd frowns at the car. "Al, as a guy, I like him, but you'd better watch yourself."

Though I have my own reservations about Justin—some have to do with his one-night-stand merry-go-round—I'm refusing to overthink it. I don't want to become a jealous shrew ever again. I used to give girls around Trevor dirty looks. If he touched the door handle, I asked him where he was going. I called his phone constantly. None of it helped our relationship—actually, probably hurt it. And I became a crueler person with every look, question, and call. Even though this is only a date, I'm not going down that road ever again.

"Slow down," I say. "He's not proposing or anything. We're just going out on a date, having fun."

Todd twists the gauge in his ear. "Fun, huh? You're not that kind of girl." He nods toward the Beemer. "But he's that kind of guy."

I let out a huff. "I can date a guy and have fun."

Todd's chin lowers as he gives me an even look. "Since when?"

"Since now." He frowns at me. "Relax. I'm a big girl."

"Who hasn't really dated since she got a divorce."

Justin gets out of the car. As usual, even dressed in jeans and a dark blue windbreaker, he's hot enough that I want to push my hands into his messily styled hair and attack.

Todd leans closer to me. "Just beware of going from zero to sixty in like three seconds," he says before walking off and giving Justin a wave.

My teeth grind. If I can be strong with Trevor, surely I can keep Justin at arm's length. Forcing the tightness from my face, I move toward Justin.

"Hey," he says, leaning in and kissing my cheek. "You look great."

Because of the chill still hanging in the March air, I'm wearing jeans, my usual boots, a hoodie, and a pink beanie. Hardly great. "Um, thanks."

"What was that about?" He nods to where Todd is getting into his car.

"Nothing, just work stuff." I slide into the seat. Hoping to end his curiosity, I add, "And I've had enough of work."

"Then no more shop talk tonight," he says, closing the door.

After he backs out of the lot and onto the street, I ask, "So where are we going?"

His sideways glance is smooth. "It's still a surprise."

I roll my eyes and he shifts the car into drive. He only goes about eight blocks, passing the center of downtown and parking on a side street near the river in front of a loud bar. I give him a questioning look. Drinking with a bunch of beer-swilling college kids is hardly a unique idea for a date. He had me all nervous for nothing. And what was with the warm clothes request?

Once we're out of the car, he grasps my hand and we head toward the bar. "Hope this is a first for you."

Confused, I let him lead me across the sidewalk. A sarcastic remark about this date being a rerun since we'd met in a bar last week almost escapes my lips. But a moment later, he surprises me. Instead of going into the bar, we enter a door on the side of the building and climb a long flight of stairs. At the thought of going to his apartment, I'm getting nervous again.

"You live up here?"

"No. I live in the dorms."

He clearly isn't in the mood to explain.

We round a landing studded with several apartment doors and climb another staircase. At the top, he unlocks then opens one of three doors, and more stairs come into view. Since this staircase is extremely narrow, he waits for me to go ahead of him. With him at my back and the unknown dark at my front, I move cautiously.

When my feet connect with a flat surface, I turn to him. "Um . . ."

A light flicks on.

We're standing in a small room filled with stacked chairs.

He smirks at my baffled expression. "Almost there."

I follow him past the towering stacks of chairs to a ladder screwed into the wall. As he climbs the ladder then pushes the hatch above it open, I realize that for whatever insane reason we are going on the roof.

Near the top of the ladder, he holds out a hand for me, and I'm raised into a deep blue starry night. "Oh," I say in awe. Watching me and not letting go of my hand, he tugs me closer to the edge.

"Oh," I say, stunned again as a cool breeze hits us.

The river, its surface dark and oily, is below us. To the right, the docks are lined with bobbing boats, more riverfront bars, and old warehouses turned into condominiums. Their brightly lit windows reflect off the water, casting long shimmering columns of sparkling yellow light. To the left, the town's biggest bridge spans the black water, and the headlights of cars moving across it gleam in the night. Above everything is the clear night sky riddled with bright stars.

Justin's thumb rubs the top of my hand. "The surprise. Your own *Starry Night*," he says, referring to van Gogh.

"*Starry Night Over the Rhone*," I say, recognizing the similarities.

"Yes," he agrees, his thumb still rubbing my skin. "I saw it at the Musée d'Orsay."

Feeling overwhelmed, I study the stars above us as the wind off the water ruffles my hair. My gaze goes back to the view of the river and bridge. "It's beautiful. Who would have thought a view like this existed in our city? I'm not sure which would be better. This or seeing the actual painting." I imagine the strings he had to pull for this. "Thank you."

His eyes are soft and liquid in the shadows of the rooftop. "You're welcome. But having had both experiences, I'd say this is far better."

My heart picks up speed as he stares at me. Feeling overwhelmed again, I turn back to the view. "Because?"

"You're here."

Geesh. Being with me is better than being in France? Desperate to lighten the mood, I say, "Where's the cheesy romance music?"

He inches closer to me. "Tonight's about art, about you."

Afraid of what he might reply next and that leg humping will ensue, I stay silent.

We stand, taking in the lovely view for several minutes until he says lightly, "There's another surprise over here." He motions behind us.

On the curling tar of the roof lies a spread-out sleeping bag. He pulls me down and we sit with our backs against the rough chimney. The ledge is less than five feet from us, leaving nothing to separate us from the incredible view.

There's also a duffel bag, which he is rummaging through. He sets a small battery-operated lantern on the blanket in the few inches between us. "Not especially romantic, but during the test run the wind blew the candles out."

My fingers pull at the material of the slippery sleeping bag. "Test run?"

"Hey, I'm going for perfection."

I watch him open a bottle of wine and don't say aloud that his version of perfection has seduction written all over it. It's also possible that he's trying to take things deeper than simple seduction. I'm not sure which would be worse.

He hands me a plastic cup of wine, then lifts his own and knocks it with mine. "To van Gogh."

"And starry nights," I say, lifting my cup.

"I'm damn lucky that it's a clear night and not raining or cold," he says, looking at the sky. Then he holds the cup under his nose and takes a long whiff. "Tell me what you smell."

I take a sniff. Then another. "Wine. Is it red?"

"You can do better than that."

I take a longer sniff. "Berries?"

He nods.

Sniff. "Cherry?"

Another nod.

Sniff. Sniff. Sniff. "Maybe a touch of something woodsy?"

"Ah, the only thing you missed is the hint of currant."

"Currant? I have no idea what you're talking about. And if this wasn't in a plastic cup, I'd think you were a wine snob."

His teeth gleam when he smirks. "Oh, I'm a wine snob. You can't go to Europe for three summers and not become a wine snob. I'll drink any crap beer but never crap wine." He takes a sip. I watch the shadows along his throat as he swallows it. "Try it. Tell me what you think."

Dragging my gaze from his throat, I take a sip. The liquid's warm and rich and fruity. "It's good. A little dry."

"Good thing I went mild."

"Mild?"

"If it were too sweet, it wouldn't go well with these." He opens a box and I'm staring at chocolates lying in silver little cups. He sets the box between us, then reaches for one. He lifts it to my mouth. "Take a bite."

Seriously shy to be eating from his hand, I take a tiny nibble. It's good. Dense. Creamy.

"Now take a sip of wine."

I robotically follow his orders, but when the wine hits the chocolate, smooth and dry meet rich and creamy—then meld into intense. "Holy crap! It's amazing."

His laugh causes his eyes to crinkle at the corners. "Wait until you taste it with the dark chocolate." He pops the bitten candy in his mouth, takes a drink of wine, and holds out another chocolate for me to bite. "Dark."

With another shy bite, my lips touch his finger. A jolt from the contact has me sitting back and gulping wine.

A boat horn sounds somewhere echoing along the river.

"Good?" he asks in a husky voice.

"Very. Better than the last. So," I say, still holding but setting the cup on my thigh, "I'm curious. How did you come up with this?" I gesture to the roof, then the view.

"It's kind of embarrassing." His eyebrows knit together as he takes a sip.

The wine and chocolate in my stomach turn as I wait for him to admit he's had sex up here or something.

"Romeo, our guitarist, has been pushing the indie route lately. We've been searching for places to shoot a video. This roof is on the list."

All thoughts of sexual escapades fly out of my head. "Why is *that* embarrassing?"

He shrugs and crosses his arms over a lifted knee. "I don't know. I guess going live on YouTube seems over the top. I like to perform.

Going national or international or whatever was never part of what I expected. We're big around here. That's always been enough."

"No dreams of filling a stadium?"

"I . . ." He runs a hand through his messy hair. "Obviously I can't speak from experience, but I imagine the connection I have with the crowd won't be the same in a huge concert. And that connection is what keeps me going sometimes."

Maybe because of his gorgeous exterior, his obvious wealth, and the harem that's apparently available twenty-four seven, I'm always surprised when he deepens the conversation. Like when he talked about his connection to the audience at his shows in the tattoo shop. My cynicism and reservations about him fade into the background. "Except for the glimpse of temper at the coffee shop, I imagined your life carefree."

He turns to me, resting his back against the brick of the chimney. "Everyone needs a bit of light to keep them from the dark, even when they live in a perfect world like me," he says with a trace of sarcasm. "But I like hearing that I'm in your imagination."

"Don't get too excited. My imagination isn't all that wild." I've become good at keeping it in check. In fact, Justin is the only guy I've met since Trevor who breaks past the barriers to enter my imagination.

Setting his cup at the edge of the blanket, he leans closer and the breeze is full of his dark, earthy cologne. "Well, I can't say the same thing."

I let out a nervous laugh. "Please don't tell me I'm running naked through your head."

"Sometimes," he admits as his lids lower and his gaze rests on my lips. "Right now my imagination is tamer."

"Oh," I say stupidly and a little breathlessly as I pull a strand of windblown hair from my cheek. He watches me as if giving me time to grasp the purpose in his eyes. I could turn away from his sensual gaze, look at the view, and end the excitement lurching in my stomach, but I don't want to.

"What I'm imagining right now is this," he murmurs. He bends and his lips brush against mine. Our odd angle against the brick, with my cheek almost brushing the chimney and him shouldered against it, means he can't kiss me fully. Still, his lips press against the side of my mouth with a slow burning heat. The rest of my body hums with anticipation, waits for him to drag me closer and deepen the kiss, but he keeps his hands still, touching me only with his mouth. The slow tantalizing caress of his lips is the drip of a powerful drug drawing me into a cocoon of lust.

Finally, he shifts and kisses me fully, yet still without any other contact. I taste the chocolate and wine on his tongue as he explores my mouth. The plastic cup in my hand cracks in my tight grip, and the sound echoes between us.

He pulls back a bit.

"Sorry," I mutter in embarrassment.

With the shadow of a smile, he takes my cup and sets it next to his. Then he moves the lantern and chocolates from between us. He scoots closer and lifts me halfway into his lap. His fingers brush over the barbells in my eyebrow in a light caress. "This all right?"

Laying across him into the crook of his arm, I let out a breathless, "Yes."

He bends and his lips trace my jaw while his other hand comes to rest on my stomach. His hot mouth slides along my jaw, then pauses below my ear. My head falls back as desire curls through me, a soft pulsating current under the palm across my stomach. He lightly sucks my earlobe, then kisses the line of my neck, the edge of my chin, and the corner of my mouth. Clearly seduction was on his mind, and I have to admit he's doing one hell of a job. I turn my head, desperate for the feel of his lips on mine, but his mouth slides along my cheekbone. He buries his nose into my hair and takes a deep breath.

Unbelievably aroused, I clutch the front of his windbreaker in a silent plea. At last his mouth finds mine. The intensity of the kiss thrusts me back, but his strong arm holds me up. Though forceful, he comes on slow and sensual, exploring me with the sweep of his tongue until I'm desperately exploring his mouth too. The long kiss immerses me completely and it's like I'm floating. Every one of my cells is melting and becoming his to shape like clay.

When his hand slides from my stomach to rest under my breast, I'm waiting, wanting, frantic for him to touch me there. He tears his mouth from mine, and his thumb finally brushes my nipple through my sweatshirt as he whispers in my ear, "What's your light from the dark?"

One word comes at me through the haze of lust. *Ben*. Ben keeps me from the dark and holds me in the light. I sit up in a rush. "What time is it?" I scramble out of Justin's lap, my knees sliding on the sleeping bag as I dig into my pocket and yank out my phone. "I have to go. It's almost midnight."

Staring at me with an unreadable look, Justin runs a hand through his hair. "Yeah, okay."

"I don't mean to . . . I'm sorry."

He recorks the wine bottle, then stands up to pack up the duffel bag. "Just don't leave a shoe up here."

I put the lid back on the box of chocolates. "You seem to know that fairy tale well," I say, holding out the box of chocolates.

"Someone used to read to me daily. Fairy tales were included." He points to the box. "Those are yours."

"Oh. Thanks," I say stupidly, and stand. "Your mother?"

"Huh?" he asks, snatching the blanket up.

"The person who read to you."

He pauses from folding the blanket. "No . . . it was my nanny."

His odd answer keeps me silent as he finishes folding, but seriously, who has a nanny? And who remembers their nanny more than their mother?

We pack the rest of the stuff except the lantern, which he carries to light our way as we head to the ladder. I give the view one last long look. "This was lovely. Thank you for bringing me. And for the wine and chocolates."

With the duffel on his shoulder and while holding the hatch open, he says, "Don't forget about the kisses."

I roll my eyes, stepping toward the ladder. "Yes. Thank you for honoring me with the glorious touch of your lips."

He pulls me into a one-armed hug and gives me a sweet, quick kiss before brushing his lips on my forehead. "Anytime."

Fun. The word springs into my head as the touch of his lips lingers on my forehead. We're having fun. With that thought, I blurt, "Let me plan next Saturday?"

A slow smile spreads across his face as he nods.

Going down the ladder, I'm yelling at *and* thanking myself for blurting the invitation.

Chapter 14
Allie

The next morning, I peek into Ben's room to find him sitting on the floor with pieces of his dump truck Erector set scattered around him. "You have thirty more minutes to play before it's time to get dressed." We always go to my parents' on Sundays, and although Ben loves his grandparents, it's best to warn him about any upcoming departure if it's going to mean pulling him away from a building project.

Without glancing up from his task of connecting two pieces, he asks, "How about thirty-*two* minutes?"

I hide a smile behind my coffee cup in case he looks up. His five-year-old perception of time cracks me up. "All right, thirty-two minutes it is."

"Good." He keeps working and I head to the kitchen. I'm rinsing cereal bowls when my phone dings. Drying my hands, I glance at the text.

Breakfast?

I can't help smiling because Justin wants to see me again so soon. I reach for my phone and type out my reply.

I wish. Super busy.

I set my phone down, but it dings again. I grab it and head toward the bathroom to shower while reading Justin's text.

What are you wearing?

I flick on the water before responding.

Cotton.

Come on.

Tank top and shorts.

White?

Was.

Was?

Getting in shower.

Are you trying to kill me?

I'd send you a picture but they say the imagination is always better.

They're wrong! Send! Send! Holy hell, send!

Gotta go. Shower's running. :)

Late Sunday night, after putting Ben to bed, I'm finishing my business class homework at the dining room table when another text comes in from Justin.

How many tattoos do you have?

A slow grin spreads across my face. Happy for the interruption, I shut my book, push it to the middle of the table, and text back.

Wouldn't you like to know.

Fuck yes.

Six.

Where?

A girl's got to have her secrets.

I'm a man on a secret mission.

I'm busy doing laundry Monday afternoon when my phone dings in my pocket. I finish loading the washer in our little hallway closet, and before I can dig the phone out, it dings again. I'm not surprised to see Justin's name.

Tomorrow. Meet me at the candy shop? Oh, I mean coffee shop.

I actually wish I could meet him. The memory of our date—and, okay, his kiss—has been sustaining me all day long, but I'm booked up with appointments through Friday. After walking into the living room and plopping down on the couch, I text back.

Perv. Can't. Very busy workweek.

Damn. It's gonna be the longest week ever. Feel like a kid waiting for X-mas morning.

Come Saturday there'll be no unwrapping.

Peeking?

You wish.

Hell yeah.

NO peeking.

Licking then?

Licking!?

The sunflower on the back of your neck. I've licked it a thousand times in my imagination.

I'll be wearing a scarf on Saturday.

Just a scarf?

Shut up.

Hours later after dinner, I tell Ben, "Time to pick up the Legos. Then hit the bathroom and brush your teeth. You've already had an extra ten minutes." He lets out a sigh but at least listens and starts tossing the Legos into a bin.

Monday bedtime sucks. I'm not sure why, maybe because it's hard to come off the weekend, but it's definitely the worst.

I finish rinsing out the sink, then wrap up the chicken, broccoli, and buttered pasta that's left over from dinner. When Holly stops in tomorrow morning to get clean clothes and pack a lunch, she'll make good use of it. My phone dings, and I'm expecting the text to be from Trevor, since we still need to make plans for him to pick Ben up from school tomorrow. But it's from Justin.

Thinking of you, wine, chocolate, and that lip ring. I'd like to suck on it right now.

Whoa. I have things to do, like putting Ben to bed and finishing a painting for class. I don't need images in my head of Justin sucking on my lip ring to distract me. However nice they may be.

My fingers fly across the miniscule keypad on my phone.

You are a mean, mean boy. Saturday is my treat, but if you keep this up we'll be going to Mickey D's.

As long as they have a play place, we're good.

Should I even ask?

Tight spaces, small tunnels, close proximity . . .

Okay, no Mickey D's.

In the shop on Tuesday, I try to focus on a sketch for a new client. I bite into a chocolate chip cookie from the pack I snatched from Todd's tattoo room and stare down at the blank paper. It's not a very nutritious lunch, but just getting Ben to tie his shoes was an impossible task this morning, and I didn't have time to pack any food before we rushed out the door. Nor do I have time to go out and get something. Tuesday afternoons were mostly dead in the winter, but now that spring is in the air, they're busy. I had to race from campus to work after class for an appointment earlier, and I have another client coming in ten minutes.

"So your brother is having Todd do his first tattoo?" Shay asks as she folds T-shirts across from my drawing table.

I nod and pull out another cookie.

"Why wouldn't he have you ink him?"

I shrug. "Probably afraid I'll exact some kind of revenge on him."

Shay gives me a funny look. "You two get along great."

"Yeah, now. But when he was fifteen and I was eleven he used to sucker me into doing his chores," I say, stuffing half a cookie in my mouth. My phone vibrates and after I read the text from Justin, I almost spew crumbs.

I keep thinking about calling you, but your voice is too sexy to endure.

I swallow the dry cookie with a gulp of coffee and text back the word that almost came out of my mouth in a screech.

What?????

Yup. It's the first thing I noticed about you.

Get out.

Nope. Before I even laid eyes on you, the sound of your voice practically got me hard.

I fan myself with a piece of paper. Shay raises an eyebrow at the manic speed with which I'm fanning myself. Dropping the paper, I smile weakly at her and then type out my reply while trying to sound nonchalant.

Are you trying to text-seduce me?

Maybe. Is it working?

Maybe . . .

My brain screams, *"Liar!"*—because it's definitely working. Already I can't wait for Saturday night. The only problem is that I can't come up with an idea for our date. Justin used my love of art to plan our night on the rooftop. I'd like to use his love of music for ideas, but since I'm a musical moron, nothing has inspired me yet.

The bell above the door rings as my two o'clock appointment strolls into the shop.

Dang.

I'm hoping I'll have time tonight to figure out something brilliant. Something to wow Justin as much as he wowed me.

Chapter 15
Justin

I'm enjoying the music blasting from the amazing stereo system in my Beemer until I see Sam pulling out his pack of cigarettes. I hit the mute button on my steering wheel and the sound dies. "Don't even think about it."

"Dude," he says. "I'm doing this for you. The least you can do is let me have a smoke."

"Forget it." I take an exit off the highway and start making the turns toward Dragonfly Ink. "You're not smoking in my car."

Sam shoves his cigarettes back in his pocket. "Fine, but I'm smoking before we go in."

"Since when do you smoke all the frigging time?"

He shrugs. "Since when do you chase chicks?"

Ignoring him, I park just out of sight of the shop window so there's no chance Allie will see him smoking. Strangely, I'm worried about her opinion. As soon as the bastard gets out of the car, he lights up. Like I want to stand around watching him smoke instead of seeing Allie.

"Exactly where do I want this tattoo?" he asks, pointing his cigarette at me.

I step back from the cloud of smoke he exhales. "I don't know. Where would you get a tattoo?"

He squints while he thinks. "My other arm?"

Maybe using Sam for this surprise visit isn't the best idea. "Then say your other arm. You've been killing too many brain cells lately. This doesn't have to be scripted out, just act like you want another tattoo."

"Man, this girl has you wound tighter than a coke fiend. You're even stalking her undercover."

"This isn't stalking." I just need to see her. Saturday is too long a wait. I have to know if this building connection between us is as deep as it feels, and seeing her is the only way to find out. I decided that hump day would be the perfect choice for a visit.

"No? We're going in there pretending I want a tattoo."

"You might after checking out her art."

"Naw. I don't like needles. The last one was a bitch to get through. Had to down half a fifth of vodka and two joints." He tosses his cigarette butt to the sidewalk. "Probably a good thing. Keeps me from injecting anything."

We start walking toward the shop. "Who the hell would ink you all fucked up?"

"Some dude. Works out of his house."

"You are an idiot."

He nods. "Must be if I agreed to this bullshit."

"Don't screw this up," I warn, opening the door.

Mandy is behind the counter on the phone. We wander over to the books of photos. Sam flicks one open and feigns interest in the pictures of peoples' tattoos. I stand next to him, scrolling through my phone.

After a few minutes, Mandy strolls over and I introduce her to Sam. She's flirting with both of us when Allie comes out from the back with a customer. She's looking cute, wearing pigtails and a backward baseball cap. Her eyes widen at the sight of me. I give her a grin. Her expression tightens as Mandy runs a nail along the tattoo on my left arm, but Allie doesn't call her employee over, instead turning back to the guy with a Mohawk and leather pants. Douche.

While Mandy giggles and checks out Sam's tattoos, I watch Allie explain after care to the customer. He's all attention, and I'm betting it isn't on what's coming out of her mouth. When he leans closer to her, I'm at the counter in seconds without a thought.

"Hey," I say, and Allie's gray eyes flick to me. She gives me a curt nod but continues to explain how to care for a fresh tattoo. My eyes drill holes into the guy's profile until he finally draws away from her. At least he's a smart fucker.

"Was that necessary?" she snaps when the guy finally leaves.

"What?" I say innocently.

Her pierced brow rises. "Intimidating my customer."

My hand spreads across my chest. "Me?"

She rolls her eyes. "So what brings you out today?"

"Sam's considering adding some more ink." I gesture toward the front of the shop. He's paging through a photo book with Mandy.

"Custom?" Allie asks.

"Yeah, that's the direction he's thinking." Sam isn't thinking shit.

She glances their way again. "Well, since you're here, can I take a picture of your back?"

My lips form a slow and deliberate smirk. "Trying to get my clothes off?"

Her balled-fist settles on a jean-clad hip. "Just your shirt."

"Whatever you want," I say, lifting the bottom of my shirt.

One of her hands covers mine. "Not here. Follow me out back. The light's always best outside."

I grab her hand and hold it tight. "Not until we're alone, huh?"

"Yeah," she says in a sarcastic tone, pulling her hand from my grasp. "Alone in the romantic parking lot."

"I like your sense of adventure."

Shaking her head, she moves toward the hallway that leads to the tattooing rooms. "Let me just grab the camera," she says.

I wait while she ducks into a small room with a desk. She comes out holding an expensive digital camera. I hold the door open to the parking lot and we walk outside together into the bright afternoon.

"Okay," she says, pointing to the brick wall. "Take off your shirt here and—"

"Here? It's kind of cold and exposed. I can't believe you want to get busy here."

She points at the wall. "Get busy? Dream on. As for the cold, it's over fifty degrees out. Models work half-naked in the Arctic Circle. So, tough guy, get rid of the shirt."

Grinning, I yank my shirt off.

She lifts the camera. "Now face the wall."

I turn around and stare at the brick. "I like it when you're bossy. So many possibilities."

"You are impossible," she mutters. I hear the click of the camera several times along with a car driving past the parking lot.

"Okay, you can put your shirt back on," she says, her voice silky smooth.

With my shirt still hanging in my hand, I turn around. "That's it?"

Eyes sparkling, she nods. "That's it."

Suddenly, Mandy whips open the back door. "School just called. Your son is sick. Vomiting and the works apparently."

Nearly dropping the camera, Allie races back into the shop while Mandy's phrase "your son" sends shock waves through my head.

Mandy ogles my naked torso. "Did she get a picture of the front too?"

I drag my shirt over my head and stagger past her into the shop's hallway. Allie is in the office throwing stuff into her bag.

"Cancel the rest of my appointments for the day," she says to Mandy. "Try to reschedule them."

I stare at her. This woman I've been trying to figure out for weeks now. Business owner. Tattoo artist. Student. Ex-wife. *Mother?* She's like a favorite song you're sure means one thing—until you find out the meaning is entirely different.

"You have a son?" I ask numbly, recalling how hard I've tried to be open and honest with her. How much I've dug into myself to make what's between us real, while she's been so obviously indifferent that she didn't even bother telling me she had a kid. A son. How did she not share that?

Passing me in the hall, Allie nods a curt good-bye, but I grab her arm.

"Why didn't you tell me?"

She shrugs. "I have to go."

Her shrug pisses me off. It's like she's dismissing me. "Why wouldn't you tell me about your son?"

"Why does it matter?"

"Because it does," I say, and anger slips into my tone.

"I don't owe you any explanations, Justin."

"Explanations? Don't use that bullshit line on me. After all the things I've told you, your telling me about your kid isn't a fucking explanation, Allie."

"Does it matter?"

"What the hell does that mean? I'm asking why you never said anything. Why wouldn't you say something about him?" With each word my voice rises.

Though her expression is furious, she asks in a calm voice, "Who do you think you are to yell at me?"

One of the hallway doors open and Mac's gray head appears. "What the hell is going on out here? I'm trying to work."

"Sorry, Mac." Her slate eyes shift to mine. "We're leaving." Allie tears her arm out of my grasp. "I don't have time for this. I have to go," she says, and bolts out the back door.

Mac glares at me over his bifocals, then shuts the door to his workspace.

I want to punch the wall. Confusion and anger flow through me. I want to race after her. I want to shake the truth out of her.

"Don't feel too bad," Mandy says. I look up in annoyance as I realize that she has been standing there the whole time. "She doesn't really tell anyone about Ben. I only know because of the possibility of school calling."

My jaw unclenches so I can say, "Didn't know I was 'anyone.'"

Chapter 16
Allie

I'm hungry," Ben says, rolling over and staring at me. His blue eyes are big under the thick lenses of his glasses. With his head in my lap and his body encased in a *Cars* sleeping bag, he appears small and vulnerable. At least his fever has come down since I gave him some kid Tylenol after picking him up from school.

I straighten his glasses. "Toast? Soup?"

He glances at the TV for a moment. Ben is a careful decision maker. Not sure where he got the skill, because between Trevor and me, he should be tremendously impulsive. I've worked hard at growing out of my impulsivity, but my actions lately prove I still need to work at it.

His lips unscrew from a tight knot of thought. "Both?"

"All right." I give his forehead a quick kiss and then scoot out from under him, using a pillow to replace my lap. As I head into the kitchen, I can't decide if I feel happy or pissed that Trevor blew us off. After he called to invite us to dinner, I suggested that he come over and watch a movie with us instead, since Ben is still sick. He declined, of course.

The idea of sitting with a sick kid doesn't appeal to him, even if the sick kid is his own son and it would mean time with me. I'm not stupid. I'm guessing a hookup is part of his motivation right now. But then again, if he really wanted that, he'd be trying to see Ben more. He's been home over two weeks and has only taken Ben four times. Apparently, he has more important things to do than visiting with his son. My guess is those things have to do with Jazz.

Regardless that I'll always wish for Ben's sake that one day we could be a family, Trevor will never grow up. He's good at inking. He's good at partying. He's good at making a girl feel like she's the center of his world, even if it's not true. Being a father? Not so much. And he definitely sucked at being a husband.

If it weren't for Ben, I'd view the years between fifteen and twenty as a total waste. But not all the memories are bad. There are good ones, like Trevor's look of awe holding Ben in the hospital for the first time, Ben smashing his first birthday cake in Trevor's face, and Trevor playing with a newly walking Ben on the beach. But Trevor never cared for the small things, the day-to-day stuff of Ben's life. Teething, diapers, reading books before bed, even following Ben on a tricycle up and down the block—things that would have taken up too much of his valuable time. Time that he could spend inking or partying or screwing Jazz.

I sigh and pull out a can of soup for Ben. As I reach for the bread, my phone vibrates on the counter. Justin's been texting me all day. Other than glancing at the first one, I haven't read any of the messages or even picked up the phone. When I find the heart, I'll erase them without reading. Then I'll have to find the courage to call him and break it off.

As I slide the bread into the toaster, I'm guessing that might take a few days.

Though I've had doubts about dating him from the start, I'm attracted to Justin—okay, really, really attracted—and slamming the door on the chance to be with him is going to hurt a little. Between his gorgeous face and his insanely hot inked body, how could it not? But his reaction today solidified all my reservations. I couldn't tell if he was shocked I never told him or filled with disgust to learn that I was a parent—either way, he pissed me off. His response also made my recent idiocy clear.

I absently grab the butter dish as I wait for the toast to pop up.

A future for Justin and me is implausible. He's a college student and the lead singer of a local college band. He parties all the time, appears to have a trust fund, and hooks up with different women on a regular basis—for goodness' sake, he has *groupies*. I'm a single mother running a business, going to school, and paying her own way. He lives a carefree life. I have too many responsibilities to count. Important responsibilities.

I glance at Ben watching TV as I stir the chicken noodle soup.

If I'm going to date, he has to be someone who is settled in life, knows where he's going, and has a sense of responsibility. I feel old and judgmental thinking like that, but I've been down the Trevor road. Both Ben and I need stability. And Justin is the farthest thing from stable.

I'm aware that many people would call me uptight. Other single mothers date regularly, and don't consider it a big deal. My reluctance is partly because the only person I've ever really dated is Trevor—from when I was fourteen to when I was sixteen. Then, when we got back together after an especially bad breakup, I stupidly let him talk me into marriage. Okay, he didn't have to talk much. I was on cloud freakin' a million after he asked me. But having wedding rings didn't make our problems go away, and less than two years later I was freshly divorced. At the time I imagined being a teenage mother would have guys crossing me off their possible lists. Once I got distance from Trevor though—and got my head screwed on right—I realized I would be crossing men off *my* list.

Shuffling a parade of men in and out of my son's life wasn't an option. And I had no interest in dating someone who wasn't interested in being part of Ben's life.

And Justin, with his harem of fans, doesn't belong anywhere near my empty list of possible men to date.

After cutting the toast into bite-size pieces and letting the soup cool, I take a tray to the coffee table.

Ben sits up. "That smells good," he says.

I'm hoping his enthusiasm is a sign the bread and soup will stay down. I open the cabinet under the TV. "You want me to put a DVD in?"

Chewing on toast, he nods vigorously.

"*The Magic School Bus* or *Sid the Science Kid*?" I ask. I'm not sure where my son got his insatiable curiosity. Except for art, I was never more than a decent student. Trevor was a bad boy in high school and his grades reflected it. But our son is going to be a scientist or a mechanical engineer or something amazing.

"*Bus*," he says through a mouthful of toast.

Done loading the DVD, I move to the couch as he splashes soup all over the coffee table. "Here," I say, sitting next to him. "Let me help."

We watch TV as I feed him soup. Done eating, he curls against me. I let him watch one more episode, then run him a bath. He doesn't play like usual, just lets me soap and rinse. Clean and dressed in warm pajamas, he leans into me.

"Can I sleep with you?" he asks, his mouth a cute pout.

After Trevor left, I let Ben sleep with me far too often. Breaking the habit had taken one hellish month. But when he's sick, I usually cave. "Just tonight," I say, hugging him back. "Tomorrow you're back in your bed."

"Tomorrow I'll feel good enough for my bed," he says firmly with a soft smile. My heart warms.

Ben always melts my heart.

I read his favorite book. He falls asleep. Too tired to do anything but brush my teeth, I trudge to the bathroom. The sound of my phone vibrating on the counter comes at me in the hall.

I ignore it and the tug at my heart.

Because if I do ignore Justin, my heart will be safe. It's not only my practical thoughts concerning Ben that are keeping me from picking up the phone. It's mostly my torn, beaten, fearful heart.

Chapter 17
Justin

"Hey, Justin," Marcus says, pressing a controller and jumping in front of a flat screen. "What's up? You want next game?"

I pause at the door of his dorm room, trying to decide if I can deal with the scene—dorks playing video games.

It has been twenty-four hours since I talked with Allie. She won't answer my texts or her phone. My reaction about her son was fucked up, sure. But her not telling me was fucked up too. And her refusing to communicate with me pisses me off. Then I get pissed because I'm pissed. I don't do this. I don't "care" about girls.

The loud sound of the video game spills into the hall, and I realize Marcus is giving me a questioning look. The guy is in the college marching band, and is one of Riley's best friends. He's been in awe of me since he moved into the dorm in August. His awe pumps my ego. Selfishly, I like my ego pumped. And it seriously needs to be pumped right about now.

"Invite him in and you'll be sitting out, bitch," Marcus's roommate, Don, says.

"Please. Here comes the boom!" Marcus yells as his quarterback throws a bomb across the screen. The receiver catches it.

"Oh, you are one lucky asshole," Don says.

"Luck? It's all pure talent." Marcus glances over his shoulder. "You in?"

"Nah," I say, shaking my head. "Just passing through." Usually I find their freshman antics amusing. Not today. I'm finding them both beyond annoying. And other than at band practice, I rarely get annoyed. I push out of the doorway. "Catch you later."

In my room, I drag my acoustic guitar out of the closet, sit on the bed, and strum the few tunes I know. I'm hoping that playing will distract me from thinking about Allie. I tried doing homework earlier but couldn't concentrate. Yet hearing the chords of the guitar echo in the room reminds me of her. Frustrated, I put down the guitar next to me and pick up my phone. No missed calls. No new texts.

Something snaps inside me, and I lose it. Before I know it, I'm smashing my guitar on the ground. Once. Twice. Three times. Pieces of splintered wood fly all over. Some hit me. Others bounce off the walls and the desk. In seconds, they cover the floor.

Breathing heavy, I'm sitting there staring at the shards of wood strewn all over when a knock sounds. After about the fifth knock, I let out a deep breath, drop the broken guitar stem on my bed, and answer the door.

"Justin!" Riley says, confusion turning her lips down. "What are you doing here?"

"Ah, I live here."

"Shut up. You know what I mean. You're never here."

"Right now I'm here."

She still appears puzzled. "Romeo in?"

I shake my head.

"Huh," she says, still looking confused. She twists her ponytail between her fingers. "He's supposed to meet me here. Can I wait inside?"

"You don't really want to come in," I say from behind gritted teeth.

"Why?"

Reluctantly I let go of the door handle and head for the bed, sitting down with a sigh.

"What is that?" Riley asks, staring at the pieces all over the floor.

I shrug. "What's left of my guitar."

After shutting the door, she takes a couple steps into the room and picks up a piece of wood. "You smashed your guitar?"

"Apparently."

"You and Romeo fighting again?" she asks, her voice low.

"Nope. This one was all me."

She picks up some of the bigger pieces and tosses them into the trash. "Must be nice to be able to afford to smash things."

"Please don't remind me that I'm a rich prick."

After staring at me for several seconds, she falls on the other bed across from me. "What's going on, Justin?"

I rub my temples. "Nothing."

"So you look all devastated like something awful happened *and* smashed your guitar for no reason?"

"Yeah."

"No."

She stares at me with a stubborn expression. Riley really is a decent person, even if she is madly in love with Romeo. But I don't talk about feelings. Because usually, other than the occasional flash of anger at my bandmates, I don't have them.

She crosses her legs. "So?"

I scowl at her.

"Why did you smash your guitar?" When I don't answer, she persists. "Well?"

"Because I fucked up."

"Big surprise there," she mutters.

My eyes narrow.

"O-ka-ay," she says, drawing out the word. "What did you mess up?"

When I'm silent, she gives me an expectant stare, drops her chin in her palm, and waits.

"I kind of lost it with this girl I'm seeing."

Her eyes get big. "You're seeing someone?"

"Kind of."

"Do tell."

"There's not much to tell."

Riley glances at the mess on the floor. She gives me a pointed look.

I run my hand through my hair. "She doesn't want anything to do with me, and I'm not taking it well."

Her expression conveys that's obvious. "Why do you think she doesn't want anything to do with you?"

"Who are you, fucking Dr. Phil?"

"What are you? A five-year-old who can't talk about emotions? Just answer the question."

The kid comment hits a nerve. I lean my elbows on my knees and sigh. "Probably my rep. And because I'm an ass," I say, hissing out the words. "And most definitely because I freaked out when I found out that she has a son."

Riley's eyes widen.

"We met like a month ago. We went on a couple of dates." There's no way in hell I'm explaining to Riley that the first one was mostly fake. "We've talked. We've texted. She never said anything about a kid. I found out about her kid in a roundabout way earlier today."

Her fingers tap the metal frame of the bed in a slow, rhythmic beat. "So she was never serious about you."

I stare at her with amazement. There are so many unfamiliar emotions warping my thoughts that Riley understands the situation more clearly than I do.

"But were you serious about her?" she asks, her tone questioning.

"I . . . She's different. There's something about her, something in her eyes. They're lonely or . . ."

Riley stares at me to the point her eyes almost pop out of her head. "I'm shocked," she says. "I'd never expect—well, you use girls for one thing, you know?"

"Yeah, and now I know why."

"Maybe you need a couple scars on that heart of yours." She kneels on the floor and starts tossing more of the broken guitar pieces into the trash. "Other than her lonely eyes, what's different about her?"

"Well, she has an ex-husband to go with the son." I bend and toss in the pieces closest to me.

Her mouth turns down in distaste. "What the—? You hooking up with a cougar?"

A sad laugh escapes me. "Not exactly. She's only twenty-two."

"Well, that's different, but how is *she* different?" Riley taps her fingers on a broken piece of wood, obviously waiting. "What else about her has you so hooked?"

"I don't know. She—when we're together, there's no bullshit between us. She makes me feel real. I haven't felt real in a long time." I rub the back of my neck. "I know that sounds stupid."

"No," she says, and shakes head. "That makes it sound like you shouldn't let this girl go."

Suddenly, Romeo is standing in the doorway, looking between us. "What's going on?"

Riley stands and brushes the knees of her jeans. "I'm waiting for you. Justin's playing rock star and smashing guitars."

Romeo glances at the mess on the floor. "What the fuck? What instrument you plan on playing next Saturday?"

"I'll get a new one," I mutter.

"Damn right you'll get a new one."

I scowl at his bossy ass.

"Come on." Riley winds an arm around Romeo's. "Let's get something to eat."

He smiles at her and she smiles back. For once, I'm truly jealous of their relationship.

"See you later," Riley says over her shoulder as they leave.

Once they're gone, I slam the broken stem against the mattress in frustration. I'm about to slam it again when a guitar riff comes out of my phone.

At the sight of the name on the screen, the stem falls from my hand.

After picking up my phone, I cautiously say, "Mom?"

"Hello, Justin," she says in a formal tone. I swear the older she gets, the more uppity she sounds. "I'm calling you back."

"I called you almost a month ago."

"We returned this week."

Not today. Or even yesterday. They got back days ago. "I'm pretty sure they have phones in Barbados."

"We were getting away."

"From your son?"

"Please quit the dramatics. What was the reason for your call?"

To talk to my mother, but the need is fading with each passing second. "Can't remember."

"Well, if your memory comes back, we're home now, but please don't call past ten."

"What if it's an emergency?"

"Then call the local authorities, that's what taxes are for. Besides, what am I going to do across the state?"

"Give a shit?"

"How lovely. Drama paired with vulgarity. Good night, Justin."

She hangs up, cutting off my response.

After tossing the phone on my bed, I forget about smashing my guitar stem against the bed and start beating it against the garbage can, trying to forget my mother's icy, nasal voice. Even more than that, I want to forget the reason why my temper exploded in the first place.

Chapter 18
Allie

I slowly climb the stairs to the apartment above the tattoo shop, pulling up my hood to ward off the cold rain. I've been putting off talking to Shay, but Trevor keeps bugging me to increase her rent. Usually, I'd agree. I tend to make decisions with a business head when it comes to the shop, but with Shay, it's a different story.

After noticing her wandering the streets one too many times—in the cold, in the rain, late at night—I started talking to her when I'd see her in the parking lot or passing on the sidewalk. Then I started inviting her into the shop. At first, it was just a few minutes at a time. I'd give her sodas or cookies or candy—Todd has a wicked sweet tooth—and say good-bye. But eventually she started showing up at the door more and more often. Within a month she was a regular at our pizza and takeout nights. And gradually her story started coming out.

Shay's mother not only parties constantly, but she goes through men like some women go through shoes. As Shay got older, the boyfriends started hitting on her. One even tried to get into her bedroom late at night. After that experience, Shay made a point of leaving the house whenever her mom brought a new boyfriend home. Sometimes she'd hang out at a friend's house; other times she'd roam the streets until four or five in the morning. Neighbors told her they'd reported seeing her out late, hoping that notifying child services might change her mom's behavior, but nothing happened.

Working at the shop was Shay's idea after hearing that I was advertising for another receptionist. When she asked about the job, she also asked about the FOR RENT sign in the window of the studio upstairs. I thought about it for maybe a total of fifteen minutes. Between her work hours and renting to a minor, the whole thing was illegal any way you looked at it, but then, Shay hanging out on the streets was dangerous. Even though we don't live in a high crime city, I knew something would eventually happen to her.

Illegal or not, I decided to hire her. The local authorities obviously didn't want to fix the problem. Between my parents and some friends, we rounded up enough used stuff for the studio apartment and Shay settled in. I didn't have the heart to charge her much rent, so we agreed on a few hundred bucks a month. She's been working for me for over a year. I've watched her change from a timid, sad girl to a happy, independent almost adult. She used to miss school regularly. Now she goes in the morning and co-ops at the shop. She loves working at Dragonfly Ink. Looks to Todd and me as older siblings, but she hates that we won't ink her until fall, when she'll turn eighteen.

I don't mind breaking a few laws but I do have my limits.

I knock once on the door and she yells, "Come in!"

"What's up, Al?" Shay turns to me from where she's standing at the tiny sink, washing dishes, and smiles. Her mother is on the couch smoking a cigarette.

"I need to talk with you about something," I say, closing the door behind me.

"Sure," says Shay.

I glare at Shay's mother. "I've told you this is a nonsmoking apartment." I've also told her if she ever brings one of her boyfriends over, I'll tear out every last strand of her bleached hair. I've never been violent in my life, but I'll go nuts on Shay's mom if she ever makes what has become Shay's safe place feel the opposite.

"Oh yeah," she says, stubbing out the cigarette onto a plate of half-eaten macaroni and cheese. "Right." The look in her heavily black-lined eyes is not friendly. She nods to Shay. "Thanks for lunch. Gotta get ready for work."

She works nights at some dive bar. Her shift won't start for hours. She's making a lame excuse to get away from me. I'll take it. To say I can't stand this woman would be an understatement. I loathe her. But she's Shay's mom.

Shay sets a dish in the strainer next to the sink. "You coming for lunch next week?"

"Sure thing, kid," her mom says, escaping out the door.

Funny, Shay's offering to cook for her mom. Funny in a sick twisted way.

I go lean against the counter and decide to get right to the point. "Trevor saw how much I was charging you for rent. He wasn't too happy."

She pulls out a towel and starts drying. "Guess I can see why."

"He wants it doubled. I agreed to increase it by a hundred bucks a month, but I can give you a raise after he leaves to make up for it."

Shay frowns. "How about more hours?"

Of course, Shay would just want to work more. "Not until you graduate." The girl has raised her GPA to a three-point, which is impressive considering where it was a year ago.

"You already pay me too much. Two dollars more than Mandy. How is that fair?"

"Mandy stands behind the counter looking pretty and you actually work. You're the only one who cleans, stocks, files, and does anything else I ask."

Shay twists the towel in her hands. "I can probably cover fifty more each month. Can you loan me the difference until May?"

I knew this was going to be difficult. It wasn't easy to get her to accept the last raise either. Between her independence and her pride, Shay can be sensitive. "Fine."

"It's only two months, right?" Shay says, trying to appease my apparent irritation. Without waiting for my answer, she lifts a pot off the two-burner stove. "Want some homemade macaroni and cheese?"

I shake my head. "Already ate, but how do you stay so damn slim?"

Scooping the gooey mess into a plastic container and capping with a lid, she tilts her head, lost in thought. "Isn't *damn* considered cussing?"

I push off the counter. "I'd better go."

"I'm pretty sure it's on the cussing list."

"What list? And they say it on TV." I turn the doorknob.

She shoves the container of macaroni at me. "Would you let Ben watch those shows? You have a pretty strict TV list when I babysit."

We stare at each other for a long moment while her lips twitch. I grab the container. "Fine," I say through clenched teeth. "I'll put five in the jar as soon as I get downstairs."

Her laugh follows me as I descend the stairway. I might want to pull her mother's hair out, but I wouldn't mind giving Shay's curls a tug now and then either.

I get to the bottom of the stairs and stand there, frozen at the sight of Justin getting out of his Beemer. Raindrops hit my face as emotions run through me: guilt, anxiety, desire. Along with a strong urge to run back upstairs.

He's over to me in an instant, "Hello, Allie."

My stomach tenses. "Hey," I say lightly, stepping onto the sidewalk. "What are you doing here?"

His gaze is flat. "Came to talk to you, obviously."

I snap at the idea of his forcing me into communication, "One would think my lack of response to your phone bombardment would make it apparent I don't want to talk." My nails dig into my palms.

He crosses his arms over his chest. "I'm not one for being ignored."

I glower at him. "I'm not one of your adoring fan girls."

"I never treated you like you were." He leans close. "So why are you treating me like a piece of shit?"

Between my awareness I have been rude and his stern, unrelenting expression, I cave. "Okay, let's talk." Not wanting Mandy or Mac to see us, I move to the side of the building even though we're getting wet in the cold rain. He stands across from me. Too close.

This isn't going to be easy. "Look, I'm sorry for ignoring you. It was rude, but I couldn't find a way to explain there isn't any point in us continuing to date."

"*Point*? What the hell does that even mean? I just wanted to get to know you. I still do. But obviously you were playing me the whole time. Why else wouldn't you say something about Ben?"

My face flushes in exasperation. "I wasn't hiding that I have a son. Between text flirting and swapping spit under the stars, my son didn't come up, but it's possible . . ."—I pause and frown—"okay, probable, that I didn't want to share that part of my life because—"

"You were never serious about me," Justin fills in with a tight tone.

Cringing, I nod slowly. "I was trying to keep things light between us. Ben is the most important thing in my life. He'll always come first," I say stubbornly.

"He should. But what does him coming first have to do with me? With us?"

I groan. Explaining what's going on in my head is just too messy. "You're the lead singer of a band. From what I hear, you're also the king of one-night stands. I know you get fan girls to do your homework." He raises an eyebrow at me. "Yeah, when I saw you at the library it was clear as day. We're at different places in our life." His jaw tightens but I can't help adding, "I have to be responsible. You live carefree."

He rests a hand next to the brick on the side of my head and leans close. I swallow tightly. His eyes roam over my face too long. "My past is my past. I can't change it, but I can tell you this—haven't slept with anyone since I met you. Not saying there weren't opportunities or I didn't consider it. But since we met, nobody compares to you. Those other girls don't have your soulful eyes. Or your sexy voice. Or that lip ring. I want you. And I've only wanted you since the first night at your shop."

The clearness of his gaze and the conviction in his voice make my breath catch. And his words about me? What girl wouldn't be awestruck by this moment? As I look up into his face, the rain falls over both of us and his one-night-stand merry-go-round fades into oblivion. The sincerity in his expression and voice make every part of me want to believe him.

"And you're right," he says, stroking a wet strand of hair away from my cheek with a gentle finger. "I'm practically responsibility free, but I'd like the responsibility of making you happy."

"Justin . . . ," I say as my knees threaten to buckle.

He leans until our noses almost touch. "I can make you happy, Allie. Don't tell me you don't feel the connection between us. Don't give me excuses about responsibilities. You can be with me and still run your shop and be a good mother. Quit trying to extinguish the possibilities between us."

He's seducing me with words and with his touch, and my entire body warms as his finger traces the line of my cheekbone. He's disorienting me and getting past all my reservations except one.

I reach up and catch his hand, pulling it away from my face. "Like possible heartbreak?"

His fingers grip mine and he gently touches his forehead to mine. "You don't think I'm confused too?" He draws in a deep breath. "You terrify me. I haven't opened my heart in a long, long time. Shit, I was sure I didn't have one. But somehow you cracked it open without even trying."

My heart tightens at his words, at his openness. Feeling completely overwhelmed, I step away. Tugging at my hand, he tries to pull me closer. "I just need some space to breathe and think, Justin."

He quits tugging but doesn't let go of my hand while calm patience fills his moss-green eyes. Raindrops trickle along the strong lines of his face and drip from his hair. He's so beautiful I can't consider anything else with him in my sight.

I glance down at our hands, and his words wash over me like the rain that's pelting down. I don't have time to make myself happy, but my heart tells me it could be possible with him.

Inside, I feel like I'm falling but I want to keep things slow. I say, "Maybe we could start over." I peer at him through rain-wet lashes. "Saturday night? Like a first blind date?"

His expression is placid as he nods gently, but his grip tightens on my hand.

"I have to go," I say. He doesn't let go. A smile escapes me as I tug. I gesture to my wet hair with the hand that's still holding the macaroni container. "Really. I have an appointment to get ready for."

He finally releases my hand. "I suppose we're strangers right now."

I laugh as we walk around the corner of the building. "Until Saturday."

The purr of the Z4's engine sounds as I enter the shop, then right inside the door, I stop short, startled. Trevor is standing in the window, watching Justin drive away. "You still seeing that douche bag?"

"It's none of your business who I'm seeing." I march past him to the counter.

He follows me. "But it is my business who sees Ben."

I whip around. "We've been on a few dates. He hasn't even met Ben. And I'm not planning on it anytime soon."

He leans on the counter. "How about never?"

"When are you going back to California?" I glare at him.

He drums his fingers on the counter. "How about never?" His smile is not warm.

I'm getting tired of Trevor and the constant reminders of our past that tear through me each time I see him or hear his voice. Though I feel like ripping open the plastic container and smashing the macaroni in his smug face, I say, "Since you're into the word *never* at the moment, let me be clear it applies to us." With that I leave him standing at the counter, looking pissed.

Chapter 19
Justin

S aturday night takes forever to come, but when Allie opens the door to her apartment, the sight of her makes the wait worth it. The smile on her face is warm and welcoming, and her gray eyes are bright. She's dressed simply in a tank and flowing skirt that doesn't reach her knees, and she looks beautiful from the top of her head all the way to her sandal-clad feet. Those bare legs are going to drive me shit-crazy all night. The nerves I tried to conquer in the car detonate inside of me at how badly I want this second chance to be perfect.

"Hello." She gestures for me to come inside. "You must be Justin."

I grin at her way of starting over and roll with it. "And you must be Allie. Your picture on the website doesn't do you justice. You're far more beautiful in person."

"Ah, thank you," she says, laughing.

Stepping inside, I hand her the flowers and bottle of wine in my hands. Sam is getting sick of me dragging him to the wine store, but by summer I'll be legal.

Her smile grows. "You didn't need to bring anything." She lifts the bouquet of sunflowers, and whatever else the florist put in there. "But they're lovely."

"There's need and there's want. I *wanted* to."

Still smiling, she shakes her head slightly. "Well, I suppose we did need the wine. I didn't have time to get creative. Busy week at work. So we're having dinner here."

"Sounds perfect."

She shuts the door and I glance around the apartment. If I keep looking at her, we won't be eating dinner.

We're in a big, carpeted room with a small dining table at one end and a leather couch across from a TV at the other. The tall tiled counter/bar behind the table opens to a narrow galley kitchen. Everything is plain and simple, from the wooden table to the cotton curtains. Except for the paintings on the walls. They're bright and vibrant. I walk to one that hangs above the square dining table. Decrepit old buildings lining the edges of the painting frame the colorful swirling sky at its center.

"This yours?" I ask as she sets the wine on the counter/bar and reaches for an empty vase near the sink.

"Yes . . . you like?"

"It's amazing." I lean closer, studying the paint strokes. "There appears to be a contrast with the deteriorating buildings and the beauty of sunset."

"Pretty much what I was going for," she says, unwrapping the flowers and turning on the kitchen faucet.

I move toward the painting above the couch. "Your son?"

"Yes, Ben at two months."

The wide-eyed baby lies in a bright blanket, with swirling colors leaping out of the painting. I let out a low whistle. "And I thought your tats were good."

Setting the flower-filled vase on the table, Allie smiles with satisfaction. I'd love to see that look in bed. "Thank you. That's quite a compliment coming from someone who has been to as many museums and galleries as you."

I glance at a painting of wilting sunflowers, obviously van Gogh inspired, in the kitchen. "You're almost too good to be inking."

"I used to think so. At first." She frowns slightly and absently rearranges the flowers in the vase. "There's just something about creating on skin. Having someone put your work on their wall doesn't compare to them letting you permanently mark their body. Body art doesn't stay home. It's carried around all the time. Forever."

"Unless it gets removed."

"Well, yes, there's that. . . ." Her lips tighten. "Though it's quite the ordeal."

From her expression, I'm guessing she might have firsthand experience with tattoo removal, but I want her look of misery gone, so I tap the large bin of Legos at the end of the couch with a foot. "These yours?"

She blinks innocently at me. "Of course. I love Legos."

We both laugh until she bites that lip ring and a ping of lust has my nerves twitching.

She knits her eyebrows together and frowns slightly at the bottle of wine on the counter. "I'm not sure I have a wine thingy to open the bottle."

I tilt my head in thought. "Well, instead of pulling it out, we could push it in."

She gasps.

A laugh bursts from me. "I'm talking about the cork, you pervert."

She turns pink. "You must be rubbing off on me."

My lips twitch as I hold in another laugh.

Her pink cheeks grow red. "Ugh," she says, with a deprecating tone. "I need to shut up. We need to eat." She moves toward the kitchen.

Digging a wine key from my pocket, I go to the bar.

Her eyes narrow on the corkscrew as I twist it in. "You are the perv. You set me up."

I give her an innocent look.

"Fine, two can play at that game. Pour yourself a big glass of wine. You'll need it after the extra spice I'm going to add to your dinner."

I lower my eyelids seductively. "I like a little extra spice."

She reaches into a colander next to the sink and whips a noodle at me. I catch it before it smacks me in the face. "I can get naked and lie on the table, if you want to eat off me."

A laugh escapes her. "You are awful," she says, turning to the stove.

After tossing the noodle back at her, I pull the cork out. "Should I have brought glasses?"

She pretends to glare at me and yanks the noodle from her arm. "We have glasses." Her lips push together and that damn ring catches my eye again. She glances around the small kitchen. "Some-where."

She searches high and low for wine glasses, bending and stretching to reach inside the cupboards until I have to look away. Never thought something so innocent would rile me up so much.

"Ah, finally" she says, reaching into the cabinet above the refrigerator.

Finally is right.

She sets two champagne flutes on the counter. I'm not about to comment on the difference between wine glasses and champagne flutes. "Why don't you go pour and I'll plate."

I reach for the glasses. "Don't forget my extra spice."

"Don't tempt me."

The table is already set for two, with bright linen and silverware. At opposite ends. Glancing at Allie busy in the kitchen, I move one setting next to the other. Allie raises an eyebrow when she comes in with two steaming plates but doesn't say anything about the new table arrangement.

She sets the dishes down. "Hope you like chicken pad thai."

I glance at the chicken, sauce, and noodles. "Never had it, but it smells great."

"You like spicy, right?"

"I think we already covered that."

She lets out a harrumph and sits. "It's too spicy for Ben, so I rarely get to cook it."

I spear a piece of chicken. "How old is Ben?"

"Five," she says. She watches me mentally doing math as I chew. "I had him at sixteen. Well, I was almost seventeen."

Fuck. That's way too young to be having a kid. Afraid I might blurt the words, I point to the food. "This is really good. Nutty and spicy." I twirl some noodles onto my fork. Then keeping my tone light, I ask, "So how does that happen?"

She blinks at me in confusion.

"I mean, I know how it happened. It's just . . . what about protection?"

Her gaze turns level.

"Shit, I'm sorry," I say, realizing how she's construing my question. "I wasn't trying to be rude. It's probably—no, *definitely* none of my business," I mumble, wondering how I'm going to dig myself out this time.

The barbells in her eyebrow drop. "Sometimes condoms don't work."

A twinge of horror runs through my body and I blurt, "Don't tell me that."

"But it had more to do with alcohol and other substances that lead to not being careful."

Still scared shitless at the thought of a condom not working—I mean, I've heard about that but never known anyone to have a *kid* because of it—it takes me a few seconds to understand what she's saying. I give her an astonished look. "You?"

"Prior to being pregnant, way too much." She shrugs. "After I got pregnant, never."

"I'm having a hard time imagining you as a wild partier."

"I wasn't until I started dating Trevor. And really, only when I was with him. Trevor ruled my world from the moment he noticed me in art class at the end of freshman year. It didn't help that he was a junior."

Trevor is the last person I want to talk about. He's the one big *if* between us. I try to change the topic in a subtle way. "Was it tough being pregnant and going to high school?"

"At first no. I was kind of in my own little bubble trying to figure out the changes happening to my body and life." She stops cutting a piece of chicken, and sets her knife on the edge of the plate. "But when I started showing, people did act a little weird, even some of the teachers, and that made me feel weird too. My life changed faster than I could mentally keep up. Trevor had already graduated, so my social life at high school was almost nonexistent except for my art friends. Then he broke up with me and got back together with Jazz."

I frown. I'd imagined they dated, had Ben, graduated, then married.

She picks up the knife again and absently taps at the edge of her plate. "The pity came at me in waves from people I didn't even know. I started hating school. All those pitying looks reminded me of my heartbreak."

Taking in her sad tone, I admit, "I would've quit."

"After I had Ben in the summer, I went back senior year for about a month. But it was stupid for me to spend seven hours sitting around with high school kids while my baby was in daycare. I decided to take the GED and go to community college for a couple of classes."

"And then marry the dick who left you," I say, unable to stop myself.

She reaches for her glass of wine but stares at her plate. "I should have learned the first time, huh?"

I do not want to talk anymore about fucking Trevor, who is obviously a major fuckhead, and the idea of his having power over her makes me set down my fork. "Allie, you're beautiful and sexy." Her grip tightens around the stem of her glass. "But everything else about you is amazing too. Your direct personality, your talent, the way you handle your business, your commitment to your son—I'm attracted to it all. The idea Trevor would leave you is mind-boggling."

Eyes wide, she lifts her glass with a trembling hand. "Um, wow, I'm a bit taken aback but thank you." She takes a sip of wine and clears her throat. "What about you? What was high school like for you?"

Since she appears a bit shaken by my revelation, I lightly say, "It was all right. I played football and ran track. Partied a lot. Got semishitty grades. The ACT saved my ass for college."

"I imagine you were popular."

Her tone is light, but I'm guessing that coming from her little art circle the popular thing bugs her. I shrug. "In some ways, but I never had real friends like you. More like a circle I partied with."

Watching me, sadness crosses her face.

Feeling like I opened up too much, I absently twirl more noodles on my fork. "So tell me about Ben."

Her face lights up. "He's in kindergarten this year. He's read over thirty books so far. Granted, they're like ten pages long, but he's really smart. He loves science and anything to do with building. He was building complicated Legos structures by the time he was three."

I don't catch everything she says about Ben. It's hard to pay attention to her words when her face is so animated and open. She's never been like this with me. We keep eating and I keep asking about Ben and she keeps talking, all the way through dessert, a rich, chocolate cake she made from scratch. She smiles, she laughs, and her eyes are a warm gray while she talks. I'm enjoying listening to her, which is something I never do. I rarely want to talk with women. There's usually far more interesting things to do with them. But watching Allie's glow as she talks about her son has me more than content with the conversation.

When she clears the dessert plates, I refill our glasses and follow her into the kitchen, where she starts rinsing plates.

She glances over her shoulder. "I just want to let them soak. I can do the dishes later."

I set the flutes down and reach for the towel lying on the counter. "Go ahead and wash them. The least I can do is dry after you cooked such a great dinner."

"Ha. You live in the dorms." She reaches for a scrubber sitting on the back of the sink, and I catch a glimpse of her sunflower tattoo. "Anything not out of a box or fast food wrapper is five stars."

"True. I should own stock in frozen burritos. But then I've eaten in restaurants across Europe, thus my compliment does carry some weight, and dinner was great, Allie."

Smiling slightly, she hands me a dripping washed plate. "Thanks."

"Thanks for cooking."

"Student exchange?" she asks, scrubbing at a pot.

It takes me a second to realize she's referring to my travels. "Vacations," I say, drying the clean dish. "My parents are quite the globe-trotters."

With a sideways glance, she studies me for a long moment while I dry another plate. "What exactly do your parents do?"

"My father's a retired surgeon. My mother's a socialite." I hold up the clean dishes and give her a questioning look.

"Set them there." Her hands in sudsy water, she nods toward the peninsula between the galley kitchen and main room. "I'll put them away when we're done." She turns back toward the sink. "My father works in a car parts factory."

The message in her tone is loud and clear. We were raised worlds apart. I dry a pan and set it next to the plates. "Did your father spend time with you as a kid?"

She gives me an odd glance as she rinses a spatula. "Of course."

"Well, mine was too busy. Then too tired. Money isn't everything."

She nods at me. "Very true." She places the last pan in the rack. "Didn't they take you to those museums?"

"My mother shopped. My father relaxed. I wandered."

"Oh, wandering alone in huge rooms full of art," she says, letting the water out of the sink. She doesn't turn around but says, "That sounds unbelievably lonely. Too lonely for a teenage boy, Justin."

At the pity in her voice, I toss the towel on the counter and step behind her. Pity is the last thing I want from her. I wrap my hand in her silky hair and drop the curls over her shoulder, then brace myself against the counter with my other hand. "I didn't have it too bad. I got to see this, right?" I touch my lips to the sunflower at the base of her neck.

"Yes," she whispers as her body trembles.

Kissing the flowering ink is all I intended to do, but the way her body trembles at the touch of my lips pushes me to move my mouth up to her hairline. "You smell like sunshine," I murmur, my lips grazing her skin.

Her entire body quivers. Her fingers clutch the edge of the counter while mine grasp her hip to steady her, or maybe to steady myself. My lips follow her hairline and brush alongside the soft skin of her ear. I take the soft lobe into my mouth. She gasps and turns toward me. That's all the invitation I need.

"I bet you taste like it too," I whisper, covering her mouth with my own. She tastes like wine and chocolate—reminding me of the night on the roof—and like I said, sunshine. The little sigh she lets out when my tongue slides into her mouth has me pinning her to the counter. She kisses me back, running her tongue along mine slowly then exploring the roof of my mouth, and desire shoots through me like lightning. I pull away for a moment, my fingers digging into her hipbone, but unable to help myself I close in again and start sucking at the corner of her mouth, then lick that sexy ring.

She gives another little moan and presses her round ass against me. I let out a low chuckle. Fuck. Something has to be released because I'm more wound up than a drummer on coke. After one damn kiss. And we're still fully clothed. Holding her hips and resting my cheek on the soft skin of her neck, I feel like the thirteen-year-old boy I used to be, all crazy and wound up after nothing more than a make-out session.

Our heavy breathing fills the kitchen. She still doesn't move, simply stands there as heat builds between our bodies. We're motionless as we press into each other, but my hands have a mind of their own as they slide up and cover her breasts. Her breath catches. The sound of it is too sweet. Shit. I need to slow down before I have her skirt up and I'm taking her in the kitchen. I do not want our first time to be in a tiny kitchen against the cupboards. But she's too damn sensitive as she leans forward, pushing her breasts into my palms, and sighing, "Justin."

The way she says my name reverberates to my gut. I can't help slipping a hand under her tank and bra. My fingers explore and caress her skin. She moans and bends farther over the sink until I almost lose it.

Oh shit, we're not going to make it to a bed, I think as my lips glide along her jaw while my other hand drops below the counter between her and the lower cupboards. Desire comes off her in waves as her body shudders. My tongue slides between her open lips as my fingers press between her legs and start to explore. She lets out a deep moan and almost bucks me away. My fingers circle and press. Her hips follow the movement. Then gripping the counter until her knuckles are bone white, she melts and trembles beneath me.

Amazed at how responsive she is, I slow the kiss, cupping her as she comes down. When she exhales, I brush her ear with my mouth. "Where's your bedroom?"

Her eyes pop open. She blinks twice then starts twisting in my embrace. Obviously, that was the wrong question. I release her and step back. She scoots to the far end of the kitchen. "Whoa, that was—that was—"

"Enjoyable?" I brace myself between the two counters and take a deep breath.

"Intense." She swipes her glass off the counter and takes a huge gulp. Her nervous eyes catch mine. "I know I came on strong the night you brought me home, but . . ." She takes another gulp of wine. "I've never been with anyone except Trevor, and obviously"—she blushes—"it's been a while. I may need time before—before . . ."

I'm stupidly ecstatic she's never been with anyone other than her ex. Though I'm still wound up tighter than a teenager, I say, "Hey, I'm not in any rush. Like a fine wine, I can wait for things to mature between us."

She blurts, "I'm sorry."

"Why are you apologizing?"

"After the way I acted the other night, I thought you might think . . . Well, especially here alone in my apartment and me being a single mother . . ." She stares at the wine in her hand.

I step forward and gently lift her chin. "I'm not going to lie. I was hoping. I've wanted you since that first night at your shop." She's frozen still as I stroke her skin with a thumb. "But I don't want you to feel pressured, and I sure as shit don't want you to have any reservations. I want it to be perfect." I lean closer until my lips almost touch hers. "It may be as tough as hell for me, but anytime you feel like we're moving too fast just tell me." Unable to resist, I give her lip ring another soft kiss. "Okay?"

She nods slightly but still appears nervous.

I've never wanted a girl's trust, but I want this girl to trust me. Bad.

My hand slowly drops from her chin. "It's a warm night. How about we end it with a walk?"

She stares at me like I have two heads but finally says, "All right. Let me get a jacket." She steps around the peninsula and opens a closet in the living room. I drain the rest of my wine in one gulp, then open the door for her. Stepping outside, she glances at me and there's a slight curve to her lips—and maybe a hint of trust in those granite eyes.

Chapter 20
Allie

With the breeze ruffling his dark curls, Ben rushes up the ladder on the slide for about the fiftieth time, and for about the fiftieth time I yell, "Slow down!"

He grins at me but at least climbs slower.

"Kid has a shit grin," Holly says, sitting next to me on the bench. She tightens the hood around her head. Dressed like a bum in sweats for a Sunday afternoon in the park and dealing with a hangover from hell, she doesn't want anyone to see her. "Reminds me of—"

"Don't say it," I warn.

She pulls her hood tighter around her head. "I was going to say you. Not asshole Trevor."

"Oh, since when do I have a sh—crap grin?"

"Used to before you became so freaking serious about everything." She opens the box between us and takes out a doughnut with thick pink frosting.

Irritated by her comment, I blurt, "I had a date with Justin last night."

The pink pastry pauses inches from her lips. "You're shitting me."

"Nope. I made him dinner. We went for a walk. We did dishes together."

"Oh really?" She lets out a loud snicker. "Did you hold hands too?"

"Quit. Things did get a little heavy at one point."

"What?" She sits back, her lips twisting. "You sat on the couch and sucked face like teenagers?"

I snatch the doughnut from her hand.

"Hey!"

I take a big bite, and through a mouthful of sugar I say, "I actually, embarrassingly, had a lovely orgasm in our kitchen."

She pulls back, eyebrows raised. "From sucking face?"

"Shut up." I toss the rest of the doughnut at her but she misses catching it by a mile.

She snatches the pink mess from the ground and picks pieces of grass from the frosting. "Went on a walk, huh?"

I shrug. "It was nice. We talked about Ben, his music, and my parents. His parents sound like rich jerks, but he isn't." Ben rounds the slide again.

Holly flicks a pebble off the doughnut.

Frowning at the pink disaster, I say, "Why don't you get a different one?"

I get the infamous Holly "duh" look. "Because this one is pink." She nibbles at the pastry, then says, "He sounds like he's really into you, Al."

My fingers flip open the box. "Yeah, I'm starting to worry about that." What I don't say aloud is that I'm worried about how my feelings for him are growing too.

"Why?"

I snag a cinnamon twist. "Everyone tells me I need to date. Everyone tells me to get out and have fun. And Justin is fun. But he's not someone for the future."

She sighs dramatically. "Just have fun. Justin's a big boy. Quit worrying about everyone else and worry about your—no, scratch that. Just have fun. No worries. You're twenty-two not frigging thirty." She pops the rest of the pink mess into her mouth.

"Twenty-two and a mother." I sigh and toss the twist back into the box. "I don't know. Guess I'm worried about things turning serious."

"News flash." Holly waves her hand in front of my face. "You're not getting married. You're not even in serious territory. You're having *fun*." She leans back. "Geez. I swear sometimes it's like Trevor sucked all the life out of you."

"Well, I'm seeing Justin again on Tuesday. To have *fun*," I say, jabbing her with an elbow. "We're meeting for coffee, okay? I'm not running away like normal."

"Coffee? How romantic," she says sarcastically.

"It's a bit hard to plan whirlwind dates when I have a child to take care of."

Holly flicks a wrist. "Go out. I'll watch the little terror."

"Thanks, but between school and work, I don't feel like I'm home enough."

"Oh, Allie, you're the best mom ever." She grabs my hand and squeezes it. "If anyone deserves some fun, it's you."

I squeeze her hand back. "I thought Trevor was fun, Holly, but look where that got me." I glance at my son climbing the slide steps. "Though I wouldn't trade Ben for all the pain in the world."

"Forget about Trevor. He's the past. And he's an asshole." She forces my hand open and shoves the cinnamon twist into it. "You're going to start living, dammit." She stands and hauls a bag of old bread out of her hoodie pocket. "Come on, Ben! Let's go feed the ducks!"

Nibbling on the delicious sugary twist, I grab the doughnut box and follow them to the mucky pond across a stone bridge covered in goose crap. We throw bread at the ducks floating in the mud-colored water and are soon surrounded by birds squawking at us for food. Holly starts backing away in terror, which sends Ben and me into a fit of giggles. She throws the bag of bread at us and we finish feeding the ducks, still laughing, while Holly retreats to a bench behind us.

The walk back to our apartment complex is along a trail that used to be railroad tracks, and it takes about twenty minutes. Ben rides circles around us while Holly whines about the killer ducks. Unfortunately, when we get to the front of our building, Trevor is there, waiting and leaning on Jazz's car. She's driven the same stupid Trans Am since high school. Good thing the skank isn't in sight.

Of course, Ben yells, "Daddy!" He drops his bike and runs over to Trevor.

"Hey," Trevor says, messing Ben's curls.

"What's with the car?" Holly asks.

He glances at her dismissively. "Mine's in the shop." His gaze roams over me. "Thought we could all go out for ice cream."

I frown at the car as I imagine how many times he and Jazz have had sex in it. "I'm not getting in that."

He shrugs. "We can take yours."

"I have homework to do, but I'm sure Ben would love to go out for ice cream."

His smile fades. "I want to take both of you."

"Yeah, Mom, you should come with us," Ben says from Trevor's side.

Bending to pick up the bike Ben left on the sidewalk, I say, "Sorry, have to paint. Holly's supposed to pose for me tonight."

Holly nods vigorously and strikes a pose with her hand on her hip, fluttering her lashes.

Trevor ignores her. "Then maybe we can bring back dinner instead. Pizza?"

Ben nods yes and I don't have the heart to say no. "Okay, but remember it's a school night."

Trevor opens the door for Ben. "Oh, we'll be back soon."

He starts the engine and I wave to them with my free hand. Through a fake smile, I ask Holly, "You can go to Jake's later right? And stay for pizza?" I need a Trevor buffer big time.

She frowns. "What? I hate that asshole."

"Half off on your next tattoo?"

She grins. "You bet your sweet ass I'm staying for dinner."

Chapter 21
Justin

On Tuesday morning, I race to the coffee shop. Finding time to spend with Allie is hard enough as it is, and now my stupid ass is running late. It took me twenty minutes to find a pair of halfway clean jeans in the piles of clothes littering my room. Wrapped up in Allie, I haven't been doing my flirtatious rounds across campus. Thus my laundry ladies haven't shown up for a week. And since I can't imagine making those kinds of rounds again—flirting with other girls kind of turns my stomach—guess I'll be hitting the basement in the dorm later.

The coffee shop is half full of students talking and studying. I notice Allie, in pigtails, sitting at a table in the back, and it crosses my mind that doing my own laundry might not be so bad. Then I notice the guy standing by her and stalk over there faster than I moved across campus. The douche bag pauses midsentence as I glare across the table at him.

"Hey, Justin," Allie says. "This is Greg Gains from my water-color class."

I don't say anything. I simply glare at watercolor boy, who is standing way too close to my girl.

He gets a clue and steps back. "Aren't you the singer for that band . . . ?"

"Luminescent Juliet," Allie fills in while giving me a level look.

"Yeah, that's it," Greg says, bopping his head like an idiot. "I saw you guys at the Razor on New Year's Eve. Great show."

I just nod.

Finally noticing the tension in the air, he yanks his beat-up backpack from a stool. "Guess I should get going."

No shit, dickhead.

Allie smiles weakly. "See you in class on Thursday."

I pull a stool close to hers as Allie glares at me.

"What?" I ask, trying to downplay my obvious annoyance.

"Don't ever do that again."

"Huh?" I ask innocently.

"You know perfectly well what."

My booted foot finds the top rung of the stool and I wrap an arm around my knee. "He was practically sniffing your hair."

Her glare continues as she turns her computer toward me. There's a row of flowery paintings on the screen. "We were looking at these and discussing them because we have to comment on them online. For class."

"Well, he didn't have to get that close to discuss, did he?"

"Justin," Allie says evenly, "I've been warding off men for over two years. I'm practically a pro at it. Do not go caveman on me. I do not appreciate it."

I lower my knee. "Caveman?"

Nodding, she twists the paper coffee cup between her hands. I give the cup, then her, a slow, assessing look. She takes a sip. "Let it go. I buy my own coffee. Women's lib and all that."

"Is that what women's liberation is all about?" I lower my elbow to the table and rest my chin in my palm. "Here I thought it was about equality and shit, but it's just about buying coffee and talking to watercolor boys."

She smiles. "Yep, it's sisters doing it for themselves."

My brows rise. "Really, whatcha doing to yourself?"

She blushes but her smile turns into a smirk. "Wouldn't you like to know?"

"Hell yes." Unable to resist, I remove the cocky grin from her mouth with a quick kiss. "You know, I don't like coffee unless it's on you."

She checks to see if anyone is watching us.

"Don't tell me you're embarrassed by a little public affection," I growl.

Her fingers grasp the edge of the table. "It's been a while. I'm not used to it, so be patient with me."

I reach for her hand. Unfortunately, a stack of papers slaps on the table in front of me before I can touch her. With fists on her hips, Lila stands across from us. "Well hello, Justin."

What the hell is this? It's like they come out of the woodwork whenever I'm with Allie on campus.

Lila gestures to the papers. "I've been carrying these around, hoping I'd run into you." Her lips curl into a sneer. "Because you can do your own damn paper." Her eyes flash from me to Allie. "Or maybe *she* can do it for you. But if you aren't going to return my calls, I'm done being your homework bitch." She whirls away in a huff and stomps out of the coffee shop.

People around us stare. I ignore them but Allie appears embarrassed. I catch her hand and hold it underneath the table. "Part of the charm of being with me, I'm afraid. My baggage might be endless for a while, but like she said, I haven't called her."

Allie tugs her hand away and rests it on top of the table. "If you weren't such a jackass, then there wouldn't be all this baggage."

I grab her hand again and bring it up for a quick kiss. Her gray eyes blaze smoke at me but I don't let go. "You need to be patient with me too. After years of being a jackass, I can't change overnight. And my past, no matter how much I want it to, isn't going to go away. But my past is past. And the future is full of possibilities. I want to be with you and only with you."

Her lips are a thin line until she lets out a sigh. "We should stop meeting on campus. Too much of your past is present here."

"You might have something there." I finally let go of her hand and cross my arms. "How about letting me surprise you again on Saturday night?"

"I can't leave work early again. And Ben's not going to my parents' as usual, so I have to get home for the babysitter."

"What about Friday?"

"Babysitter again."

My arms tighten across my chest. "Sunday?"

"No, we're going to—" She stops abruptly.

I can't help think she's going somewhere with Trevor, which has me crazy insane. My chin drops as I glower at her. "What's going on Sunday?"

Her gaze flicks to the screen of the computer still open on the table. "Nothing. After church and dinner at my parents', Holly and I usually do something with Ben on Sundays."

"Oh." When we went for a walk the night she cooked dinner, she explained why she doesn't want Ben to meet me until we've dated for a while. I get it. Kids need stability. And I'm willing to spend time together around her time with Ben and work. Yet being last on her list makes me feel like she punched me in the gut or something.

She frowns as she watches me.

The dejection inside of me grows. I'm used to it. Trying to hide my obvious hurt expression, I ask, "How about I make you breakfast next week at your place? Monday?" I add, knowing it's her day off.

After nodding, she bites her lip ring while she slowly closes her computer. "Maybe you can meet up with us on Sunday? Like, pretend to run into us and I can introduce you as a friend from school?"

I really do want to meet her son since he's the most important part of her life, but I don't want to push her. "I thought you wanted to wait a while."

"It's not that I don't want him to meet *you*." Her fingers drum on the table. "I don't want him to know we're dating. Things like that are a big deal for a kid."

"Where are you going?"

"State park, to explore some trails and picnic."

"Wouldn't it be a bit odd? Me running into you out there?"

She shakes her head. "Ben's smart, but he's five, Justin. He wouldn't find it odd at all."

"All right. Nature's not my thing, but to see you, I'll explore it to the fullest."

Allie is smirking at me when Riley plops her backpack down on the table and sets a huge blueberry muffin on top of it. "Hey, Justin." She looks from me to Allie, eyebrows wiggling. "Who's your new friend?"

I'm guessing Allie thinks that Riley is another blast from my past, based on the sour expression on her face.

Unable to stop a grin, I say, "This is Allie. Tattooist extraordinaire. And this is Riley, ex-drummer of Luminescent Juliet and our guitar player's girlfriend." I shoot Allie a smug look that says, *See? I haven't screwed the entire female population on campus.* Sure, at one point I did make a move on Riley, but that was to get Romeo's perfectionist panties in a twist more than anything. It was obvious he had it bad for the girl from the first moment she walked into our audition. After a couple of band practices, it was clear she had it bad for him too. I pretty much knew from the start it was a no go.

Allie's expression softens as Riley scoots onto the stool across from us. "As of now, I'm the current drummer of the Bleached Blondes, the best two-member band you've never heard of. Or maybe we'll be called Rowdy. Or possibly the Brassy Dolls." She frowns. "Obviously, the name is a work in progress."

I frown. "What are you talking about?"

Riley grins slyly. "I'm starting a band. Romeo's helping me with auditions. I'm hoping it will be an all-girl band, but hey, if that doesn't work out, boys may be welcome. As long as they like loud and fast."

"All-girl sounds cool," Allie murmurs.

"Why the hell would you do that?" I ask, slapping my hand on the table. "Why don't you come back to us?" I'd love to get rid of ass-wipe Gabe.

Riley pauses from tearing the paper wrapper off her muffin. "You worried about the competition?"

"Ha. No. I'd like to get rid of the dick behind the drums. I'd rather deal with you and Romeo making out in between sets than him."

Riley's head shakes and her ever-present dark brown blonde-streaked ponytail swings behind her. "I'm not doing that to Gabe."

"Why not?" I snap.

"Because you and Romeo would be at each other's throats again if Gabe wasn't around, so I can't take his spot. Besides, you should give Gabe some credit. He's been working really hard, Justin."

"At being an asshole," I say under my breath.

Riley tosses her muffin paper at me. "We're not going to be anything as serious as Luminescent." She catches the paper I whip back at her and turns to Allie. "So how long have you been inking?"

"Over six years."

The muffin pauses on the way to Riley's mouth. "You must be good."

"She's better than good. Check this out," I say, turning and lifting my T-shirt.

Riley lets out a low whistle. "That is awesome. If I ever get the courage, I know where to go."

Allie digs out a card from her bag and slides it across the table. "With the right artist, it's not *that* painful."

We spend the next half hour talking ink and music and school. Riley doesn't leave, which is on the verge of irritating me. I don't get to spend much time with Allie as it is. But in the end, it's not too bad. I like Riley, and miss her being in the band, and she and Allie have hit it off.

When it's time for both Riley and me to take off for afternoon classes, Allie packs her stuff too and walks us out. After saying goodbye to Allie, Riley goes to read the message board outside the shop. The kiss I give Allie feels way too quick, and I promise to call her.

As I'm watching her walk toward the parking lot, Riley comes to my side. "I really like her, but you'd better not screw this up with your manwhoring ways, Justin."

"Rile, I'm a changed man."

She lets out a harrumph of disbelief.

I hoist my backpack to my shoulder. "Since I met her I've been as celibate as your man was back in the day."

Riley's eyes just about pop out of their sockets. "No shit?"

"No shit," I say, understanding her skepticism.

"Huh." She lets out a low whistle and glances at the empty sidewalk where Allie had disappeared around the corner. "Maybe I should be worried about you."

"Huh? I thought you wanted me to stop my manwhoring ways."

Forcing a smile, she says, "Forget it. Come on. We're both in the Lit building."

"Bullshit," I say, following her. "Why would you say that?"

She shrugs. "You've never been close enough to someone to get hurt."

"Why are you assuming she's going to hurt me?" My tone is exasperated.

Just as we separate to avoid a group of students in the middle of the sidewalk, she says over her shoulder, "I'm not, but things don't always work out like we want them to."

When we rejoin on the other side of the little crowd, I let out a huff. "Just because you and Romeo have had problems doesn't mean everyone will."

She adjusts the backpack on her shoulder with a bounce. "Here's the thing, except for a shaky start, Romeo and I worked. It was everything else that wasn't working."

"I'm not Romeo. Allie's not you."

"Justin, you're not dating a college coed whose biggest worry is her social calendar, GPA, and hair color. Allie has a son, an ex-husband, and a business."

"So she can't date?"

"Sure she can date." Riley lets out a sigh as I open a door to the Lit building for her. "But even though you've pulled a three-sixty, she has bigger commitments than a boyfriend—and you need to be aware of that."

"I'm aware."

"Okay, just don't smash any more guitars," Riley says. Starting up the stairway, she adds, "Catch you later."

As Riley disappears around a landing, thoughts of Trevor hit me. I'll never forget the look on Allie's face at the art show when she saw him. Though I have a hard time believing she'd toy with me if she was still in love with that asshole, I haven't known her long. She doesn't seem like the type of girl who would lead me on or use me to fill in for her ex, but Trevor *was* the reason she went out with me on that fake first date.

Chapter 22
Allie

I step out of my car and stare into the dark antique shop window, wondering if this is a good idea. The muffled sound of loud music comes from above as I lean against the driver's door. After Justin told me where they practice, a place not too far from my shop, the thought of stopping by and seeing him before going home had stuck with me all day long. Now, standing here, the entire idea seems rather stupid because, essentially, he's at work. Yet I want to see him if only for a minute or two. Hearing his voice later while we talk on the phone won't be enough to sustain me until Sunday, still three long days away. I try to ignore that he's starting to fill my thoughts all of the time. Which means I *really* should not be here.

The music ends and I tap my fingers on the roof of my car. This would be the perfect time to make my unofficial entrance, but I don't move. Suddenly a door at the far end of the old building opens and Sam steps out. After lighting a cigarette, he glances over and catches me leaning on the car.

He blows a stream of smoke. "Allie, right?"

Pushing away from the car, I nod.

"Looking for Justin?" he asks, running a hand over his buzzed hair.

"I wanted to say a quick hi, but if the band is too busy . . ."

He grins. "I have a feeling Justin will never be too busy for you. Give me a minute and I'll take you up."

I hesitantly step onto the sidewalk. "If you're sure I won't be interrupting."

Sam blows out smoke with a laugh. "Romeo's a slave driver. Trust me. We all look forward to interruptions." His head tilts as he studies me. "Tell me something. If I showed up stoned, would you ink me?"

I blink at him, then slowly say, "Ah no. You would need to be fully sober."

He tosses his butt in a can by the door. "Knew you were going to say that," he says, hauling the door open. He waves a hand in a rolling gesture. "Ladies first."

With a deep breath, I step inside and ascend the long, narrow staircase.

"What if you didn't know I was stoned?" Sam asks from behind.

Been there, done that. "I'd know," I say over my shoulder.

He chuckles. "Well, I wasn't expecting that."

At the top of the stairs, I step into a room illuminated by naked light bulbs hanging from the ceiling. The place clearly hasn't seen a contractor since it was built. Justin stands with his back to me, leaning against the rough slats of a wooden wall and studying a sheet of music. The floor is made from worn, rough boards. With his profile almost hidden in the shadows, and dressed in faded jeans and an old T-shirt, he blends in with his surroundings. The image of him has me wishing I had a camera to perfectly capture the sight and re-create it in a painting.

"What the hell, Sam? You know the rules." The voice comes from the direction of the drum set. The guy behind it is glaring as he tightens a knob on the front of the kit. He impatiently tosses his head to get his longish light brown hair out of his eyes.

I turn back toward the stairs at the harsh sound of his voice, but Sam wraps an arm around my shoulders. "She isn't here to see me. She's here for lover boy."

Justin looks up and his green eyes widen in surprise.

A tall, dark haired guy steps out of the shadows at the far end of the room. He snaps a phone shut. His jaw hardens, and I realize he's the guitar player, Romeo. The slave driver. "It doesn't matter who she's here to see. She doesn't belong up here."

As his dark eyes flash to Justin, I'm ready to fly down the stairs, but Sam's arm is tight around me. This was an awful idea. "I'm sorry. I just—"

"No need to be sorry, Allie," Justin says, his voice even lower and more steely than Romeo's. He shoots a cold look at Romeo first, then at Gabe. "Get your arm off her, Sam."

Sam chuckles, but he releases me.

"I should go," I say. I wonder if a room can combust from angry stares as the band members glare at one another.

Tossing the sheet music on a box, Justin says, "Not a chance."

"Justin," Romeo says in an obvious warning tone.

Ignoring him, Justin comes to my side—close enough that I can smell his dark, earthy cologne—and wraps an arm around my waist. "This is Allie. You've met Sam." He gestures to the drummer. That's Gabe." He then nods toward the guitarist. "And that's Romeo." Obviously done with introductions, Justin drags me across the room. "Give us five," he says, pushing a small door open and then pulling me into the darkness.

"I should have called," I say, but before I can get anything else out, he shoves me against the back of the door and covers my mouth with his. With his body pressed into me, his hands wrapped in my hair, and his mouth devouring mine, the kiss is hot and luscious. For several minutes, instead of oxygen, Justin is the air I breathe.

He pulls away slightly and I nearly sigh in disappointment.

His thumbs brush the skin of my neck and I shiver. "This is a nice surprise, but why are you here?"

Both his touch and voice are amplified in the darkness. Searching for the belt loop of his pants, I say, "Just wanted to see you." I tug him closer until he's pressed to me again. "And I guess I wanted this too," I say. I tug his head down and kiss him as hotly as he kissed me, exploring every crevice of his mouth with my tongue.

He pulls away with a gasp. "Damn, you picked a hell of time." His lips slide along the skin of my cheek and I instinctively wrap a leg around him. He cups my butt and slides me over him. At the hard feel of his desire, lust sizzles through me. We're wrapped around each other and both heavily sucking in air. Why, oh why, did I slow things down the other night?

"Think they'd hear us?" he whispers hotly into my ear, and I can feel the chuckle he releases.

I rock against him and he groans into the skin of my neck. "I don't care."

"Shit, Allie. You have to stop or I'm not going to be able to."

Not only do I not stop, I push my hands under his shirt, grasp the muscles of his back, and touch my lips to the hollow between his collarbones.

"Allie," he says in a warning tone while groaning.

As my tongue darts out to taste his skin, a knock sounds at the door. "Ah, Justin?" Sam loudly says.

Our bodies pause while intense desire flows between us.

"Out in a minute," Justin yells, untangling himself from me.

Separated from him, I feel the fog of lust that's blanketing my brain clear.

Embarrassment at what we'd been doing while Justin's band members were on the other side of the door rushes through me. Slapping my own forehead, I groan—but mine is entirely different than his was minutes ago.

Without touching me anywhere else, Justin leans his forehead against mine. "I'll be done in less than an hour."

I shake my head. "I have to pick up Ben from my parents'."

Justin draws in a deep breath. "Can you stay for one song?"

The idea of facing his bandmates on the other side of the door, much less watching them for an entire song, isn't too appealing. "I don't think they want me here. I should go."

"Justin!" Sam bangs on the door again.

"Just one song, then I'll walk you down."

Bang. Bang. Bang. "I'm going to come in there!"

"One song," Justin repeats.

Bang. Bang. Bang.

"Fine," I say. "One song."

He yanks open the door and pulls me out of the weird closet or room we were in. Three sets of eyes stare at me. Sam stands next to us with a smirk on his face. Lifting a guitar strap over his head and letting the guitar hang from his neck, Romeo appears irritated. Gabe sneers from behind his drum set. A telltale blush warms my face and I try to escape Justin's embrace, but he holds me tight.

He nudges me toward a line of folded chairs along the opposite wall. "She's going to stay for the next song, then I'll walk her out."

Romeo's hand clenches the bottom of the guitar strapped around his neck. "Justin, I told you about bringing—"

Justin releases my shoulders as he whips toward Romeo. "One song, and don't even say what I think you're going to. She's not like that."

Gabe leans across his drums. "If anybody would be able to tell, it would be you."

Justin's fists tighten and he takes a step forward, but Sam comes between him and the drum set while I'm seriously thinking of sneaking down the stairs. For a group that plays awesome together onstage, I'm surprised at the animosity hovering over this dusty room.

"Leave it alone, Gabe," Sam says, for once sounding serious. "She doesn't know our rules. She just stopped by. J. didn't invite her, so quit acting like a dick."

Gabe continues to sneer but sits back without saying anything.

Justin turns to find I've taken a couple of steps toward the stairs. He comes over to me and says, "Don't worry about them. You came to see me." He gently pushes me onto a chair. "Just one song," he repeats.

Deciding to ignore the hostile atmosphere, I nod. "Okay, but get playing so I can go."

He gives my hand a squeeze, then moves toward his bandmates.

"What song did you have in mind?" Romeo asks him in an irritated tone.

Justin steps to the microphone in the middle of the room. "How about 'Echo'?"

Romeo rolls his eyes but says, "Fine." He nods to Gabe, who lifts his sticks and hits them together several times. Romeo starts playing a soft and slow but driving melody. Justin wraps his hands around the microphone and leans in as close as possible. I move to the edge of my seat.

Justin takes a deep breath and starts singing. His gaze meets mine and I hardly hear the words as I watch him intensely sing to me. Despite the shadows, his eyes bore deep inside me and I feel like I'm not only connected to him but also open to him. I notice the rest of the band only after Justin closes his eyes and sways to the music. Romeo watches his hands move across the stem of the guitar. Gabe nods as he plays the drums. And Sam has a content, almost sleepy look as he plucks at his bass.

Justin's eyes open and take hold of me again as he sings. Whenever he sings, it's like he's singing to me. Well he actually is this time, but he makes the song seem like it was written for us. His piercing gaze ensnares me, pulls me into the song until we're connected and riding the same wavelength of emotion. For this brief moment, I'm reminded of what he said in the shop—that we understand each other. Both of us recognize the longing, physically and emotionally, floating between us.

The song ends and his gaze devours me.

I'm instantly on my feet, ready to leave. And Gabe's and Romeo's irritation isn't the only thing pushing me toward the stairs. The sense that my soul has been opened up, and read, adds to my desperation to flee.

Taking the first step, I murmur, "Thanks, bye."

Justin follows me down the narrow staircase. As we step out into the cool night, I can finally breathe.

He pulls me into an embrace. "Thanks for coming," he says into my hair. "You made my night, and don't worry about them. They take this whole band thing a bit too seriously."

He's warm and a rush of lust shoots through me, but I brush the ring in his eyebrow with my fingertips and say, "You're welcome, and I must say you sing beautifully, but I really have to get going."

"All right." He gives me a soft, lingering kiss, sighs, and steps back. "See you Sunday."

With a nod, I move around to the driver's side of my car. I ask, "By the way, what was that song?"

He smiles flirtatiously, showing his dimples. "'Echo' by Incubus."

"Huh, well it was lovely."

Still smiling, he watches me as I get in the car and start the engine. Since he's standing on the curb, I offer a quick wave and drive away, but after the first turn, I pull to the side of the road and yank my phone out. It takes me only a few seconds to find the lyrics to "Echo."

After reading the words several times and recalling his singing "Iris" to me weeks ago, I lean back into my seat with a hand to my chest. Both songs hint that Justin wants me to see beyond his playboy image. Instinctively, I understand he's trapped in the persona. But I've seen the real him. I'm attracted to playboy Justin, but the real Justin is the one who keeps me coming back.

I bang my head back against the seat in frustration. This isn't supposed to get serious. Justin and I should just be having *fun*. But his heartfelt plea is melting my resolve and I already know that it's turning us into something beyond superficial. Recalling the intensity of him singing, I realize he has caught me. And despite all the responsibilities on my shoulders *and* reservations in my heart, it feels right. More than I ever thought possible, I *want* to be caught.

Chapter 23
Justin

Though I'm following the instructions Allie texted me, all the state park trails appear the same. Trees, plants, wood chips. I open her text and read it again. *Start at the north trail. Left, right, right, then wait at the fork. Be there around two o'clock.*

It's past two and I'm standing alone, surrounded by trees. Wasting time is a little ridiculous considering I have a paper to write and three exams to study for just enough to attain the parent-aggravating average C. I slap at my arm—bugs. All to meet a five-year-old, and to see Allie. At least the sight of her will be worth the unwanted nature hike.

I'm about to text her when the sound of giggling comes at me from the left. Hopeful, I jog toward the sound as it grows louder. The first person to come around the corner is a small boy with curly hair and thick glasses. Seeing me, he stops walking *and* kicking wood chips. He glances over his shoulder nervously as I continue jogging toward him. Holly and Allie round the bend. Allie's too cute, sporting a backpack and a baseball cap.

She plasters a look of surprise on her face as I stop my jog a few feet away from them.

"Justin! What are you doing out here?"

I bend and pretend to catch my breath. "Sunday afternoon jog. Nothing better than running on nature trails." Yeah, right. I like to run on a treadmill with a TV in front of me. I draw in a deep breath like I've been running for miles. I'm dressed for deception in Adidas running shoes, a hoodie, and running pants. "You?"

Holly shoots me a mocking look.

"Out hiking," Allie says, putting her hands on the small shoulders in front of her. "Ben loves to hike and study nature."

I give Ben a grin. "Hiking's cool."

He stares at me, and I slowly realize this kid has got to like me because if anything would be a deal breaker for Allie it would be her son. Yet even though I know next to nothing about kids, being fake isn't going to work. Kids can smell the "nice grown-up" scam a mile away. At least I used to be able to, if memory serves me right.

Holly crosses her arms and grins wickedly. "It's been a while since we hung out, J-dog." My teeth grind at the nickname. "Hanging out with you is the best. Remember that time in band camp?" she asks with a giggle.

Crossing my arms, I say, "How could I forget band camp and your . . . instrument?"

Holly lets out a loud laugh. Allie nudges her with an elbow, telling her without words that she's overdoing it, but Holly lifts the cooler in her hand and her eyes sparkle mischievously at me. "You should join us on our hike. We're, like, picnicking and everything."

I clear my throat. "Picnic? Sounds great." I look at Ben. "Do you mind if I join you?"

He shrugs and stares at a folded paper in his hand.

Allie's forced smile is wide. "Of course he doesn't mind. And you can help us find all the plants in our scavenger hunt." She leans over Ben. "Show him the next couple we're searching for."

Still silent, Ben opens the brochure in his hand and points to several pictures of weedy green things.

"Neat, huh?" Allie says, gesturing to the brochure. "They give them out at the ranger station."

I try to appear impressed. "Very cool. How many of them have you found so far?"

"Twelve," Ben says, at last speaking. "We have eight more."

"Okay," I say, glancing at the brochure. "I'll make sure to look out for the one with the little yellow flowers."

Ben's expression stays flat, but he nods in agreement.

Mother and son walk ahead of Holly and me. She keeps bumping me in the leg with the cooler. Then she points at Allie's butt. "Quit looking at that and spy some flora and fauna."

My response comes out with a smirk. "Can't help it."

Shaking her head, Holly smirks back.

Of course, I don't find shit. Neither does Holly. Allie spots two of the plants and Ben the rest. Each time they find one, Allie pronounces the Latin term and Ben repeats it, then she reads the properties of the plant, which Ben also repeats. In the span of forty-five minutes as we walk through the swampy part of the trails, I'm thinking the boy is a supergenius and unlike any other five-year-old walking the planet.

The trail ends at a wide-open beach on Lake Huron. Growing up on the other side of the state on Lake Michigan, where the water is rougher, I can't help but notice how the vast expanse of blue water appears calm and serene under the warm April sun.

Ben runs to the edge of the water and is about to dip a tennis shoe into the slight wave rolling onto the beach.

"Don't even think about it!" Allie shouts. She glances at me as Ben backs away from the water. "I don't like yelling, but sometimes it's unavoidable."

"Soakers do suck," I say in agreement.

As she unzips her backpack, it finally hits me: The woman I'm dating is a mother. As in, she had a baby. As in, she's raising a child. Of course, I knew this, but seeing them together makes it somehow more real, and gives me a glimpse into the reality of her responsibility, which I'm suddenly understanding is huge. I've been in my own little Justin world for so long that the whole thing kind of blows my mind. I'm aware I suck at understanding other people. Never used to care though.

Allie spreads out a blanket and then dumps the contents of her backpack, a collection of Hot Wheels, onto the sand while Holly unpacks the cooler. In seconds Ben is pushing the cars around and finally acting his age. I sit on the corner of the blanket closest to him. Feeling totally out of my element, I pick up a red sports car and lift it to get a closer look.

"Now this is a cool car."

He pauses from pushing a tiny dump truck and says, "That's a Viper. Fourth generation, Phase Two ZB. Zero to sixty in three-point-four seconds. Highest speed two hundred and two."

My mouth falls open and I blurt, "Damn, kid, how do you remember all that?"

His little shoulders shrug. "Remembering is easy."

"Do you even know how long three-point-four seconds is?"

His gaze turns pensive. "Not really."

"Good," I say. "I was starting to feel like a dumb ass."

He grins at me.

"Justin," Allie says in warning, handing me a wrapped peanut butter and jelly sandwich that reminds me of elementary school. "We're trying not to use bad words in front of Ben. He likes to repeat them, especially in front of his teachers."

Ben mouths "dumb ass" when Allie turns around and reaches for a juice box.

I put one finger to my lips, but he mouths the words again. I'm starting to like this genius little shit instead of considering him only as a way to get to his mother's heart.

The thick peanut butter sticks to the roof of my mouth. The sweet apple juice does little to clear out the texture of the sandwich. And every now and then, I crunch on a grain of sand. But despite the awful lunch, I'm enjoying myself. Pushing cars through the sand, carving out hills and roads, and enacting massive car crashes with Ben turns out to be fun. Never would have thought I'd be one to get along with a kid. But I'm having such a great time—there's a bit of a jog down memory lane into my own childhood happening—that I almost fail to notice Allie observing us with a pleased expression. As Holly sits next to her and drones on about her boyfriend, Allie appears to watch us more than listen to her friend.

Obviously a pro at kid manipulation, Holly challenges Ben to a race along the beach. Once they're off and running, I say, "He's great, Allie."

"He is," she agrees, stuffing empty juice boxes and sandwich wrappers into the cooler.

"You said he was smart, but he's, like, a genius."

She closes the cooler and plops down across from me. "It's awesome he's so smart, but keeping up with him can be a challenge sometimes."

I can hear the strain in her tone, the constant self-questioning if she's doing everything right. "From what I've seen, you're a great mom, Allie."

"Thanks." She sifts sand obsessively through her fingers as she watches Holly and Ben race farther down the beach. "I hate remembering my freak-out when I realized I was pregnant. I was terrified and miserable about . . . well, having to grow up overnight."

"Shit, Allie, you were what? Sixteen?"

She nods.

"Give your teenager self a break. Becoming a parent must be terrifying. It scares the shit out of me now. Can only imagine at that age."

"I was young but my meltdown feels selfish now. I wanted to go out and party. I wanted to be pretty and sexy instead of fat and pregnant. I thought my life had stopped. Then Ben was born and all of those wants went away. Well, mostly," she adds with a frown. "Unfortunately, I didn't grow up overnight."

"Hey, you don't have to be the world's most responsible adult to be a great parent. Hell, most people act like idiots regardless of age." I get what she's trying to tell me, but even my dumb ass knows having a child doesn't have to stop you from living. "None of those things are wrong to want, even now. You can be a sexy mom who goes out once in a while, especially since you had to grow up so fast."

She shrugs. "Those things lost importance over time."

Leaning back on an elbow next to her, I snag a truck from the sand. "I'm not trying to argue my own case, but the truth is you've got to live a little." I run the small vehicle along her thigh.

She lifts an eyebrow at the toy. "You saying I'm uptight?"

I roll the truck across her knee. "Too driven?"

Giggling, she swats at the toy. "Stop it—that tickles." I roll it over her other knee and she snatches it out of my hand. "I have to be driven. I have a child to take care of. My job keeps the roof over his head." She tosses the car back into the pile and glances down the beach to where Ben and Holly are digging in the sand with sticks.

"I'm always amazed he came from two underage, partying tattoo artists."

"Hey, I've met some sharp inkers. There's one in particular I know. She's not only smart but damn sexy too."

The breeze blows a lock of hair loose from her hat as her lips curl seductively. "The smart reference should be what gets my attention, but I do like that you find me sexy."

Staring at the ring in her mouth, I say, "Oh, I do, trust me. I find you the epitome of sexy."

"If we're admitting things," she murmurs, "then I must say you're quite sexy too." I warm from the inside out at her words. After she glances at the specks of Holly and Ben running together far down the beach, she suddenly leans forward and kisses me. It's quick and hot, especially when she sucks on my lower lip.

She breaks it off and sits back, wrapping her arms around her knees. "So you're cooking me breakfast tomorrow."

Oh, hell yes. "Quiche," I say, pushing up from the blanket toward her luscious lips.

She shoves at my chest and jumps up. "They're coming back."

Fuck. I like the kid. Shit. I even like Holly. But I like Allie and that ring curling around her bottom lip a whole lot more. I reluctantly stand and help her fold the blanket, then toss the sand-encrusted cars into her backpack. She wears a soft smile that I want to kiss from her mouth, but now that Holly and Ben stand mere feet from us, tossing rocks in the lake, it's not going to happen.

All four of us walk back along the beach, and we take turns skipping rocks into the lake. Luckily for my male ego, I'm the only one to skip a rock four times. Growing up on Lake Michigan, I spent a lot of time skipping rocks by myself as a kid. When we finally get back to the parking lot, Ben makes a beeline for the small play structure off to one side. Allie pushes him on a swing while Holly and I sit on top of a picnic table.

"You'd better not hurt her," Holly says. Her expression is light but there is a threat in her voice. "She's not a one-night-stand kind of girl."

"You think I'd come out here for a walk through nature and a peanut butter lunch if a quick hookup was all that was on my mind?"

"No. But guys like you have a hard time changing."

I pull back and give her an assessing look. "Guys like me?"

"Come on, J-dog. It's common knowledge you're a user."

My teeth grind because it is and I am. "She's different and I'm different with her. Shit, Holly, I haven't dated since high school. I haven't wanted to until now."

"Okay," she says, tilting her head. "I'm just warning you. I'll round up every biker who comes to the shop to ass-whip you to the highest degree if you cause even one tear to fall out of that girl's eyes. Trevor's caused enough for a lifetime, and I never want to see her like that again. She doesn't deserve it."

My entire body tightens at the thought of Allie's ex. "What's with Trevor anyway? Are they talking? Is he still here?"

Her lip curls as she nods. "Not sure why, but yeah, he's still in town."

"Allie has feelings for him?"

She taps her foot on the picnic-table bench. "You're going to have to ask her about Trevor if he's got you worried. I can't say for sure, but even if I could, that's her business to share."

Remembering Allie's response to Trevor, first at the shop and then at the art show, my teeth grind again and my chest becomes strangely heavy. If it weren't for their past—for their son laughing and swinging under the April sun—I'd claim Allie in a heartbeat and pound Trevor into oblivion. "Can't ask," I say. "I'm too afraid of her answer."

Holly watches me until I grow uncomfortable under her stare. "Listen, J-dog, she let you meet Ben. You wouldn't be here if she didn't think you two had somewhat of a future."

Holly's words make enough sense that I'm able to relax again. She's right. If Allie were seriously contemplating getting back with Trevor, she wouldn't have let me meet Ben. The nagging fear that has been at the back of my mind since Riley shared her worry about my getting "hurt" dissipates for the most part. In fact, Holly's insight has me beaming like a kid because Allie's letting me meet Ben implies we're far more serious than she's ever let on.

I watch Allie's bright smile as she pushes Ben.

Somehow, without my even considering it, I've come to want serious too.

Chapter 24
Allie

It's a relief to be in the car alone. All morning I kept the lustful thoughts from my head as I dutifully got Ben dressed, fed him breakfast, and dropped him off at school. Now driving back home, I'm very aware that Justin is in my apartment cooking breakfast. For me, for him, for just the two of us. Alone. The possibilities of us alone in my apartment roll through my mind. As I park the car, my thoughts can't be contained. They should be, but they are like thrown blobs of paint—messy and vivid and lingering, running down a canvas.

I could blame my pent-up lust on the fact I haven't been with anyone in over two years, but the reality is that I can't resist Justin. His tall, lean muscled frame. The ink covering his body. Those green eyes. Those dimples. But mostly what gets me is the way he yearns for me to know him. And I'm beginning to want to know him in every way possible. The topography of the surface of his skin *and* the man beneath that skin.

The scent of bacon hits me as soon as I open the door. Standing at the stove behind the counter, he glances over his shoulder. "Breakfast will be ready in about five."

I shut the door and whip off my shoes. Food is not on my mind. Feeling as sexy as he claims I am, I round the table and step into the kitchen. He's moving bacon around a pan with a fork. Faded jeans hug his tight butt, and his right biceps ripples as he moves sizzling strips to a plate.

Lust and apprehension fight a war within me. This wouldn't be confusing if there were nothing between us, if I knew that being with him would be safe and emotionless. But there are feelings between us. Lovely, growing feelings I shouldn't but want to give in to. Even knowing this is a huge step—maybe a wrong step, I can't help myself from sliding close behind him.

Wrapping my arms around his waist and pressing my body against his back, I say, "I don't want food right now." Beyond the bacon, I breathe in his sexy scent and then press my lips between his shoulder blades. His entire body freezes. "I want you even more than bacon," I say, trying to lighten my brazenness with humor. "That's a lot, you know, because bacon is really, really good."

He stays frozen for a long moment, then flips off the burner, shoves the bacon into the oven, and turns into my embrace, his hands wrapping around my waist. "Say it again in that smoky voice of yours."

I wonder if it will be harder with his hot green gaze boring into mine, but it isn't. "I want you," I repeat without hesitating.

His eyes flutter closed while he pulls me tightly against him. "Shit, Allie." He bends and kisses me softly. I try to follow his lips but he pulls back. "I've been waiting since the first night we met."

His words excite me more, because I know he's telling the truth. I kiss him while backing up toward my bedroom. Lucky for us, it's the first stop in the hall, right across from the kitchen. As our tongues slide together, I pull up his shirt and then lean back to see all his glorious inked skin on display. Holy wow. My hands itch to touch him. He hauls the shirt off over his head and drops it to the floor but steps into the hall.

"What?" I say in a rush, suddenly fearing rejection.

He smiles deep enough for a dimple to show. His fingers encircle my wrists and he draws my hands to his naked chest. I almost shudder at the touch of his skin. "It's been a while for me too. We need to slow down or I'm going to devour you whole. Let me lead. Let me make this good for you," he says, propelling me forward, then kicking the door shut behind us.

My room is dark and inviting. Though I would never have admitted it this morning, I had shut the blinds and drapes before taking Ben to school in preparation for this.

"The days don't seem long enough, and the moonlit nights even shorter," he sings quietly into my ear, brushing the sensitive skin of my earlobe with his lips and making me almost stumble. "*Without you.*" His hands slip under my sweatshirt and whatever he sings next, I don't hear clearly. I'm electrified as his hands skim my ribs and settle below my breasts. His thumbs brush the sides of my bra and my breath catches.

He turns and we sway into the small space between the bed and the dresser. "Since you're my girl, I can't help but be true," he continues singing with a slight twang, then his teeth scrape a path down my neck.

"Are you singing me a country song?" I ask with a gasp.

His lips slide along my collarbone. "You don't like country?" he asks, and his breath heats my skin.

Though I've never been a fan, I don't hate it. But as Justin continues to hum while pulling me close, I'm thinking country is kind of sexy. A minute later I'm thinking it's *very* sexy. "I'm starting to," I say, letting out a heavy pant without meaning to.

We sway and he keeps singing. His hands slide across the full-ness of my breasts as he peels my shirt off then draws me back to him. The contact of skin on skin—the cold metal of his nipple ring pressing into the tender skin above my bra—makes my heart thump to the tune he sings into my ear. His strong hands span my back as our slow dance turns into just the slow grind of our hips, with his melody controlling the rhythm of our movements.

I'm melting, and I give in to his seduction completely.

In a graceful sway and then a half twirl, he twists me around away from him, singing the chorus. His hands settle on my hips and his warm, heavy muscled chest slides along my back. As my head rests on his shoulder and the deep timbre of his voice fills me, he somehow loosens the clasp of my bra. Caught between his voice and his touch, I'm listless when he tugs at the straps and my bra drops to the floor.

The line "Make my heart tremble wild" has me opening my eyes. Then his hands cover my breasts. His palms caress me, and I tremble with want, then try to turn toward him. But he holds me tight, singing and swaying, the length of our bodies touching.

"Since you're my girl," he sings possessively in my ear. At the last "I can't help but be true," he turns me around and devours my mouth, his tongue plunging into me. My fingers move over his back. The contours are as marvelous as I imagined while inking him. I'm so lost in his kiss and the sensation of his skin that I'm almost startled to find myself lying on the bed when he tears his mouth from mine.

"Since you're my girl," he repeats in a whisper. He licks my lip ring and lowers his mouth to my breasts. I'm grasping and squirm-ing while he sucks my quivering skin. His fingers find the band of my yoga pants and he yanks them off.

When his hand slips under the silk of my panties, his teeth let go of my nipple. "Say it."

His hovering fingers have me panting as I try to understand what he wants.

His fingers brush me with the softest touch but don't offer relief. "Say it," he demands again.

Desperation offers enlightenment. "I'm your girl."

"Don't ever forget it," he says roughly, and drags my panties down. After skimming his fingers from my ankle to my inner thigh, he touches me and my hips jump at the contact.

As he leans over me and turns my desire into pure fire, I twist and squirm from his touch. Even as his mouth stays fastened on my breast, I clutch his forearms. "Take off your *pants*," I insist. The last word comes out as a gasp, and he chuckles while his fingers continue to circle, slowly torturing me.

"Soon."

I reach for the waistband of his jeans. "Now."

"Soon," he repeats, then kisses me while his fingers wreak havoc until I'm simply clutching at his belt loops and panting. Finally, he pushes off the bed, digs in his pocket, and peels his pants and boxers off in one smooth move. For a moment I study the beauty of him, then I tear open the condom he tossed on the bed and reach for him. The planes of his face constrict at my touch, but he lets me roll the rubber on. Then he's kneeling over me and I'm breathing hard in anticipation.

His hands cup my jaw. He leans forward and sucks my lower lip, runs his tongue over my lip ring. "Tell me you want me again."

My fingers slide across his tattooed chest and find solid muscle. "I want you."

He gently widens my legs and in one smooth move, he's inside and on top of me with all his glorious weight. "You've got me."

I can't verbally respond, only moan.

Teeth clenched, he moves and my entire world becomes him above me. His body, his tattoos, and those deep green eyes that won't let me look away. There is kissing and touching and straining and sighs, but mostly there's a connection between us I never imagined possible. Past the lust, past the eruption of my climax, then his, is the feeling with each thrust that he's touching my heart from the inside.

* * *

Afterward we lay in a tangle of sheets, each tracing the other's tattoos. He's lying on his side. I'm on my back. Thoughts and questions run through my mind. I trace the Japanese letters along his tight abdominal muscles. "What does this say?"

He glances down as if he'd forgotten he'd been inked there, then murmurs, "Just always be waiting for me."

"Just always be waiting for me," I repeat slowly, staring at the sharp black letters. Maybe Justin wasn't always on the one-night-stand merry-go-round. Maybe he deals with heartbreak in reverse from the way I do. Instead of staying away from the opposite sex, he overindulges.

His fingers absently stroke my shoulder. "It's from *Peter Pan*," he says. "The book at least. Not sure if the line was in any of the movies."

"*Peter Pan?*"

"My nanny used to read it to me," he adds and his gaze turns wistful. "I used to say the line to her every night after she tucked me in."

"What did she say back?"

"Forever."

I wistfully imagine him as a little boy. "She sounds wonderful."

"She was, still is. But what about you? There's this one," he says as his fingers follow an olive branch etched on my arm. "That's the big one." He traces the cursive *Ben* on my other arm, and my fingers pause on the tribal swirl on his chest as I realize he's counting my tattoos. "With the sunflower that makes three."

He pulls at the sheet. Not wanting my entire body open for his perusal even in the shadowy confines of my room, I drag my leg out from under the sheet and show him my thigh. He leans close and reads the words along the top aloud: "*We can only make our pictures speak*. Who's that?"

"Van Gogh. Last letter to his brother before he died."

"You and that ear slicer. I'm almost jealous," he says teasingly. His fingers follow the curl of ink. "Any others?"

I twist around and show him my lower back.

He traces a wing. "Dragonfly Ink, huh?"

"It was my first."

"Should I ask who did it?"

"Probably not."

It's hard to miss the sudden way his eyes narrow. "What other ones did he do?"

"The one on my thigh." I roll over to my back again, not wanting to talk about the name on my shoulder that was removed. "Todd's done all the others. But you're here in my bed, and I don't want to even think about *him*."

He glances at my body covered with the sheet. "That's it?"

I lift my leg and show him the tiny dragonfly on my ankle.

"So that's it?"

"Yup. That's it."

Wrapping an arm around my sheet-covered waist, he grins slyly. "Would have thought there'd be more ink on such a badass tattooist."

I shrug. "Between raising a kid, going to school, and inking everyone else, the ideas I have for me keep getting pushed to the side. But once I get my degree, I'll have more time."

"You're keeping the shop?" he asks in a surprised tone.

"Is there something wrong with that?"

"No," he says, shaking his dark blond head. "I'm just confused why you're going to college at all."

"The shop does decent, but if things ever change, I want something to fall back on. And learning about business can only help."

His nod is thoughtful. "What about your painting?"

"I used to consider painting and tattooing separately, but really they're both creating. And having someone hang something on their wall isn't as thrilling as them letting you mark their skin for life."

"You said something like that before. Your paintings are awesome though."

"Well, I can always do both. I'm kind of planning on it. What about you?"

His eyebrows raise and I lift a finger to brush the gleaming metal of his piercing.

"Why a communication degree?"

"Thought it would be easy, and useful for law school."

After closing my mouth and blinking at him, I ask, "You're going to be a lawyer?"

"Is that hard to believe?"

Thinking of his BMW and his clothes, no. But then there's him onstage. Hot. Sexy. Magnetic. "I hope you'll still sing and play guitar in the courtroom."

"The whole band thing happened because Romeo and I are roommates. I never considered being in a band before I met him. He was starting one, heard me sing, and the rest is history. But in my family, you're a doctor or a lawyer. No way in hell would I ever be a doctor. So law school here I come."

"But do you want to be a lawyer?"

He shrugs. "I'm not the driven type. I'm more the laid-back type who wants to enjoy life." His gaze wanders over my face. "But you make me want to be ambitious, to catch the stars on a starry night and pull them down for you."

I turn toward him, my expression serious. "I don't want you to be anything for me. I want you to just be you."

Tugging at a curl brushing my shoulder, he lifts his head. "Sometimes I'm not sure who I am." He kisses me so softly I lean forward, hoping for another touch of his lips. "Except when I'm with you, pretty Allie." Our mouths are so close his words are a light breeze on my skin. He blows gently on my lips. "Be with me?"

My fingers dig into the skin of his ribs as I scoot closer to him. "Can't seem to help myself."

He chuckles deep in his chest. "Quiche for lunch?"

I lean down to give his pierced nipple a wet kiss and his pectoral jumps. "Yes, definitely—later though." I give the ring a soft jerk with my teeth.

"Maybe not even later." He groans. "Food can wait. Exam week too."

Chapter 25
Justin

All four of us are crowded into a small room to the left of the stage as the stagehands finish the sound checks. Sam is bouncing up and down. Idiot likes to wind himself up before going out. Romeo is going over sheet music with Gabe one last time. He's become Gabe's mentor over the past couple of months, and once the stubborn prick stopped resenting being told what to do, his drumming improved immediately. Not that he sucked, but he wasn't anywhere near our first drummer, and not even in the same galaxy as Riley.

Except for Gabe, who's new, playing live has become almost easy for the band over the past two years. We roll through gigs onstage effortlessly. That's why we do things like adding songs with violins, or me finally learning guitar. Shit can get boring without a challenge. Can't say the studio stuff is easy. I'm not looking forward to our final session next weekend.

But outside of the band, life has become something to grasp with both hands and hold on to. Instead of or searching for what I can take, I want to give. Give everything to my girl. Take away her worries; erase the little crease that sometimes etches her forehead. And make her as happy as she makes me.

But Allie's life is full. She's got her son, her business, and school too. I don't like it, but I accept the crumbs of time she can give. We talk over the phone late at night about art and music and Ben. We send each other dirty texts. We squeeze in visits when we can. Even though I did some studying for exams over the past week, I found time to stop by the shop to visit her twice. Between the slices of her life, we are building a relationship, something I never imagined wanting so badly, but with Allie I want everything.

That she'll be here at our show tonight has me feeling pumped. She's coming after work, halfway through, and I know once she shows up I won't even notice the rest of the audience.

Some guy with stringy long hair stops by to tell us the stage is ready. Romeo reminds him to make sure the lights are turned low. Romeo has a thing for theatrics, likes to open with a boom.

Once the lights are low, we file out and take our places. A hush pervades the crowd in the sudden darkness. We wait about half a minute to let the anticipation build, then Gabe hits his sticks and Romeo cranks out a screeching riff. The lights come on. The crowd roars. Energy fills me. Romeo hits a hard synthetic-sounding riff then makes his guitar screech again. I move my head to the beat, throw out an arm at the third screech, step to the microphone, and sing into the fourth screech.

The crowd's energy rises as I start singing.

Standing in front of the microphone, I move to the music and sing in a low, crooning voice. When we hit the chorus, I release the mic and let loose, bending and shouting the chorus.

"Chalk Outline" by Three Days Grace is a dynamic song. It mixes low, raspy singing with a forceful shout in the chorus. The lyrics describe a man's anger after being dumped. I've never really understood the meaning until now. If Allie left me, I'd be a mess. My newfound knowledge lends more emotion to my singing, and

I can tell from Sam's and Romeo's glances that this is definitely the best I've ever sung this song.

During the instrumental, I sway next to Sam and give Romeo the spotlight, then go back to the edge of the stage, belting out the chorus and bending over the crowd.

Once the song is over, I shout into the microphone, "You guys ready for some rock 'n' roll?" The crowd roars at me. "Let's see how you like our new original, 'Bleak Moon'!"

Gabe rolls out a drum fill, Sam gives us a baseline, and Romeo joins in with a booming riff. I open with a fast vocal. The crowd beyond the stage moves in one huge, surging wave. I'm immediately high on the adrenaline of the masses.

We roll through two originals and five more cover songs. During the last song prior to our break, I fist bump half of the people standing in front of the stage—and by the time we finish it, the crowd is in a frenzy.

I leave the stage for our break reluctantly. If it were up to me, we'd keep playing. But we don't have a choice because for the second set we're doing acoustic. The stage needs to be changed over. I'm not big on the acoustic crap like Romeo. Given the choice I'd take blaring guitars every time. But other than a few trips to the Detroit area, we only play at about six different clubs and bars in the area, most of them at least twice a year. Though I hate admitting it, even internally, Romeo's right. We have to mix it up or we'll get old.

In the tight hallway behind the stage, Romeo is again mentoring Gabe. Sam has disappeared. He'd better not be off sucking shit up his nose. Partying is one thing, doing it while we're performing is a completely different scenario that would cross the line even with me.

The waitress who brought me a beer is trying to talk to me, asking if I want something else. A shot? Or . . .? I glance at her and almost laugh. There was a time, not so long ago, when her casual invitation would have had my brain running in all kinds of directions. The girl is attractive, dressed in tight shorts and a tight T-shirt with the bar's logo. Her short hair is spiked, and the thick chain around her neck would have gained my interest in the past, but not anymore. I've got nothing to say to her and zero interest. And strangely, I'm even kind of shocked at who I was less than two months ago. That I would have been considering the possibility of going home with this girl now seems kind of skeevy. What was wrong with me? And why would girls let me use them like that? After being with Allie, the whole thing feels empty and heartless.

I lift my beer. "Thanks, but I'm set with this."

Her lips push together as she obviously thinks of some other way to make an offer.

"Really, I'm good."

"Sure you don't want another beer at least?" she asks, trying to save face.

I shake my head. "Got to sing. Acoustic. Easy to mess up," I add with a grin.

She grins back, then goes and asks Gabe and Romeo about a beer. Romeo declines. Gabe accepts.

Leaning against the wall, I finish my beer and reach for my new acoustic guitar. This acoustic shit does rattle my nerves. I've been playing for only about four months. Four months is not enough to feel invincible onstage. But then, the nervousness adds to my energy high, and that's my addiction.

As I strap on the guitar, the stagehand with long hair tells us the stage is switched over and ready. Romeo goes over the lighting with him again, and Sam finally comes back—and the four of us head out to start the set.

The crowd goes wild when they see us. There's one stool in the middle of the stage. For my lame ass. Still new to playing, I like to sit if possible. Romeo and Sam go stand at their microphones. Romeo is holding a mandolin. Sam is playing his electric bass for this one. Gabe sits in the back with a tambourine and access to the bass drum.

Even though I've practiced the shit out of this one since I play lead, I take a deep breath. Not only do I have to play, singing with acoustic music doesn't allow much room for error. A second after I strum, the rest of the band yells out the first words of the Lumineers' song "Ho Hey." The crowd recognizes the lyrics and starts stomping, clapping, and singing along wildly. Instead of making me more nervous, their exuberance helps calm me down.

Strumming and singing, I relax into the performance. Gabe pounds on his bass drum and bangs his tambourine. Then Romeo adds the mandolin. I scan the crowd for Allie even while singing and playing an instrument I've only recently conquered.

We're in the chorus for the second time when I spot her shiny auburn hair at the back of the crowd. Smiling and clapping, she looks so happy and into the music, my newly awakened crazy-ass heart swells.

With my eyes mostly still on Allie, we finish the song.

We play three of our originals next, which are fast, folk, and bluesy. Romeo and Sam do most of the guitar work. I only have to strum a few cords. The crowd is still into us, and I'm still flying high from the energy, but my attention continues to wander toward the back of the room. To Allie.

We end the night on a song we have been practicing forever. I don't play this one, only sing. If Romeo could have his way, I'd have learned the keyboards for this song, but I told him to back off. I can only conquer one thing at a time. My first priority is singing, then the guitar. Piano is a long way off. He wanted to hire a keyboardist for this song, but the rest of us put a stop to that. "Wish You Were Here" by Pink Floyd has enough power to carry it with just vocals and guitars. When the drums come in halfway through, they kick the intensity up a notch.

After the first few guitar notes, the crowd goes crazy, and I sense a bit of surprise.

Yes, you happy fuckers, we are singing Pink Floyd.

Still sitting on the stool, I watch Allie through most of the long beginning instrumental. Musically clueless, she doesn't join the the crowd in humming along and swaying with lifted arms. I concentrate on doing the classic song justice and sing the shit out of the lyrics, high for this awesome crowd.

I glance at Allie only a few times.

Then we're bowing as the rowdy fans scream for more, and exiting the stage with our instruments.

Lucky for us, there's a stage crew that hauls our equipment out back. Usually, I take my sweet-ass time helping out, but tonight I'm all business and efficiency. So much so that Romeo's raising his brows. "Who slapped your ass?"

Before I can tell Romeo to eff off, Sam says, "His new lady friend is here."

Romeo's brows rise even higher. "You're serious about this girl?"

For one stupid moment, I'm embarrassed, like I'm whipped or something, but then I proudly say, "Very."

Romeo gives me a curt nod and we finish loading the van.

Afterward, I rush inside the bar and start making my way over to Allie, ignoring the people who try to get my attention or stop me. She's leaning against the bar, talking to the guy next to her. A twinge of jealousy erupts in me, but then I remember her caveman comment from a few weeks ago and push aside the possessiveness. It's an initial reaction but one I can ignore. Allie's not that type of girl. Shit, I was the first guy she'd been with since her divorce.

"Well hello," she says as I step in front of her and put my hands on her waist.

"Hello, pretty lady. I couldn't help noticing you back here all by yourself." She's hot in her standard tank, jeans, and boots, but tonight her hair is in two braids. The ends lie right above the soft expanse of her cleavage. Very nice.

She smiles seductively and that's all the encouragement I need. I kiss her long and slow, showing her mouth all the things I want to do to her body.

When we part, the guy who was talking to her closes *his* mouth and turns toward the bar.

Allie lets out a rare giggle as her hands tighten around my waist. "The show was great. I didn't know you played acoustic so well."

"I really don't. I only know a few songs." I reach for her hand at my back. "Come on. Everyone's in the back room."

"Holly's coming," she says. "I should wait for her."

"Just text her to go to the back room."

"Oh, okay," Allie says, pulling out her phone.

I walk behind her as she texts, touching her waist but wanting to touch even more.

When we get to the back room, it's full. Even Romeo and Riley are here tonight. I introduce Allie to Riley's best friends, Marcus and Chloe, who ooh and aah over her sleeve tattoo. Riley gives Allie a wave, but of course doesn't leave Romeo's side. At the end of the table, Gabe sits as usual with his girlfriend in his lap.

The two of us grab the seats at the middle of the table, and then share the beer that's there waiting for me. I order two more.

It's different and nice to just talk instead of trying to lay the moves on someone I hardly know with the expectation of whoever it is taking me home. Allie and I laugh at Sam's story about going out for a smoke, then getting locked out of his apartment for four hours while the girl he'd brought home slept off the body shots they did. Chloe, Riley, and Allie talk school and classes while Romeo drones on to Sam and me about next Saturday's recording session.

I'm arguing that I'd rather break it into two more sessions instead of an unbearably long one when I notice Allie is gone. Chloe picks up on my confusion and tells me Allie went to get Holly. After a thankful nod in Chloe's direction, I continue arguing, but after more than ten minutes pass without Allie's returning, I get up and go to inspect the busy bar. I finally spot her across the room. With Trevor. Even from this distance, I can see the grip of his hands on her arms. He's leaning over her. She's leaning back as her face turns fearful.

Pushing people out of my way, I'm across the room in seconds.

Chapter 26
Allie

As I walk through the crowded club to meet Holly at the bar, the giddiness that has pervaded my mood since watching Justin onstage doesn't dissipate. As he performed, all I could think was, *That wonderful, sexy rocker up there is mine.* I'm not sure how it happened, when exactly I opened up to it, but there's no denying that I'm out-of-control into him now. I feel exactly like I should, a twenty-two-year-old out at the bar with her boyfriend. I feel young and carefree.

And I like it.

Holly and Jake are waiting for a round of shots at the bar, so I hit the restroom. On the way out, I'm still on my Justin cloud nine when someone steps in front of me. Startled to see Trevor, I stumble backward. He appears a bit menacing in all black: jeans, T-shirt, boots.

"Thought you weren't into this guy. Thought it wasn't serious," he says, sneering so much the tats on his neck stretch. He's also yelling in my face because of the loud music blasting through the speakers. "Making out in the middle a bar screams serious, Allie."

For a moment I'm too stunned to reply, but I slowly put two and two together. I'd been talking to Mark Beech, a Dragonfly customer who'd known Trevor forever, when Justin came up to me at the bar. Obviously, the jerk had called or texted Trevor after we left for the back room.

I stand with my fists clenched but calmly say, "It's really none of your business who I date, kiss—or how serious it is. We're divorced, Trevor."

His blue eyes blaze and he reaches for my arm. "We have a kid and a business together." He pauses and leans low. "You'll always be connected to me. Always. No douche bag singer is going to change that." He starts dragging me toward the door.

For one quick second, I remember the past, the constant aching over Trevor. Then I imagine a long, sad future of constantly pining for Trevor. Of never feeling loved. Of sick jealousy over Jazz. Oh, hell no. That won't be my future. I jerk back from his hold and brace myself.

"We are divorced," I repeat, trying to pull away from him. "Let me go. Now."

His grip grows tighter. "What's going on with you and this guy?"

"Let me go," I say under my breath, noticing people watching us.

"Are you fucking him?"

"Now," I say through clenched teeth.

"Are you?" he says, shaking me.

His shaking me hits a major nerve. "Screw you! I'll fuck who-ever I want! Let me go!"

Fury fills his face, and he lets me go with a shove that sends me colliding with a nearby table. Unfortunately, it isn't empty. Drinks fly and crash onto the floor when the table nearly tips. The people at the table jump up, yelling, "What the hell?"

I'm finding my footing as Justin gently helps me upright and searches my gaze. "You okay?"

Before I can answer, Trevor whips him around. "Don't touch her!"

"Why? So you can push her again?" Justin's expression is furious as he shoves Trevor.

Trevor's mouth twists as he stumbles backward. "Fuck that," he snarls. He lunges forward and punches Justin in the jaw.

Justin's head snaps back, but his feet stay planted. He whips his head around, his gaze livid, as Trevor raises both fists in an aggressive stance. Justin takes a quick step back, and punches Trevor in the middle of his face before he can lift a fist. Jaw slack and eyes wide, Trevor staggers against the wall and slides to the floor.

Things are moving fast. Yet it feels like I'm watching a fight through a lens in slow motion.

Scrambling up from the floor, Trevor bull-rushes Justin, who ducks just in time to jab Trevor in the ribs.

People crowd around us—some screaming, some yelling, and some cheering. Their voices reverberate in my head as I move forward, intent on pulling Justin away from Trevor's reach, not caring that I'll end up in the middle of their fight.

As I reach for Justin, Gabe flies out of the crowd at Trevor, who cuffs him in the side of the head. The punch does nothing to stop Gabe. Fists flying, he beats Trevor to the ground. Even amid the shouting around us, I can hear Gabe repeating, "Men don't fuck with girls. Men don't fuck with girls. Men don't fuck with girls."

Strangely—or maybe not so strangely since it's obvious that Gabe is in a rage—both Justin and I work at dragging him off Trevor. After nearly getting pulverized by Gabe's elbows, we finally have him standing between us. He's breathing hard, eyes still murderously trained on Trevor, who's rolling across the floor and covering his face.

Gabe tears from our hold and lunges again, but Justin yanks him back by the waist. "Whoa, he's down. Leave him be."

The music in the bar is suddenly cut off.

Romeo breaks through the crowd. "What the hell is going on?"

"He"—Gabe points a shaky finger at Trevor, who's sluggishly pushing himself up off the floor—"pushed her into a table."

With rage etching his features, Romeo is obviously about to lay into Gabe with an embarrassing reprimand, but some guy dressed in a button-up shirt and pressed slacks breaks through the crowd around us. A nametag on his chest and the ring of keys on his belt loop signifies he works here. He holds a hand out to help Trevor up. "Back off, people!" Supporting Trevor, who's swaying as if drunk and cupping his bloody nose, the guy yells, "Get away or get out!"

People start dispersing. Justin tugs Gabe away from the scene.

The man helping Trevor points to us. "You two, stay put. The cops are on their way."

"The cops?" Gabe gasps, finally pulling his rage-filled gaze from Trevor and struggling to get out of our grip.

Romeo is instantly in Gabe's face. "Don't even think of taking off," he says from behind clenched teeth.

Gabe visibly deflates, and Justin lets him go and wraps his arms around me.

"Tell me you're okay?" he whispers in my ear.

"I'm all right," I say into the skin of his neck, breathing in his earthy, comforting scent. "Your jaw?"

"A little sore, but forget me. When I saw that prick push you I feared the worst."

"I'm all right," I repeat, though the side of my thigh is throbbing where it hit the table. A bruise will definitely be there in the morning. "Just shook up and shocked. He's never been like this." I can't tell if Justin believes me, but it's true. Sure, Trevor has always been a jerk, but he's never gotten physical with me. Something was off about him tonight, though, and I'd been close enough to him to know he wasn't drunk.

Justin's arms tighten around me. "I almost wish we'd let Gabe continue."

Shaking my head, I hold on to him and let his embrace calm me down. Holly is suddenly next to us. "I can't believe this. He pushed you?"

I can only nod at her.

She sneers at Trevor, who still appears out of it.

Behind us, we can hear Romeo lecturing Gabe. "Three years of playing and this is the first time this type of shit has happened. This shit is never happening again, do you hear me?"

As Justin turns and holds me close by one arm, Gabe mutters something under his breath but keeps his head lowered. I notice the group from our back room table standing at a distance and watching the aftermath unfold. A few tables over, the man I assume is the manager has Trevor in a chair and is crouched in front of him, holding a towelful of ice to his bloody nose. The sight irritates me. Even though Gabe went overboard, Trevor is not the victim here.

Romeo keeps bitching at Gabe. Now he's talking about losing the club.

Justin shoots Romeo a cold look and says, "Honestly? This isn't the time to be an asshole."

Romeo stares at Justin with eyes that flash daggers.

I'm starting to feel awful. If I hadn't come, none of this would have happened. I'm aware the guilt isn't entirely mine, but I can imagine the rumors that will spread over the next week: *The singer and drummer of Luminescent Juliet got into a bar fight over one of their girlfriends.* The thought makes me cringe.

As the guys continue to argue around me, my gaze finds the instigator of the evening's fiasco. The manager tries to help Trevor up, but he brushes off the man's hands and heads toward the bathroom. The manager then comes to stand by us, probably hoping to stop anything else from erupting, Trevor turns back and his hostile gaze finds me. I don't flinch. Instead, I stare right back until he disappears into the bathroom.

A few minutes later, the police arrive. My shock over the fight escalates when, after talking with the manager and several bystanders, the two policemen cuff and arrest both Justin and Gabe. Justin looks shocked too. Gabe's face is impassive. Startled, I'm at the policeman's side in an instant.

"They didn't start it." I've already told them this, but I have to do something before they haul off Justin. "My ex-husband was the first one to throw a punch."

The cop glances at me. "This isn't elementary school, miss. If someone hits you, it doesn't give you the right to beat them senseless."

My hands clench at my sides. "He kept the fight going, after he shoved me into a table and almost knocking it over." I've already told him this too.

The cop directs Justin toward the door. "You can post his bail tomorrow morning. After that, it's for the judge to determine who, if anyone, was in the right."

Justin glances at me over his shoulder as he's dragged out of the building, and I have to stop myself from following them.

The least shocking thing of the night? Trevor is nowhere to be found.

* * *

Between the three of us, Romeo, Sam, and I managed to collect the seven hundred dollars for Gabe's bail. It turns out this isn't Gabe's first run-in with the law. All Justin has to do for his release is sign a personal recognizance bond—something about promising to return and appear in court. Justin will pay us back on Gabe's behalf once he gets out, but I'm not too worried about money at the moment.

We arrive with the money at the police station at dawn, and while Romeo and Sam go inside to pay, I sit in my car. I'm looking forward to putting this sleepless night behind me. I've been consumed by guilt while also wishing I'd punched Trevor myself. I really don't understand why he came last night. Sure, he's been hinting at getting back together with me since he returned but he hasn't been persistent. And he showed no signs of being completely freakin' nuts about me with Justin until last night.

I've been waiting in my car for over half an hour when Romeo and Justin finally come out of the building, with Gabe and Sam following behind them through the revolving door.

Even though this is stupidest—I'm blaming it on lack of sleep—time to be obsessing about appearances, I'm kind of wowed by the four men coming at me. Of course, with his dimples, green eyes, and swoop of dark blond hair, Justin's brand of hotness is the most devastating. But Romeo, who's as tall as Justin's six foot two, has this dark, sensual thing going on. Then there's Gabe. Tall too, maybe just over six foot. He's all wiry muscle, with piercing eyes and a jaw so hard it's like someone cut it from marble. Last is Sam, who is all energy and handsome cuteness with his buzzed dark hair and muscles bulging, even at seven thirty in the morning. Geez. You'd think they were models instead of bandmates.

After a few fist bumps, Justin, Sam, and Gabe come over to my car. Romeo has to get to work at the family center where he volunteers, so I offered to drive everyone else home when he and Sam and

I met up this morning. Up close, the two who got sprung appear the worse for wear, with red eyes and exhausted expressions.

"Hey," I say as Justin gets into the passenger seat. "You all right?"

He reaches for my hand and smiles softly. "Seeing you, I'm doing a shitload better."

When Gabe and Sam get in the back, my car is overloaded with testosterone.

After a few minutes of arguing—everyone wants to help everyone else on this bleary Sunday morning—it's decided that I'll take Gabe home first, and then he'll take Sam home. Really, I could take them all home, but it's obvious they're trying to leave Justin and me alone.

Gabe's directions land us in one of the few seedy areas in town. The houses are rundown. Yards are overgrown, and junk covers almost every porch. As I pull in front of Gabe's house, an older man opens the broken door and wobbles out onto the first step. Between the wobble and the beer can in his hand, he appears half-drunk.

Pointing at Gabe with the hand holding the beer, the drunk shouts, "You know I've got a scanner, you little piece of shit. I told you the next time you get arrested not to come back! Your shit's going to the curb!"

Getting out of the car, Gabe gives the man the finger.

The man points his own middle finger at Gabe. "Come in this house and I'll break that off and stuff it up your ass, you little fucker."

Gabe ignores him and goes straight to the driver's side of his truck, which is parked on the curb.

Sam gets out next and bends down to Justin's open window. "See you guys later," he says. The man on the porch yells something else and after glancing over his shoulder, Sam adds, grinning, "Hopefully, we'll make it out of here in one piece." He gives Justin a soft punch on his shoulder, then runs to the passenger side of Gabe's truck while the old guy on the porch continues yelling obscenities as he whips his beer can at the truck.

Not wanting to witness any more drama, I take off just as the can hits the truck with a thud.

Keeping my eyes on the road, I ask, "Do you want to go back to the dorm? Or you could come to my house. I'll just have to take you home by two, when I pick up Ben."

"Got a washer?"

My glance at him is questioning.

"I have to get out of these clothes. Jail stank."

"Ah. Yeah, we've got a washer and dryer in the hallway closet."

"Then your house it definitely is."

Turning a corner, I say seriously, "I'm really, really sorry about last night."

"Why would you be sorry?" His tone is incredulous.

"If it weren't for me, Trevor wouldn't have come and ruined everything."

"Shit, Allie, you don't have any control over that asshole. Although after last night, you should file a restraining order against the prick."

His words surprise me. "I hadn't thought about that."

"You should. But as for last night, don't be sorry. He pushed you, and Gabe . . . Well, obviously, he has one crazy-ass temper." He watches the passing scenery out the window for a moment. "I've always thought Gabe was a prick. Still do. But in the last twenty-four hours, I'm starting to understand why. He has one screwed-up life."

"You guys talk last night?"

"A little. The shit he told me wasn't pretty. After getting her ass kicked numerous times, his mom left him with that asshole on the porch when he was six." He rubs his forehead. "I was seriously clueless about the shit life he has. I mean, we're all aware there's abuse and sick shit out there, but it's totally different seeing it."

I shudder at the thought of the person on the porch taking care of anyone, much less a six-year-old. I was really hoping the guy wasn't related to Gabe. I was hoping for distant stepfather or maybe his mother's awful new boyfriend.

"People like Gabe make me realize that my anger at my parents isn't shit."

I park in front of my apartment building, but don't make a move to get out of the car. "Why are you angry at your parents?"

He shrugs. "Because they've always been too busy for me. Except when I fuck up. Then they stop their precious lives for about five seconds to bitch. But I've always had everything I needed and they've never been abusive." He rubs a hand down his face. "Shit, Allie, did you see that house? Can you imagine if that was your father? I can't imagine what Gabe has been through. Six years old . . ."

Yes, the glimpse we just got into Gabe's life is heartbreaking. But the idea of Justin growing up and being ignored by his parents saddens me too. I reach for his hand and brush my thumb over his bruised knuckles. "You're probably right. Gabe's life has been far less pretty than yours, but that doesn't excuse your parents' negligence."

"Forget about my parents," he says, gripping his knees. "I can't believe I'm saying this, but I'm worried about Gabe. They're going to slap me with a class C misdemeanor if anything, but Gabe is going to get nailed without a lawyer. This is his third assault charge. The only way I'm going to get him to accept my paying for a lawyer is if I get one and he represents us both."

"Can you afford a lawyer?"

"Yeah, my parents may not pay attention to me but they shower me with money."

His tone is bitter, but since he doesn't want to talk about his parents I simply say, "Then that sounds like a good idea."

Nodding, he stares out the window, but I'm aware he's not seeing anything.

"Hey," I say, and pull him toward me. "How about a shower, then some sleep? You'll have time to consider everything later. You need rest now."

He covers my hand with his. "Damn. I got lucky when I walked into your shop."

I grin at him. "Damn straight."

Chapter 27
Justin

I'm exhausted. I'm wearing a pair of pink running shorts that are too tight and too short. I look like an idiot. I've been arrested and spent the night, awake, in jail. But as I step out of Allie's bathroom and almost trip over a basket of toys, I'm feeling happy.

I don't have to wander far into the apartment to find her. She's at her dresser, putting away clothes from a basket on the floor. The room is small, with a double bed and done in all white: walls, furniture, and bedding. Except for her vibrant paintings on the walls and the long brown-speckled curtains on the window.

"Hey," I say softly, moving behind her.

She smirks at me in the mirror above the dresser. "Nice shorts."

My eyelids lower.

"No, really." She turns and runs a hand across my chest. Her fingers find the ring in my nipple. "I like them." Her finger circles my ring as her smoky eyes wander over my body. "They don't leave much to the imagination."

The tiny shorts are about to get tighter. "You're making my imagination run wild." I jerk her toward me by the waist and lower my mouth to hers. Neither of us is slow. The kiss doesn't build to hot. It's instantly heated and fierce.

Desperate for the feel of her skin, my fingers seize the bottom of her shirt and lift it.

She pulls away and reaches for a curtain, drawing it closed.

The blinds had let the morning light in, but the closed curtains cast the room in shadows.

I yank the curtains open. "I want to see you."

She yanks them shut. "Maybe I'm not ready for you to see me."

Confused as all hell, I blurt, "What does that mean?"

"I'm a little shy?"

I tilt my head in thought as I recall our time together. "Not that much."

She leans against the dresser, eyes downcast. "I've been pregnant."

"Huh?" I shake my head in confusion, like a cartoon character, as I realize she doesn't want me to see her in the light. "Allie, you're smoking hot. Trust me. I've watched you for months now. For shit's sake, I've been with you." I open the curtains. "I'm dying to see you."

"I've been pregnant," she repeats softly, eyes still cast downward. "I have stretch marks, okay?"

I'm 100 percent out of my realm here. I can't recall seeing any scars the last time we slept together. Though it *was* dark. And we were doing more touching than looking.

Her lips form a thin line and her fingers dig into the white wood at the edge of the dresser. "Trevor—he didn't like them. He wanted to tattoo over them, but we weren't together long enough."

Ass. Fucking. Hole. I lean my forehead against hers. "Listen to me. You're beautiful to me. Every single part. Any tiny flaw you have because you carried a baby is beautiful too."

She blinks at me as if trying to believe my words.

I'd like to punch Trevor again. Twice. Allie's never self-conscious. And she's never been preoccupied with appearances. But this is obviously something Trevor made her feel inferior about. While she was just a teenage girl.

"You have to trust me about this," I whisper as my fingers reach again for the bottom of her shirt.

She gives a slow and tentative nod, and lets me peel the shirt from her body.

With a plan of making this slow and sensual for both of us, I place my hands on her ribs—and she shivers as I turn her toward the mirror.

Her apprehensive gaze meets mine in the glass. My eyes sweep over her body. She's slender but not too thin. Her pale skin is a lovely contrast to the bright ink on her arm along with the shine of the auburn curls falling below her shoulders. The soft swell of her breasts above her plain cotton bra lifts in a deep breath as I run my fingers up her arm and down the middle of her torso. There's not a flaw in sight.

"Gorgeous," I say, dragging my lips along her shoulder. She shivers again. I let her bra clasp loose then with a hook of my thumbs tug it off at each strap as she watches. "So gorgeous," I repeat at the sight of her firm, high breasts.

As I cup her breasts, she falls against me with a soft sigh. Keeping one hand on her hardening nipple, I move my other hand to the button of her jeans and her gray eyes open wide. Not letting her back out, I unzip her jeans. She trembles. I push them down and they crumple to the floor at her feet.

Long waisted, with a sweet curve to her hips, she could be a swimsuit model, at least for the guy magazines. She's much hotter than the ridiculous bone-ass-thin models in fashion magazines. Her flower-dotted panties ride low. Right above the red waistband, a faded slash curls inches below her belly button. Another faint scar is barely visible closer to her hip. Her gaze is fearful as she stares at the faint marks.

"You are so beautiful," I groan. "And this"—my fingers trace a path along a shiny, thin puckered scar—"doesn't take anything away from your beauty, and certainly not from how much I want you."

When her body doesn't release its tight line of tension, I kneel, yank her jeans free from her feet, and turn her sideways. Hands gripping her hips, I kiss and then run my tongue along each faint scar visible above the line of her panties. Releasing a sigh, her body finally relaxes and she thrusts her hands into my damp hair. My shoulders loosen. So intent on her response, I hadn't realized the tight coil of my own body.

Finally, oh fucking finally, I slowly pull her panties off, and as soon as her feet are free, I press my lips and tongue to the place I've been wanting to kiss forever. She gasps and bucks, but I hold her still by the hips. When her climax hits, I watch her face in the mirror. Head back, lips parted, she's more beautiful than I could ever explain to her.

I stand slowly, then quickly shed the pink shorts and even more quickly lead her to the bed. She still appears dazed as I lay her down. But when I reach for my wallet, miraculously—or not, since it appears Allie had made plans while I showered—on the nightstand, her hands come to my chest.

"Wait, wait. Let me touch you."

Though I'm not sure how much longer I can wait, I lie on my side and let her hands slide over me. Her fingers trace my tattoos and the muscles on my chest. Her hands wrap around the hot length of me, and my eyes roll into the back of my head. The movement of those hands has me hissing through my teeth, "Get the fucking condom."

Twisting toward the stand, she giggles. "Yeah, that's what it's for."

I snatch it from her fingers, tear it open with my teeth, and pretty much slap it on. The curve of her mouth turns into an O as I push her onto the pillows and roll over her. Poised above, holding her face in my palms, I know it's too early, too damn early yet, but my heart is overflowing. "I'm falling in love with you," I say, entering her.

Her eyes widen into gray pools of shock, but as I deepen my angle, she gasps. I drink the gasp from her lips, her legs wrap around me, and we rock into mindless oblivion.

Chapter 28
Allie

With his arm around my waist, Justin falls asleep almost immediately. I stare at the ceiling while his words, *I'm falling in love with you*, echo in my head. After his breathing evens in a deeper sleep, I untangle myself, grab my robe, and flee into the bathroom.

I sit on the closed toilet and try to get a grip. My arms tighten around my knees.

Just have fun. Just date. Just get laid.

Why didn't they tell me to jump off a cliff?

Because Justin's words have me feeling like I'm standing on the edge of one.

Deep inside, I'm elated, because his words feel right. Yet I'm not ready for them, and I can already feel the weight of them crushing me. Between Ben and the shop and school, I have too much on my shoulders already. Now Justin's heart has been added to the list. Though Holly keeps saying that Justin is a big boy and that I should worry only about myself, I can't ignore his words.

And what about my heart?

I can't even contemplate the issue of love. It's too much.

I never wanted things to get to this point. It was supposed to be just *fun*. This sudden deep emotion is suffocating me.

Unable to deal with all the emotions swirling through me, I stand and turn on the shower. For over a half hour, I let the spray of water wash away my thoughts. By the time I step out, I've run through all the hot water and my mind is nearly empty. I put my hair in a bun and dab on a bit of makeup, then go change the laundry before getting dressed. I roam around the apartment, mindlessly straightening up and tinkering in the kitchen. I build a wall between those words and me, and try to relax. I pretend for the moment that they don't exist, that they were never spoken, and that whatever is between Justin and me is just fun.

And instead of acting freaked out, I'm going to have fun for once, dammit.

Once the apartment is spotless and Justin's clothes are dry, I toss his jeans and boxers at the end of the bed. He sits up still sleepy eyed despite having slept for hours.

His blond hair is a wild mess and his jaw is covered with a dark scruff. The white comforter around his waist contrasts with his coppery skin and the black tribal art and Japanese-lettering tattoos. He is absolutely delectable. Releasing a yawn he asks, "Where's my shirt?"

"I thought you could hang out in your jeans until we leave."

The ring in his eyebrow rises. "Oh, I'm your eye candy now?"

"Absolutely. No better eye candy around."

He jumps from the bed and lunges at me. Laughing, I step into the hallway. "Get dressed. I started making lunch." I leave him shaking his head and reaching for his pants.

Since I usually cook for Ben, my kitchen is stocked with kid basics. Holly rarely eats here and hardly ever shops. So after searching the cupboards and refrigerator three times, I decide we don't have many choices besides grilled cheese and tomato soup.

I'm slicing cheese as Justin wanders into the kitchen. I pause to take him in wearing only jeans, with a strip of his boxers showing. Screw Todd. Tribal tattoos are hot. Justin is hot. I want to forget about lunch and have him instead.

He glances at the pan on the stove and the items on the counter, then bumps my hip with his. "Let me cook. You did the laundry."

"How about you do the soup and I'll make the sandwiches?"

His lips turn down. "Why do you get the good part?"

I set the knife on the cutting board. "Fine. I'll make the soup."

Picking the knife up, he says, "Prepared to be awed by my grilled-cheese-making skills."

"I've already been awed by your spinach quiche." I dig in a drawer for the can opener. "How did you learn to cook so well?"

"The housekeeper had weekends off. My parents were usually out and about."

I pause from opening the can of soup and watch him butter a piece of bread. "All weekend?"

"My mother had luncheons and fund-raisers. My father had a car-collecting hobby that filled every weekend. He could spend all Saturday and Sunday searching through car dealerships in a hundred-mile radius. I went with him once. Once was enough. He also dragged me to a few boring car shows."

"What about at night?"

"They usually met up for dinner at some fancy restaurant. Sometimes I went along. By the time I was thirteen, I opted to stay home. Something like grilled cheese"—he pauses from buttering bread and grins—"tasted better than seared foie gras."

"What exactly is foie gras?"

He picks up the spatula and spins it. "The liver of a duck or a goose that's especially fattened to make it a delicacy."

My nose wrinkles. "Yuck."

"Thought so too at thirteen, but I tried it again in France. It's not too bad. Pretty good with a glass of red wine." He flicks on a burner.

I shake the can of soup into the pot. "Ah, France," I say dreamily.

"We should go someday."

"Did you forget I have a son? And limited resources?"

He drops a sandwich in the waiting skillet. "I have resources, and why not take Ben?"

"You make it sound so easy."

"*Il pourrait être.*"

The can in my hand nearly clanks to the floor. "You speak French?"

"*Un peu, et pas parfait.*"

He's too hot, standing in my kitchen half-naked but speaking French? He's hotter than hell. I almost fan myself. "What did you say?"

"First?" He pushes a strand of wayward hair from my bun behind my ear. "'It could be.' Then 'A little, and not perfect.'"

Still dumbfounded by him, I spend a moment figuring out his responses. "Nothing's easy with a five-year-old." I stand next to him, brushing his arm with mine as I stir the soup. "Did you learn to speak it while you were there?"

He flips a sandwich. "Mostly. I took two years of it in high school but a month there was worth more than two years in the classroom."

"So you don't know Italian."

"*Le basi.*"

I tilt my head in question.

"The basics."

"Like?"

"Spaghetti, Parmigiano, prosciutto," he reels off in a heavy Italian accent. *"Chianti, Frangelico—"*

My laugh cuts him off. "That's all food and alcohol," I say, nudging him with my hip.

He hip-nudges me back. "That's the important stuff."

We're standing there grinning at each other when the apartment door opens behind us.

Though I'm startled that someone is coming in, I'm thinking it's Holly. Turning, I drop the tomato soup–covered spoon and it clanks on the tile as my heart drops to the tile too.

My father and Ben stand in the doorway.

Justin steps away from me and crosses his arms over his naked chest.

"Dad! What are you doing here?" Oh, crap, crap, crap. Oh, big-time crap! Why didn't he call to say that he was dropping Ben off early? Why didn't I give Justin his dang shirt? Because I'm a hormonal idiot who's now preoccupied with *fun*. I'm completely mortified by my father's harsh expression at seeing me with a man. A half-naked man at that.

My father's expression turns harsher as he stares at Justin. "Your mom and I have a retirement party this afternoon. She's not cooking today."

"Oh." Why don't people tell me this stuff? "Um—"

Ben tosses his backpack on the dining room table then points to Justin. "What's he doing here?"

"Um . . ." My shocked brain is coming up with nothing.

My father's jaw grows tighter.

Justin's face appears serious. "Your mom called me over this morning to fix your leaky sink. She offered lunch as payment."

Ben scoots onto a stool in front of the peninsula. "So you're a . . . plumber? Don't they wear shirts? Why aren't you wearing a shirt?"

Justin twirls the spatula. "It's in the dryer. Got wet while I was working."

Ben's forehead crinkles. "Where are your tools?"

"In the trunk of your mom's car."

Okay, Justin's kicking butt here, at least with Ben. My father is a totally different story. Though I'm relieved Ben's still clueless about us, the lies coming out of Justin's mouth have me a bit worried.

"So you're good at fixing things?" Ben asks, tilting his chin.

Justin nods with an air of indifference. "Almost the best."

After adjusting his glasses, Ben jumps off the stool. "Then you gotta come to my room and help me."

"You need something fixed?" Justin asks him but looks to me.

I nod an okay as Ben yells from the hallway, "Something super important!"

Justin turns the burner off under the grilled cheese. "Be right back."

Once they're gone, my father comes and stands on the other side of the peninsula. Obviously upset with me, he's even more intimidating in his Sunday khakis and a button-up dress shirt. He usually wears jeans and a flannel over an old T-shirt.

"It's not what you think. We've been dating for a while," I say, wishing I could melt into the floor. If there's one person I don't like letting down, it's my father.

He lets out a sigh. "I'm not judging you, Allie. It's not my place, but haven't you been down this road? I was hoping you'd wait for marriage this time around."

Staring at the counter, I can't think of anything to say. I wanted to wait, but Justin blew into my life like a new song I became obsessed with overnight.

My father comes around the peninsula and lifts my chin gently. "For others to respect you, you have to respect yourself the most. Think about that." He kisses my forehead and I tremble as he walks back to the door. "Take care of my boy," he says like he always does when he leaves.

I stand in the middle of the kitchen until I notice the smell of burning tomato soup and notice that it's bubbling and spitting all over the stove. I move the pan off the burner, wipe up the mess, and lean on the counter. The day is only half over, and so far it's been a roller coaster of emotion. After a few deep, calming breaths, I find another can of soup and the ingredients for another grilled cheese for Ben.

My father's words echo in my head as I turn the heat on again under the sandwiches and stir the soup. Though I do believe Justin respects me, I'm aware we are moving too fast. I dated Trevor for over a year in high school, then four months prior to getting married. Obviously, I should have taken more time then too. But with Trevor, I always had a desperate obsession with holding on to him, as if our connection were something that could slip through my fingers if I looked away for even a second. My obsession with Justin is entirely different. I want to be with him. I want to know everything about him. I want him to know everything about me. But I don't have the need to hold on to him with a death grip. Because our connection feels mutual.

I'm about to get Justin and Ben, whom I suspect are working on the bridge Ben has been trying to create with his erector set, when my phone rings. Trevor's number flashes across the screen. Knowing he'll keep calling, I force myself to answer it.

Before I can even get out a hello he says, "Do you know how pissed I am?"

Imagining his bloody nose and battered face, I can imagine. My jaw clenches at the aggressive tone in his voice. "Just get to the point."

"I'm getting a lawyer on Monday."

"Good, you're going to need—"

"And getting custody of my son."

I clutch the counter so I don't fall. The kitchen rug, the world,— actually, even gravity—feel ripped from under me. *Breathe, Al. He's angry and spouting crap.* "What are you talking about?"

"Then I'm getting the shop back."

The shop isn't even on my radar. "Why would you even think you could get custody? He hardly knows you. You hardly know him," I snap. Now I'm getting angry. "Is this your deranged idea of revenge?"

"You want to be a bitch?" he hisses. "You want to date some douche bag? Then I'm going to fuck your world up."

"Are you threatening me?"

"Douche bag and his buddy better not press charges against me."

"Or what?"

"Think about what I said," he growls before hanging up on me.

Fury pounds through me as I stare at my phone screen. Custody? He's lost his mind.

Furious, I call him back. Of course he doesn't answer.

I'm about to destroy my kitchen—throw soup against the wall and smash grilled cheese under my feet—but instead lean against the counter and take deep breaths.

The soft murmur of conversation comes to me from the hallway as Justin and Ben make their way toward the kitchen.

I take in one last gulp of air and say pleasantly, "Lunch is ready. Go wash your hands, Ben."

With a scowl etching his face, Ben turns back toward the bathroom. Justin studies me for a long moment. "Everything okay?"

Forcing a smile, I nod.

Inside, I'm a screaming mess.

Chapter 29
Justin

We're all sitting around Allie's drawing desk on Monday afternoon. Todd's on his third piece of pizza. Shaya is on her second. Allie is still picking at her first. We'd planned this lunch last week, but Allie was surprised when I showed up with two pizza boxes. Todd and Shaya had been ecstatic.

Allie has also been quiet and distant.

Yesterday, after our surprise lunch with Ben, she'd been quiet too as she drove me back to the dorm. I chalked it up to Ben's non-stop chatter and that she was freaked out her father walked in while I was there, shirtless no less. When I texted her late last night she seemed fine, but today I'm wondering if there's more going on than her Dad's disapproval.

I can't help blaming her quietness on my big fucking mouth. I should have never told her I was falling in love, but in the heat of the moment, the words felt so right. So true.

Never said them before.

Now they're biting me in the ass.

Beyond tense, I roll my paper plate and force myself to listen to Todd's story about a customer from last night.

"So I'm kickin' it to third," Todd says, still chomping on pepperoni and sausage. "Pounding skin when the fucker passes out." He swallows and then laughs. "Almost falls out of the chair."

I'm guessing pounding skin means he was inking at a high speed.

Shaya giggles, causing her curls to bounce. "He says it calmly, but he screamed like a ten-year-old for me to get in there last night."

Allie's forehead wrinkles. Though she hasn't said more than two words so far, she asks, "Why would you push ink like that?"

"Well, he came in at five to nine."

Allie glares at him. "We take work until nine."

"Yeah, but this ass wanted a three-hour job and beyond that his back was already almost entirely engraved. How was I to know he needed a pussy ball?"

At my raised eyebrow Shaya explains, "A tennis ball to hold for pain."

Todd folds another slice of pizza in half. "He was fine until the fainting thing."

Allie gives me a weak smile, then her mouth curls in a scowl at Todd.

"Hey, he finished," Todd says.

"Our first wrastler!" Shaya says with a giggle.

"What's a wrastler?" I ask.

Allie drops a nibbled-on crust on her plate and glares at Shaya. "It's not funny."

Shaya rolls her eyes. "Somebody who faints but finishes," she replies in a tone that declares the meaning should be obvious.

"Todd," Allie says irritably, "unless it's one of your regulars, do not ever kick it to third on someone again."

Todd scrunches his nose at her, reaching for another slice of pizza. "I'm not a hacker, Al."

"Then don't act like one," she snaps.

Other than the ever-present music playing, the shop is quiet while Shaya and Todd stare at Allie like she's grown two heads. Apparently, her snapping at them isn't normal. Finally, Todd shrugs and stuffs pizza in his mouth. Shaya turns to me.

"When can *I* come and see your band?"

"Not anytime soon," Allie says, tossing cups in the trash by the counter. "He plays at bars."

Shaya's forehead wrinkles. "So?"

"So you're not even eighteen much less twenty-one," Allie says with a tone of finality.

I clear my throat. "Just tell me when you turn eighteen. We sometimes have gigs that are eighteen and over."

"Sweet," Shaya says, sounding like she hangs out with Todd too much.

Allie pauses from picking up plates to frown at me, but she doesn't say anything.

I start helping and when we meet at the trash bin, I say in a low voice, "I'll make sure it's a mellow show."

Not looking at me, she just nods.

Fuck. I want to ask her what the hell is wrong, but I'm terrified it's the oh-shit-Justin's-in-love-with-me thing and the shop is definitely not the place to talk about it.

A hardcore, thrashing guitar riff suddenly competes with the Paramore song coming out of the speakers behind the counter.

After tossing his plate on the drawing table, Todd digs in his pocket and yanks his phone out. He answers with a "What's up?"

I could care less who Todd is on the phone with, but the instant stillness of his body, the scowl creasing his face, and the way his eyes flick to me catch my attention.

His scowl grows. "Yeah, so what?"

Allie stops cleaning and watches him too.

"You know me better than that," Todd says. "I don't take sides." He sags onto a stool. "Dude, don't even think about it. It's not a good time."

Allie moves closer to Todd, partially obstructing my view of him. He watches her as she apparently mouths something, then nods his head yes. I push away from the counter and step behind her. "Is he talking with Trevor?" I ask.

Her eyes are imploring. "I have an appointment soon. Can I walk you out?"

Even knowing Trevor's on the phone, hell if I can say no to those eyes. "Ah, sure."

Outside, we stand on the sidewalk in front of my car.

I turn to her and force myself to say calmly, "Tell me he's not coming here. Tell me you got a restraining order on him already."

She crosses her arms. "I'm not sure what I'm going to do."

"You're not going to get a restraining order?" I ask in an incredulous tone.

She glances at the ground.

My stomach does this strange little drop thing I've never felt before. "What the hell, Allie? He basically attacked you on Saturday."

"Listen, Justin, things are complicated. He's my son's father. I own a shop with him. Todd and Shay, even Mandy and Mac, they all rely on me. I have rent and bills to pay. I can't make a decision based on what's good just for *me*."

The image of Trevor shoving her flashes through my head. "Good for you? He's dangerous."

Her chest rises and her arms tighten. "He's just a jerk, but no matter what, he'll always be part of my life. I can't get around it."

My head spins with incomprehension. I'm not sure what to make of this. On our nature walk, Holly had set my mind at ease about Trevor. I'd believed what she'd said—that Allie wouldn't allow me to meet Ben if she still had feelings for Trevor. But if that's true, then what Allie is saying makes no sense.

"What is going on between you two?" I ask, my jaw tight.

She rears back, blinking in confusion. "Nothing. He just . . . can make things difficult."

I'm trying to wrap my head around what she's saying. "So you let him control you?"

She shakes her head and lets out a sigh. "Of course you don't get it. You have no responsibilities. You go to school and play in a band, while your parents . . ."

"Throw money at me," I finish for her.

Biting her lip, she stares across the street and wraps her arms around herself. "I need some time, Justin."

The entire world fades away as I stare at her while those words slowly seep into me.

Her pewter gaze lifts to mine. "I need to think some things through."

"What are you saying?" I ask, refusing to believe what it sounds like she's saying.

"Things are hard right now. I need some space."

"From me?" I ask hoarsely.

Digging the tip of her boot into the cement, she nods.

"Allie, don't push me away." I reach for her, but she steps back. My newly awoken heart cracks like the damaged concrete on the sidewalk below us.

"Just give me some time."

"So I'm supposed to wait?" She doesn't answer, just stares at the sidewalk. Anger jolts through me. "What the fuck am I waiting for?"

"I need to straighten some things out."

"Will you quit talking in riddles? Is this because of what I told you yesterday?" I finally ask.

Her expression is conflicted. "Partly."

I step closer to her. Close enough our bodies almost touch. "I can't take those words back because they're true. But they were given freely, without any expectations."

"I get that," she says with a nod. "But those words are still weighing on me. *Everything* is weighing on me right now."

"Does 'everything' have to do with Trevor?"

"I don't want to discuss him much less think about him right now." She reaches for then squeezes my hands. "Give me a few days, okay? I need some space to get my head on straight."

She pulls away but pauses after taking in my desolate expression. "This isn't the end or anything, Justin. It's just a break."

"A fucking break," I murmur, trying to control my anger as it spikes again.

Her mouth tightens. "Please don't make me feel guilty about this. I have enough on my mind right now."

Though it's harder than hell, I force down my anger, and hurt, and keep my face neutral. "A few days?"

She nods and tugs open the glass door. "I'll call you soon, okay?"

I nod but as she steps into the shop, this break feels like it'll be more than a few days. It feels like the beginning of the end.

Chapter 30
Allie

E ven though I work only until eight, I haven't taken a Friday night off in ages. But on this occasion, it's Ben's spring play at school, which is not something I'm willing to miss. Along with my parents, Holly and I have front-row seats. My father readies the video recorder while we wait for the kids to come onstage. I'm a little worried Ben might not show since he's not too keen about performing onstage. Acting is one thing I can say is not in my son's future. Which is why I was reduced to parental bribery in the form of ice cream. He does come on though—and afterward I applaud until my hands hurt.

It's just a short drive from his school to the local diner near our apartment, where Ben insists on ordering a massive banana split.

While kneeling on the booth's bench seat and diving into the ice cream, Ben says, "I thought Dad was going to come."

"He must have gotten tied up with business stuff," I say carefully, not wanting to give away how much I hate Trevor right now. "Grandpa got it on video. You two can watch it together and laugh."

Ben smiles. "I said my lines funny, huh?"

I wrap an arm around his shoulders. "You said your lines perfect."

"Dude," Holly says from across the table, "your performance was Oscar-worthy."

"Who's Oscar?" he asks.

"Not a who but a what," Holly says, snagging the cherry from the top of the mound of ice cream while Ben frowns at her. "Every year a bunch of people get together and give out trophies called Oscars to the best actors."

Ben pushes his lips together. "So where's mine?"

Holly throws the cherry stem at him. "You have to wait for Oscar night."

He throws the stem back and it lands in her hair. "When's that?"

"Next winter," she says, digging through her blonde locks for the stem.

He gives her a long glare, then digs into chocolate ice cream. "The banana split is better."

"Way better," I agree, skimming off some fudge sauce.

Even with three of us, we don't make a dent in the massive mountain of ice cream in front of us. Holly, refusing to take no for an answer, pays.

We get home late. Well, late for Ben—it's almost ten when he gets into the tub. I keep an eye on him through the open bathroom door while I pick up his room. Holly, with an overnight bag on her shoulder, pauses in the doorway.

"Just look at tonight. Trevor would never win. Stop worrying about it."

She's referring to Trevor's continued threats about custody and the tight expression I've worn all week. The expression I'm wearing at the moment.

"You're right. He probably wouldn't." I stuff a dinosaur book onto a shelf. "But he'd probably get joint custody. Courts are big on joint custody. The thought terrifies me because he's just doing it just to get back at me. It would be different if he actually wanted to be a father."

"Come on, Al." She steps into the room to help pick up and bends to snatch a little coat off the floor. "You know he's just yanking your chain. He doesn't want to take care of Ben, even part-time."

"Think about it, Holly," I say sarcastically. "How can I not be bothered? It's every divorced mother's with a craptastic ex's nightmare."

"Okay, okay I get it," she says, dropping the coat on a hook next to the dresser. "He's freaking you out. But you have to get over it. Don't let him rile you up like this."

I toss socks into a hamper. "I'm trying but it's easier said than done."

Her gaze grows skeptical. "What's going on with Justin?"

Shrugging, I chuck a Hot Wheel into a bin on the floor.

"Don't tell me you broke it off with him."

"I'm taking a break, thinking things over."

"Oh hell, Allie. He's got it bad for you, and I'm pretty sure you've got it bad for him. And I'm not just talking about in between the sheets."

"I can't deal with a relationship right now."

She shoves some toys under the bed with the toe of her shoe. "Oh, and when's a good time?"

I drop the Hot Wheel bin on another shelf with a thud. "Trevor has showed up every day at the shop. He's not only talking custody, he's talking about buying me out or taking me over or whatever. Every day his plans get more demented. Mac just about punched him in the face because he thinks he's the boss now. Shay is scared she's going to lose her job and be forced to move back in with her mom.

Todd is threatening to quit if Trevor comes back. My mom has been giving me the third degree all week about the half-naked man she's never met being in my apartment on Sunday. Ben was crying before he got in the tub because his dick of a father didn't show up for the play and—and . . . ," I stutter, falling onto Ben's bed with a plop. "Justin told me he's falling in love with me."

The bag on Holly's shoulder drops to the floor.

I dramatically throw an arm out. "On top of everything else, I can't deal with him right now. Thinking about him makes me crazy. I can't do crazy with Trevor breathing down my neck."

Dropping next to me on the bed, Holly wraps me in her arms. "Did you ever consider Justin might be someone to help you with all this shit, someone to lean on?"

"Oh, Hol, I'm not going to use him. I called him on Wednesday, but it was just short and awkward with my head caught in a mess." I wipe my face, surprised that it's wet because I hadn't even known I was crying. "I'm super confused with all this Trevor crap."

Shaking her head, Holly leans on my shoulder. "I should have never tried to get you to just have fun. It's always all or nothing with you, isn't it?"

As I rest my head against hers, a self-deprecating laugh escapes me because she's described me perfectly. She lets out a sad chuckle too as we sit there leaning on each other.

"Why are you crying?" Ben asks from the doorway. He's dressed in a fuzzy robe but still dripping water on the floor, his face frozen in a fearful expression.

I try to stand but Holly keeps her arm around me tight. "Sometimes mommies get sad too," she says. "Everyone has sad days. You know those days when everything seems to go wrong?"

Ben nods.

"Your mom's having one of those days. Why don't you come and help me hug her?"

He nods slowly before rushing across the room and jumping in our laps.

After a long group hug, Holly bends until her nose is almost touching Ben's. "Should we tickle her?"

"Yes!" Ben says.

Their attack is so fierce I fall back on to the bed. In a few minutes, I'm laughing and gasping, "Stop! I'm going to pee the bed!"

Ben scoots off the bed like lightning. "Yuck!"

Holly stands and heaves her bag from the floor. "When someone's threatening to pee, my work is done." She pauses at the door. "Unless you want me stay in tonight?"

I wave a hand. "Jake's waiting. See you later."

"All right, but call me if you need chick flicks, booze, and an assortment of Little Debbies."

Zebra cakes and rum? Hard to resist but I wave my hand again. "Go. Jake's waiting."

She gives us a wicked grin before taking off.

After she's gone, Ben crawls back into my lap. "Why are you sad?"

Running my hand though his damp curls, I try to find an explanation that doesn't have to do with his father or with Justin. "Things were crazy this week at work. I'm a little stressed out."

"Stressed out?" he repeats slowly, obviously trying to understand the word *stressed*.

"Yeah, like worried all the time." I tug on the belt of his robe. "I don't want to worry anymore tonight. How about you get your pajamas on and then we can read and relax?"

"That sounds good," he agrees, and scrambles off my lap.

We read books until he falls asleep. I tuck him in, remove his glasses, kiss his soft forehead, and wander through the silent apartment. I fall into the chair next to the window and look outside. It's almost eleven now, and a few people are coming and going. Some hold hands; others have their arms around each other. The silence grows. It booms loudly through me. Beyond the booming silence is loneliness, the dull ache I've grown used to and accepted over the past few years. But tonight it's more crushing than usual.

Unable to take the loneliness anymore, I move to my easel in the corner and attempt to work on my most recent painting. The shadows get deeper along the street, but that's all I can extract from my imagination because thoughts of Justin are filling my mind.

I've refused to think of him all week, but after talking with Holly, he's all I can think of. His masculine scent. The bright flash of his dimples. The seriousness of his green eyes searching mine. The sound of his sexy voice singing in my ear. The desperate way he wants to prove himself better than his reputation or his past. The lighthearted way I feel when I'm with him. Memories, images, and emotions swirl in my head until I'm rushing to the closet and yanking out a clean canvas.

I don't visualize, just let the swirl in my head inspire me while I paint and paint and paint.

Sometime around four in the morning, I step back from my easel.

I'm shocked at the sight.

A picture's supposedly worth a thousand words.

Mine depicts many, but mostly . . .

The truth.

Chapter 31
Justin

Of course, the last studio session is hell. Romeo is on a perfectionist tear. Sam is hungover. Gabe, as always, is being an asshole. And I'm a depressed piece of shit. Perfect time to play some music and record it. At least there will be an edge to our sound.

After four hours of playing, we take a breather to eat the Chinese takeout Sam ordered, declaring he needed some grease to help his hangover. I pick at gong bao chicken and pork pot stickers. The windowless break room is essentially a basement, but at least it has several round tables and is large enough that we can also take a break from one another. I'm sitting at a table alone, picking at my food and doodling in a notebook, when Romeo decides to join me. The ass is obviously dense. I'm not in the mood for company. I go to the pop machine for a drink. When I get back to the table, he's reading over the bullshit I've been writing since the drive this morning.

I plop down at the table. "Didn't know you were such a curious fuck to invite yourself into my shit." I hold out a hand. "Give it back."

"This is pretty good," he says, continuing to read and ignoring me.

My hand reaches to tear the notebook out of his, but he leans back. I fly up and my chair hits the wall behind me. "I'm not fucking around."

He still doesn't look up. "I'm not either. This is really, really good."

"Romeo," I say through clenched teeth.

"I've been working on a tune this would be perfect for." Ignoring me, he mouths the words from the paper and nods his head, obviously thinking in music notes. "A few tweaks and we could have one hell of a song."

With one step around the table, I snatch the notebook away. "I didn't write if for your album."

"It's our album and that could be our first single."

"Oh, awesome. Tear out my heart and put it on display for the world. That would make a great song."

Being a business asshole he says, "What do you think? That great songs come from lame-ass poets sitting in the parks under trees?" He shakes his head. "They come from real people writing about life and what matters to them. And those"—he points to the book—"are awesome lyrics because they're real and they're heartfelt."

My hand grips the notebook until it scrunches. "My fucked-up personal shit is not making it into a song."

Still digging into a white takeout container with his chopsticks, Sam comes to stand next to Romeo. "He's right. Fucked-up shit usually makes the best songs."

I glare at Sam.

He shrugs. "Just saying."

Romeo leans across the table. "How about this? After we work on the music, give me three practice rounds with it, then on the fourth we'll record. Then if you say no, I'll let it go."

I'm trying to ignore their hopeful faces when from across the room, Gabe says, "Quit being a pussy and just sing your pussy shit."

"Fuck you," I say, glaring at Romeo. "Four times. That's it."

"Give me the notebook and your pen." He reaches for his chopsticks. In between shoveling in food, he writes out an arrangement using the lyrics. Feeling nauseous like some nervous schoolboy on his first date, I toss my half-full container of food in the garbage, then stare at the wall while drinking pop to wet my suddenly dry throat. I can't believe I agreed to this shit. And I'm all too aware of the words he wants to use for the chorus. Words from my mutilated heart I'll have to belt out in front of everyone.

We head back into the studio and my nervousness intensifies. I watch them learn the song over the next hour. Romeo was right. His simple melody matches my lyrics perfectly.

But when I join them, I can't sing it. Even after three times through.

Romeo glares at me. "Are you kidding me? Are you doing that shit on purpose? Everyone else has it but you."

My jaw clenches tighter than his. I'm not kidding, singing this is killing me. I'm not sure I *can* do it. "I said I'd sing it. I didn't say I'd do it well."

"We all know you can sing way better than that. Get your shit together or I'm going to assume you're screwing up on purpose, especially since this is not only the fourth time but our last session."

"Lovesick pussy," Gabe sneers from behind his drum set, and Sam snorts.

"Just start the song," I snap.

Snickering now, Gabe hits his sticks together.

They play through the chords twice. I take a breath and start singing. This time I let myself think of Allie while I sing, and the words somehow come easier with the vision of her in my head.

They're about her, and I sing them to her. My voice comes out not only clear and in tune but also wrapped in emotion.

The studio is quiet once we're finished. Even the two guys behind the soundboards, whom we pay a ridiculous hourly rate to, are quiet. Finally, Romeo says, "That will work. He glances at the clock above the glass. "We should be able to get two more in. Let's do 'Trace,' then 'At the End of the Universe.'"

We're all shocked by that. Romeo had planned four more songs. Dropping two songs without a Romeo tantrum is unheard of. Since we've done the next two songs so many times, it only takes a couple of plays for each before we call it good. While we pack our stuff, Romeo goes into the sound room, playing back and reviewing the stuff we did for the day.

We all pause when the new song comes on. I almost don't recognize my voice. It sounds raw and emotional, and completely different than I ordinarily sound. I usually work hard at hitting all the right notes and that's about it. Hearing myself so emotional kind of sucks. Essentially, it really sucks because now I can *hear* how I feel like shit.

"That is going to go viral," Sam says, clasping his bass case shut. "No doubt. That one is blasting us onto the charts."

At the thought of my heartache turning us into real rock stars, I snatch my guitar case and a snare drum from the floor, then march out to load up the van. I should have never agreed to do the song. I'm going to have to relive that shit every time I sing or hear it. The album comes out in a couple of weeks. That song might not be on it. The rest of the band will be pissed at me, but I'm not sure I'll be able to sing about Allie over and over again if we're through.

The ride home is quiet as usual. Sam sleeps on the bench. Gabe sleeps in the passenger seat. Romeo drives. And I lie in the back surrounded by equipment, scrolling through pictures on my phone. I have three of Allie. One from the beach on the day of the nature walk. Another of her at the coffee shop. And the last is of her at her apartment the night she made dinner. I look at each long and hard as the highway rolls under me.

She wanted time. She wanted space. But it has been six days since she asked for space, and all we've shared is one short phone call during which we talked like strangers muttering hellos. The longer I wait, the more it feels like her needing time and space will last forever. I want so badly to see her, to know what she's thinking, yet I want to respect her wishes even though they're killing me.

Back at the dorm, I'm left alone staring at four walls when Romeo heads over to Riley's. I never used to hang out in my dorm room. Lately I don't leave it. I clean some of my shit up. Something I never do. Try to read ahead for my communication class for spring term, which starts this week. Toss a tennis ball at the wall. Stare at the wall. Resist the urge to punch the wall.

Feeling caged, I grab my keys—and without realizing it, I'm driving on the highway, driving home. The two-hour drive takes me a little over an hour and a half, but lucky for me I'm not pulled over. I just listen to music and let the drive empty my turning mind.

My parents' home, just north of Grand Rapids, overlooks Lake Michigan. The house is empty of course. It's large and professionally decorated, the only warmth inside coming from the sight of the sun setting over the lake framed by the floor–to-ceiling windows.

Ascending the steps to my old bedroom, I dial my mother.

Surprisingly, she answers. "Justin, we're in the middle of a charity dinner. Please make it quick."

Miss you too. "I was wondering what time you were getting home."

"Why?"

"Because I'm here."

"Here?"

"Home."

"Oh . . . we should be home a little after eight. See you then," she says quickly, and hangs up.

Though my room's the same as it was when I left for college almost three years ago, it's always strange to come back to it. Except for once freshman year when I saw my parents for all of five minutes, I don't come home on weekends. Yet as I lie on the bed and watch the waves roll onto the beach, I feel less confined than I did in the dorm. Still, the solitude eats at me.

Eight o'clock comes and goes without my parents returning home. Desperate for someone to talk to, I call Olivia. The one true love from my childhood. My nanny.

"Hello, Justin," she answers in a bright cheery voice.

"Miss Olivia." Though she's been married for over six years, this will always be my name for her.

"Well, this is a lovely surprise."

"Not too late to be calling?"

"Never too late for you, love. To what do I owe the pleasure?" I religiously call my former nanny on Christmas and on her birthday, but otherwise I'm too busy. Doing what, I'm not sure. But besides that, she has a family now, a husband and two children, and I don't want to suck up her time. I already sucked up almost ten years of her life.

"Just needed to hear your voice."

"What's the matter, Justin?" Her voice sounds worried and caring. After all these years, she still has a wonderful English accent. I loved listening to her read to me as a child. The simple sight of a childhood book brings back the sound of her voice in my head.

"There's this girl I met," I say, clutching my phone and watching the dark waves roll in.

"Someone doesn't love my sweet boy? How can that be?" she says heatedly, and I'm imagining that if she knew how I'd used women over the past three years, her attitude would definitely change. "Tell me about this girl who has you so devastated you're calling your nanny."

I spend the next half hour describing Allie. How her ex hurt her and how I scared her away. Olivia asks questions every now and then, but mostly she lets me talk. Staring out over the rolling water, I realize how much I just needed to talk.

When I'm done, she says, "It sounds like she needs you as much as you need her."

My sigh echoes in the empty room. "She said she needs time."

"What she needs is to know you're there for her. Unlike that other boy."

I almost laugh at her calling Trevor and me boys. "Maybe . . ." Hopefully. "I'm not sure what to do."

"Listen to me closely, Justin. Love isn't fear. It's courage. Courage to trust, courage to give, courage to fight. Be fearless and fight for this girl. It's obvious to me—even from miles away—after forty minutes of listening to you talk that you're in love. Use your love to be courageous."

"Damn. You have me feeling like the pussy Gabe called me," I blurt.

"Words and manners, Justin," she reminds me, like I'm still five.

"Ah, yeah. Sorry."

"Now tell me, what are you going to do?"

My mind reels. "Go to her? Talk to her? Tell her how I feel?"

"That's a start." Her cheery tone has me imagining her smiling into the phone.

Before we hang up, Olivia makes me promise to visit her this summer. I went to Maine once when I was twelve and felt out of place, but Olivia had only a boyfriend then, not an entire family I'd be invading, But I tell her I'll visit before hanging up, then getting off my bed and snagging the keys from the dresser.

As I'm walking down the stairs, my parents come in the front doors. They're dressed to the nines. My mother recently turned fifty, but she has been dressing like a politician's wife for years. Perhaps that's her true calling. My father wears expensive tailored suits, but with his graying blond hair down to his jaw, he will never look like a politician.

"Justin!" she says, staring at the keys in my hand. Her forehead scrunches. "Are you leaving?"

"Yeah, got tired of waiting." I plop onto the marble bench across from the doors and reach for my shoes.

My mother sets her tiny purse on the entryway table. "Well, we're here now." She frowns at me. "You made it sound like an emergency on the phone."

Yes, an emergency you rushed home to, I think sarcastically. I glance at the large modern clock at the end of the entrance. It's nine thirty.

Behind her, my father takes off his shoes and opens the entryway closet. Like her, he doesn't so much as offer a hello.

I shrug. "Just needed to get away and clear my head. It's clear now so I'm going," I say, sounding even to my own ears like a pissed-off teenager.

"Mix me a drink, darling?" she asks over her shoulder. Turning back to me, she shakes her head. "When are you going to grow out of the melodrama? You're almost twenty-one."

My father steps past me and mutters, "Perhaps his emergency had to do with three Cs and one B." He's referring to my winter semester grades, which he has access to online.

Irritation shoots down my spine. My hands clench the edge of the bench. They haven't seen me since Christmas. Though I never come home, I show up unannounced and this is the bullshit they spout? Wrapped in their own little superficial world, they are so clueless, so selfish.

I'm about to blow. My fingers dig into the marble. Anger swells in my chest until I slowly release my grip, and with it I let go of the need for their attention. My body and mind instantly lighten.

As usual, I hate admitting it but Romeo is right. I need to grow up. I got dealt a shitty hand when it came to parents. But it's time for me to step up to the plate of life. First of all, there are people out there like Gabe, whose cards are far shittier. Second, there comes a time when you have to let go, man up, and let your actions speak for you instead of letting the past or your parents or any other bullshit define you. A man needs to define himself.

My parents are my parents, not the worst, sure as shit not the best, but there's no fixing them. But there's a girl who I'm madly in love with. I need to talk to her, be with her, and prove myself to her. Wasting anger or time or emotion on something I can't change suddenly makes no fucking sense.

Ice clinks in the kitchen as my father mixes drinks. I slip on my boots, then face my mother as she crosses her arms. "Guess I got homesick for a minute, but I really have to study tomorrow." I bend and kiss her cheek. "See you in July." And with a newfound feeling of freedom, I close the heavy front doors on her startled face.

Chapter 32
Allie

I t's almost midnight by the time I get home. Like Todd last
weekend, I got burned with a walk-in just before cutoff time
at nine. The guy's eagle took me until almost eleven o'clock to
ink. Normally, I don't mind late walk-ins, especially since Ben stays
at my parents' house on Saturday nights. But this week has been
crazy. After dealing with Trevor's antics all week, I'm drained.

Alone finally, I'm debating if it's too late to call Justin. All day
I've been thinking of how to explain the realization of my feelings
through the painting I made last night.

Yet no sooner are my boots off and my butt on the couch when
a knock sounds at the door. Having an awful suspicion about who's
on the other side, I stay on the couch, but the knocking grows loud
enough to irritate my neighbors. A look through the peephole con-
firms my suspicions.

Trevor flies in as soon as I release the dead bolt.

"I've been driving past your place all night," he says almost too
fast for me to understand the words. "You're lucky you're not out
with that douche bag." As he leans on my dining room table like he
owns it, I notice his wrinkled clothes. His bruises have healed and
without them to distract me, I notice the dark circles under his eyes.

"You should have tried the shop," I reply. "I had a late walk-in." Pushing the door closed with my foot, I ignore his gesture for me to sit in a chair. I'm not sitting. The sooner he's gone the better. "Why are you here?"

"First off," he says, yanking an envelope from his back pocket and waving it in the air, "I got this in the mail today."

I cross my arms. This riddle talk has been coming out of him all week. "Am I supposed to know what *that* is?"

"It's a court date. For my arraignment. You were supposed to tell douche boy not to press charges."

"We haven't been talking much lately, but I doubt that has anything to do with Justin. The police came. People were arrested. The state or city or whatever is pressing charges."

He folds his arms over his chest. "Well, that's good news."

"What?" I'm confused why he would be happy that charges are being pressed.

Pushing out his chest, he steps toward me and places his hands on my shoulders. "I've decided I want to work out things between us. I want you, Ben, and the shop back."

Part of me feels like he has socked me in the gut. Another part is pissed. We're divorced. That he believes I would take him back is beyond egotistical. A third part of me is completely confused. Trevor has been halfheartedly pursuing me in his own twisted way since he got back. I assumed his main purpose was to get me in bed. Trevor has always used booty calls to boost his ego. But the old connection we used to have is dead. It's almost like he's been going through the motions. Now this? And including the shop in his statement? Who includes business during a conversation about getting together with their ex-wife? Suddenly, I recall his child support payments. They've always been erratic. I never count on them, just put half in Ben's college fund and the other half in an emergency fund, but it's been months since his last payment.

My hands ball into fists on my hips. "What's going on?"

His expression turns sly as he grabs my upper arms. "I want us to be together, babe."

Ugh. The "babe" has come out. I tear away from his grasp. I've always feared a part of me would want Trevor. He was my first love. My first heartbreak. And second. He's the father of my son. He was my husband. But since last night's revelation while painting, I can say without a doubt I do not want to be with Trevor ever again. I'm finally totally over him. However, even if I wanted him, there's obviously something going on here I'm unaware of.

"What about your tattoo business in California? And your girlfriend there?"

He reaches for me again, but I sidestep him.

"I broke up with Lexi before coming here, and California isn't for me." He clasps a hand across his wrinkled shirt over his heart. "You and Ben are for me."

His blue eyes are strangely dark. I look closer. Because his pupils are huge. Maybe I don't want to know what's going on with him. In the end, it doesn't matter.

"We're not getting back together. Ever."

Confusion fills his crazy-looking eyes and his jaw tightens. "Why?"

Because I can't stand you. Because there's someone else. Rather than either of those truths, I say, "It was over when I filed for divorce. Two years ago."

He steps closer to me. I step around the table. He steps around the table.

"We belong together. We have Ben and the shop. We belong together," he repeats rapidly with confidence.

I step away again. Between the sidestepping and his ridiculous chanting, I'm getting dizzy. "It would be best if you left."

He takes a huge step and towers over me. "We are getting back together."

"We're not," I say firmly. "And you need to leave."

He breathes on me like a dog, huffing into my hair. "Are you being a bitch because of that douche bag?"

I point at the door. "You need to go."

"I'm staying."

I'm getting angry. He's basically been bullying me all week and this is the bully cherry on top. "We're not getting back together. There is nothing left to say. Leave." I point past him again.

He leans closer to me and says through his teeth, "We're working it out."

"Do I need to call the cops?" I ask, backing away from him.

He lunges, grips my arms hard, and shakes me. "Quit being a bitch!"

My anger erupts. "I'm never getting back together with you. I can't stand you. Get out of my house," I hiss.

His face twisting in rage, Trevor lets go of me as the door creaks open behind us, but before I can put any more distance between us, he snarls, lifts a tattooed arm, and backhands me. Hard. My jaw and mouth scream in agony as I fly across the room, bang into the wall, and slide to the floor.

Pissed, humiliated, and in pain, I peel myself from the carpet while grunts, crashing, and cursing erupt behind me. With my entire body shaking, I stand and then see Justin and Trevor circling each other in my living room. I clutch the back of a chair, afraid I might crumple back to the floor.

What the hell is happening?

After Trevor's slap, I'm completely dazed. I can't understand how or why Justin is here.

Trevor rushes at Justin. They end up locked together in a furious embrace that neither is willing to break, shoving at each other and knocking over chairs. The coffee table tips over, and the rain of Legos spilling everywhere sounds amid their cussing.

I'm still clutching the chair, trying to think of what to do, how to get them apart, as Justin slams Trevor against the wall. His hands clamping on Trevor's shoulders, Justin slams him into the wall two more times, causing the entire room to shake. Appearing as dazed as I am, Trevor lets Justin wrap him in a headlock.

With a heave and teeth clenched, Justin drags him across the carpet, throws him out of the apartment, and clicks the deadbolt into place before leaning against the back of the door. Still shocked he's here, I can only stare at Justin as he wraps his hands in his messy hair and bows his head. "I want to kill the mother fucker."

Trevor bangs on the other side of the door while shouting obscenities.

Justin lifts his gaze and his eyes blaze at the sight of my face, which has to be marked. "I'm going to kill him," he says, breathing hard.

Building tears finally break free. I let out a sob and stagger toward him. My hands cup his lovely face. "He doesn't matter." I'm shaking. He's shaking. "That you're here is all that matters. You came is all that matters."

He gently brings a trembling hand to my face but doesn't touch me. "You're lip's bleeding. There's a red welt your face," he says through clenched teeth.

I'm probably lucky Trevor didn't hit the side of my face with the ring in it because the blow would have torn my lip, but I'm trying not to think of that right now. "Forget it. Forget him." I slide my hands around Justin's neck and inch closer.

He finally pulls me to his chest. My fingers grip him, a raft in a swirling, angry ocean. We stand there for a long moment, holding each other, leaning on the door that pulsates with Trevor's rage.

Justin's fingers tangle in my hair as his other hand holds me tighter. "What the hell is going on?"

Shaking my head, I bury my face in his chest. "I think he's on drugs," I mumble into the softness of his T-shirt.

"Drugs?"

"Talking fast. Huge pupils. Thinks he rules the world."

"Sounds like coke." He gently lifts my head and wipes at my tearstained face. "I should have kicked his coked-up ass to hell." His lips thin. "I still want to."

I'm about to tell him again to forget Trevor, but we both pause at the sudden silence.

Listening, Justin cocks his head to the side.

My fingers loosen their grip on his shirt.

His green gaze comes back to me as a different rap sounds at the door along with the muffled word: "Police."

Justin's brows lower.

I step back. "He couldn't knock with so much control, but check the peephole."

After pressing his face to the door, Justin opens the door to the waiting officer.

The next half hour passes in a long, slow blur. One of my neighbors called the police. Not sure if it was the screaming, fighting, or door banging, but someone had enough. Finding Trevor still beating at the door, the police hauled him down to their car. After an officer takes my statement and pictures of my face, while Justin rotates between hovering and cleaning up the mess of my living room, we're finally alone.

He sits on the arm of the couch and hands me a glass of water and two Tylenol he must have found on the top shelf of the bathroom vanity. Suddenly feeling guilty and strangely shy, I can only glance at him as I lower the wet washcloth from my lip and reach for the water and pills. "Thanks." I swallow the pills, then set the glass on the coffee table. "I'm beyond grateful you were here, but why did you come?"

"You weren't answering your phone and"—he drags a hand through his hair—"I needed to talk with you. Luckily, the door was open."

Not wanting to think of what would have happened if he hadn't shown up, I say, "With Trevor's call and text bombardment, my phone's been on silent, but I was going to call you."

He stiffens beside me. "Why?"

Realizing he's imaging the worst, I shift toward him. "Because—well . . ." His expression constricts as I fumble for the right words. This was much easier expressing with paint.

A quick *rap-rap-rap* sounds from across the room.

My gaze snaps to the door. "You've got to be kidding me."

"Let me," Justin says, standing. After looking through the peephole, he turns toward me. "I think it's that girl . . . from the gallery night. Is she Trevor's girlfriend?"

"Jazz?" I ask incredulously.

Frowning, he nods. "Do you want me to answer it?"

Jazz knocks harder.

I rub my temples. "Might as well before the neighbors call the cops again."

Standing in the doorway and dressed in a cropped leather jacket and the shortest skirt in the world, Jazz glares from me to Justin twice. "Where's Trevor?" she asks me.

Still rubbing a temple, I say, "Probably in a holding tank downtown."

"What?" she wails, and rushes into my apartment. "Why?"

I pull my knees to my chest and wrap my arms around them. "Oh, maybe because he was disturbing the peace, yelling obscenities, and hitting me." I wave a hand across my injured face, showing her the damage.

Jazz abruptly stops in the middle of the living room, finally noticing my bloody lip and marked face. "What did you do?" She arrogantly flips her long platinum hair over her shoulder. "He's never been violent with me."

Still standing at the door, Justin closes it while I try to contain my dislike for the woman scowling at me. I've disliked her for so long, it's hard to keep the emotion off my face. "Guess you don't say no."

Her lip curls in disgust. "Bullshit. He came over here to talk to you about the shop and Ben."

"And about getting back together."

Now Jazz looks like *she* wants to hit me.

Guess it's my night.

"Whoa," Justin says, moving in front of her and pointing at a chair. "Sit down and talk or leave."

Jazz gives him a hard glare but moves to the chair by the window. She crosses her legs and one red cowboy boot bounces. "You know he's been staying with me this whole time, right?"

Justin sits back down on the arm of the couch, almost a foot from me. Too far away.

Suddenly, I'm tired. Tired of Trevor. Tired of arguing. Tired of hating this girl across from me. "Yes, I gathered he was staying with you." My arms loosen around my knees. "You know what, Jazz?"

At my blunt tone, Jazz pauses bouncing her cowboy boot.

"I think Trevor is in love with you." She visibly deflates and falls back into the chair. "I'm just what he thinks he needs. Now and then. In fact, he's probably always been in love with you, but he loves himself more because you've never been good enough for him. Not when we were in high school. Not when he went to California. And not now when he's obviously desperate enough to try and force me to take him back."

She opens her mouth, closes it, and wraps her arms around her waist. "He's broke."

I sigh. "I figured as much."

"He lost the shop in California."

"After tonight, I was guessing that too."

"He, he is—"

"Snorting all his money up his nose?" Justin says sarcastically.

Her nostrils flare from evident anger. "Things are tough for him right now."

"Quit making excuses for him," I say. "He's been walking all over you since you two were twelve. He walks all over everyone."

Her heated eyes flash at me. "You don't know what he's been through. What his childhood was like. Going from foster home to foster home sucks. Trust me, I know."

Justin leans forward. "So that gives him a right to treat you like shit?"

"Like you've got room to talk," Jazz spits at Justin.

"You're right." Justin leans back against the wall and folds his arms. "But that all ended when *I* fell in love."

A burst of warm emotions hits me as Jazz stares slack-jawed at Justin. She snaps her mouth shut and turns to me. "What are you going to do?"

Still fuzzy from Justin's declaration, it takes me a few seconds to understand her question. "I'll be filing a restraining order *and* pressing charges."

"You wouldn't." Her hands clasp her knees. Red nails dig into her skin. "Why would you do that to your son's father?"

"Ben is my reason," I say. "As much as I'd like Trevor to rot in hell, he's my son's father. He needs to get off the drugs and get himself together. Or he won't be seeing Ben. At this point, if it weren't for Ben I wouldn't care if Trevor snorted coke until it killed him. But because of Ben, I'm going to do everything in my power to make sure Trevor has no choice except to get clean."

"When did you turn into the judge and jury?" she sneers.

"When I became a mother."

"You can't take Ben from him!" she says, flying out of the chair.

Justin stands too. "Okay, we're done here." He goes to the door and opens it. "Allie's been attacked enough for one evening."

Jazz glances from me to Justin's stern face. "Fine, but you'd better rethink the whole Ben thing, Al." She pauses at the door. "Or Trevor's going to be really, really pissed."

Like I care.

As soon as she steps out the door, Justin shuts it and turns the lock. His lips form a grim line as he walks toward the couch. "Match made in heaven there."

"Yeah, you could say that."

Instead of sitting on the couch, he perches on the coffee table across from me. "How are you feeling?"

I summon a slight smile. "All right. Better."

"You need to lie down?"

I shake my head.

He swallows tightly. "So . . . about that call."

My arms tighten around my knees. "I kind of had a revelation last night. First let me say I'm sorry about getting weird this week. I was overwhelmed. Between Trevor's antics and my own reservations, everything was too much."

His hands grip the edge of the coffee table, but his face is expressionless. "Reservations?"

A sigh escapes me at the thought of explaining, but he deserves to understand. "Over the last couple of years, I've built up this image in my head of who I'm allowed to date. Someone older. Someone with a career. Someone financially stable. The list is never ending. Probably because no man would fit all my requirements, then I wouldn't have to risk getting hurt again. Thing is, I'd held on to my conditions for so long I couldn't see past them."

"You're right." He looks away toward the kitchen, and I finally catch the emotion on his face. Hopelessness. "I'm not good enough for you."

My knees drop and I lean toward him. "Not even close. I realized last night you're nearly perfect."

His startled gaze meets mine.

"No one has ever treated me like you do. The roof, the wine, breakfast . . . Just the way you look at me makes my breath catch." I put my hands on his knees and it appears as though I'm making *his* breath catch. "When we're together, I feel like the girl I used to be. You've broken down the wall I built around myself by being caring and sweet and so patient with me. Those words you told me Sunday were lovely, and I was a fool to panic. Your actions have shown me your feelings loud and clear, but I was too scared and blind to see the truth in them." Though his face is full of wonder, it's also tight with confusion. I stand and tug his hand. "Let me show you the truth."

He lets me lead him into my bedroom, which is where I moved my easel this morning. I flick on the lamp and gesture toward the almost-done painting sitting at the easel at the end of my bed. "I'd been fighting my feelings for you, but when I let myself go, the artist inside of me created this."

His wide eyes focused on the canvas, Justin falls on the end of my bed. He traces the swirls of the painting's center. On the canvas he stands tall in all his muscled, tattooed glory, wearing only jeans, in front of a painting. He's reaching out, grasping my hand and pulling me from the painting inside a painting, freeing me from its confines. Though done in my favorite style of modern impressionism, the painting depicts both of us in washed-out colors instead of the bright hues I usually use. Except for the growing burst of color at the focal point where our hands connect. There the painting is bright, the colors vibrant along the skin of our arms.

"It's beautiful," he says in a short breath, dropping his hand and leaning back on the bed.

"It's true." I lower myself, kneeling on the floor. "You free me from all my insecurities, take away the loneliness I'd grown to accept, and make me feel like the young woman I forgot I was." I reach for his hand and hold it in mine. "I'm not falling in love, Justin." He flinches and my hold tightens on his hand. "Look at the painting. I'm completely enamored, head-over-heels, already there. It's impossible for me to be more in love with you."

His eyes turn into wide green pools as he glances at the painting and then at me.

I lift his hand and touch my lips to his knuckles. "Yes, you. I want to be with you. I want you to keep pulling me back into life, into you."

"Damn, Allie." He heaves me up, draws me between his legs, and presses his face to my chest. He holds me tight. "I'm going to hyperventilate."

I slide my hands into his hair. "Now who's freaking out?"

He groans. "I was hoping you weren't going to kick me to the curb." He tilts his head up and studies me. "That you love me is . . ."—his hands clasp my back, gripping me tighter—"so damn amazing. I want to deserve your love."

"You do," I say with conviction.

Shaking his head, he gently kisses the side of my mouth that isn't injured. "It's like I've landed in another dimension. My own imaginary, perfect dimension."

"You're here." My hands tighten in his hair. "With me."

He glances at my swollen lip and sighs. "Let me sleep with you? Hold you? Help me find solid ground."

I smile at him. It hurts my lip a little, but I don't mind. He's so beautiful. It used to hurt sometimes to look at him, believing we could never truly be together, but now he's all mine. I push him back onto the bed and fall on him with a laugh.

"Yes. Yes. And please."

Chapter 33
Justin

I wake to bright morning light. I wake to the face of the most beautiful, sexiest woman in the world. Her auburn hair spills across the pillow and my shoulder. Her leg is wrapped around mine. She's soft and sweet in my arms. Digging my nose into her hair and breathing in the exquisite scent of her, I realize I love her with every cell in my body.

That she loves me too is nothing but a miracle.

Until I met her, I'd been a shallow, immature self-centered boy. She's unknowingly made me a man. What's important in life has finally clicked together like the last piece of a puzzle. And it's in my arms.

After watching her sleep for a while, I carefully untangle myself and make a quick trip to the bathroom. In minutes I'm back under the covers, content to hold her. As I'm thinking about how good it is lying here with her, Allie's eyes flutter open. She blinks at me, then presses herself against my body and smiles sensually. "Morning."

"Morning to you, beautiful." I grin. Here I'd been thinking I'd never spent this much time in a bed with a woman without sex, and it was great. But as her hand slides across my chest, I'm thinking sex would make it better than great.

She pushes up on an elbow. "Give me a minute to go—" She pauses, noticing something beyond my shoulder. "Is it really eleven?"

I crank my head around and glance at the clock. "Eleven fifteen to be precise."

"Oh no!" She flies out of the bed. "I'm supposed to be at my parents' at twelve for Sunday dinner." She rushes out of the room, which leaves me staring at the empty doorway.

Dejected but understanding, I'm sitting on the edge of the bed, pulling on my shoes when she stands in the doorway a few minutes later.

"You're coming, right?"

"To your parents'?" I ask incredulously.

She gives me a don't-be-an-idiot nod.

The idea of meeting her parents disorients me. "Ah, I don't have any clean clothes."

She shrugs. "Just throw your shirt in the dryer for a few minutes."

"What about Ben?"

She comes over and starts tugging my shirt up. "With my feelings for you, it seems wrong keeping you a secret from him." She yanks my shirt over my head. "We'll have to take it slow in front of him." She smirks at me, running a thumb over my nipple ring. "No sleepovers when he's home."

Though I'm overwhelmed by the step she's taking, her hands on my skin are making me forget everything else. "Keep undressing me on your bed, and we're going to be late."

"I should have set the alarm," she says wistfully.

Taking in her tone, I ask, "Breakfast tomorrow?"

Grinning, she curls her fingers around the waistband of my pants. "Oh, definitely."

Fearful of hurting her lip, I press my own lips to her forehead. "Go get ready. I'll take care of my clothes."

Studying my body with a glint in her gray eyes, she stumbles back toward the dresser. "Okay."

Our gazes meet in the mirror as she hauls out clothes. She lets out a laugh and then a wistful sigh before heading to the bathroom. After taking turns—I was tempted to join her, but then we would definitely be late—in the shower, we're out the door at five to twelve.

In my car, Allie gives directions and then plucks out the small vial of cologne from the cup holder. As I'm turning out of her apartment complex, she opens it and breaths in the scent with her eyes closed. A dazed satisfaction comes over her features. I almost hit the curb, watching her.

"What brand is this?" she asks almost drunkenly.

"No brand," I say while mentally storing the image of her expression.

She cocks an eyebrow at me.

"It's custom made from a perfumer in Paris. I reorder it about once a year."

"Holy shit, Batman!" she says, and the sound of her cursing has me smiling. "Isn't that expensive?"

I shrug. "One day soon I'm going to take you there. Not that you don't smell fantastic . . ."

She frowns. "I don't wear perfume. Probably just smell like soap and body lotion."

"Like linen and flowers," I say, nodding. "A scent I've come to love. I'll ask them to start with those two things."

She lets out a self-deprecating laugh. "You know I'd love to go to Paris, but I can't let you take me."

"Why not?"

"That would be overboard for even you."

"In less than two months when I turn twenty-one, I come into the money my grandparents left me. I plan on investing most of it, but a trip to Europe won't even put a dent in it. And whether I deserve it or not, it's mine. Let me share."

Her mouth drops. "You're twenty?" she asks, almost making me laugh that my age is shocking her more than my inheritance. "I assumed twenty-one at least, with all the wine and bars."

"Almost twenty-one, but being in the band I rarely get carded."

"I'm two years older than you? That's crazy."

I turn into the driveway of the address she gave me while she giggles.

Putting the car in park, I turn to her. "You turned twenty-two a few months ago—it's not even a year and a half."

"But still older," she says, laughing as she reaches for the handle and pushes the door open.

I don't reach for the door handle next to me. I've never met any parents, and I know this is a huge step for her. "You sure about this?"

Pausing, she studies me and then closes the door. Leaning across the console, she gently grips my face. "I love you, Justin. I want you to be part of my life. No one, not even my parents, can change that." She leans closer.

I pull back. "Besides your lip, we're in your parents' driveway."

"I don't give a crap, just kiss me."

Though her fingers pull at my hair, I keep the kiss soft and gentle, but between our lips and tongues, there's the soft whisper of everything to come.

As we break off the kiss, I smirk. "Okay, let's do this."

Allie brings Ben out on the porch while I wait a few feet away on the stairs. He sits on the swing, picking at his shoelaces while she explains we're dating. Her explanation covers that sometimes she and I will go out to dinner or the movies on our own and sometimes with him.

His expression turns pensive. "Do we have to see kissing movies? I don't like those."

While Allie laughs, I say, "Naw. We'll let you pick. I'm not into those either."

Ben nods slightly and says, "Okay then."

Inside, the small house is homey and laced with the smell of something fantastic cooking. But the sight of her father with his arms crossed, standing between the living and dining room, is not as welcoming as the house. Dressed in jeans and a flannel shirt, he glares at me in the same way he did when he found us making lunch in her apartment. Her mother, on the other hand, is giddy with excitement and rushes into the living room from the kitchen. With her graying auburn curls and wide smile, it's easy to see whom Allie takes after more.

I apologize for being late. Her mother waves a hand, saying Adam is always late. Before I can ask who Adam is, he comes through the door. I keep the surprise from my expression as I'm introduced to Allie's brother and his wife, Veronica. Allie has never said anything about a brother. Other than wavy auburn hair, they look nothing alike. He shakes my hand while grinning at his sister.

Her mother rushes everyone to a table covered with food. After a prayer—I'm late to fold my hands together; my family never prayed before dinner, and heck, we rarely ate dinner together—everyone talks and passes dishes. During the meal the talking continues. Adam has a new job. Ben was the star of his play on Friday. Allie's mother is training a new secretary at the insurance office where she works. Allie might be taking on another tattooist at the shop. Her father describes fishing with Ben yesterday. Forks are pointed. Napkins tossed on plates to make points. Hands slapped on the table. On and on they talk and eat, comfortable and open with one another.

Though I feel slightly out of place, I realize this is a normal, loving family. Something I knew existed outside of the cold, refined lives of my parents, but not like anything I've ever witnessed. I also realize how much I don't know about the girl I'm in love with.

After laughing at her father's story about Ben tangling their fishing lines, she glances at me and then reaches under the table to squeeze my hand. *You okay?* she asks with the press of her fingers. I give her a smile and press my fingers against hers. The future of learning everything about her flashes through my mind.

The future looks endlessly bright.

Chapter 34
Allie

Across from me, Holly fills my beer and winks at me. Jake puts an arm around her. We're standing at a tall table, waiting for the band to come out. After two pitchers of beer, they're giggling and cuddling together. In a bar. At a table in front of the stage. Surrounded by people. Dorks. I take a sip of the beer, wishing Justin were here to cuddle with me so I could be a dork too. Though he's probably backstage by now—Romeo called an emergency meeting before this show.

It's been two weeks since Justin had dinner with my parents. We've been together whenever possible, but there's never enough time for us.

With everything going on in my life, we've been slowly figuring things out. We've had breakfast—well, actually lunch, since breakfast never works—a couple of times over the past two weeks. He's come to the shop with takeout for dinner. We took Ben to a movie together. We tried to study—we both have spring semester classes—but that didn't work out very well. We just studied each other.

Besides my busy life, he has the band, and we've both had appointments with lawyers. Mine is confident all my demands with

Trevor will be met, especially after his two court dates and the temporary restraining order I asked for. Justin's lawyer is pretty certain he'll be fined, but he's hoping to get Gabe off with probation and court-ordered anger management. Justin *did* have to drag Gabe to the lawyer.

I take another sip of beer and try not to feel too envious when Holly and Jake start kissing.

Though the venue is small, this show is big. Luminescent Juliet's indie album launches tomorrow, and tonight is the kickoff. Justin has been grumbling all week about Romeo's decision to do a small show to get the word out. But Romeo would not change his mind about keeping the gig invitation only.

They're playing only original music. There's a team of volunteers, from the visual department at our university, that will be recording the show. Most everyone here has agreed to flood Facebook and Twitter and anything else across the Internet with show clips over the next few weeks. Romeo is obviously taking this seriously. I'm guessing Justin just wants to sing in front of a boisterous crowd.

Her own camera ready, Riley waves to me from the side of the stage. Next to her, Chloe waves also. I raise my beer in a toast and they laugh. Justin invited me backstage too, but I like being in front of him. Sometimes when he sings, even in a roomful of people, it feels like it's just the two of us—and the current of emotions between us.

The lights dim and the crowd's murmur swells as it pushes toward the stage. High-pitched whistles compete with loud shouts and claps. The stage stays dark and my stomach flutters with the anticipation of seeing Justin perform.

The lights slowly come on and the band stands silent in front of microphones, except for Gabe, who sits behind the drums. Then they break into "Midnight." One of my favorites. Justin has been loading their original songs on my iPhone and I have been listening to them every chance I get.

Stepping to the microphone, Justin breaks into the fast, bluesy tune with his powerful voice. He's looking hot in distressed jeans and a form-fitting black T-shirt that melds with the ink on his arms. My eyes devour him, and for a few seconds I don't notice the music. Just Justin. Dark blond messy hair. Intense gaze. Hard jaw. Flexing inked biceps as he reaches for the microphone. Those eyes find me, and burn into me. Wow. I'm wishing the show were over and we were at my apartment. Alone.

That's it. I'm not letting him in next time unless he has his guitar.

Next to me, Jake holds Holly while she sways in front of him as the band rips through one song after the next. Justin's gaze finds me more than once and I can't help smiling at him. People press behind us and bounce to the music. It's kind of amazing, but the band sounds as good live as in recorded music on my phone.

Partway through their performance, they change instruments and go acoustic. Justin has shared his fear of playing live acoustic songs with me, and though I know he's nervous, they sound awesome. His voice is rich and deep, then lush and even. Riley once said something about his vocal range, which I didn't understand at the time, but now hearing the changing pitches he effortlessly sings, I get it.

Cameras move back and forth in front of the stage the entire time. The crowd is wild and totally into the music. Onstage, the band moves and plays like professionals. During the whole show, I can't help believing tonight is the springboard for something huge. Tonight is going to catapult Luminescent Juliet into the mainstream.

The thought leaves me bubbly and excited as I sway to the music.

Justin strums the last notes of a fast song with Romeo, then removes his guitar from his shoulder. Dressed like a forties pinup girl in a short, black dress that hugs her curves and a veiled hat, Chloe comes and takes it from him. Several sharp whistles ring out as she carries it off the stage.

Justin adjusts the microphone. "Playing for you guys tonight has been fucking awesome. We've played a few new things, but we're going to close it out with the newest." His gaze finds me. "I hope you like it."

Romeo and Sam start a slow, haunting rhythm that isn't familiar to me. Gabe breaks in with a soft, pounding beat. Justin wraps his hands around the stem of the microphone, closes his eyes, and leans forward. He begins to sing in a clear, deep tone:

> *Got lost and found what I wasn't looking for*
> *She smiled and I fell into her a million miles an hour*
> *Brought the stars down from the night sky*
> *Just to drink in her soft sigh*
> *Fell into her a million miles an hour*
> *Again*
> *But the needle dropped*
> *Inked my heart and scarred my skin*
> *Inked my heart and scarred my skin*

Though Justin's eyes are open, he doesn't look up as the band plays the soft melody between the lyrics. And I'm not sure I could handle him looking at me while the emotion and pain of the lyrics have my knees buckling. I'm not only aware he wrote the lyrics but also know I'm the confused, messed-up source of them. Guilt rips through me and I grip the table edge as his eyes close again.

Empty days go on and on
Bright memories won't let me sleep in the dark
I want to taste her sigh once more
Suck it in and take her pain
But she's silent wrapped in a gray-eyed storm
That holds her in and keeps me out

Fell into her a million miles an hour
Again
But the needle dropped
Inked my heart and scarred my skin
Inked my heart and scarred my skin

Romeo plays the instrumental, but Justin still doesn't look up. My stomach rolls while his lyrics burn into my mind. Forced to face how my self-preservation hurt him, I feel ill. When he sings again, I want to cry, grieve, and beg for forgiveness all at the same time.

The space between us grows
While I wait on hope
And survive on memories
Waiting for the day that breaks through the gray skies
Kills the pain and everything inside

Fell into her a million miles an hour
Again
Still she inked my heart and scarred my skin
Leaving me here alone to breathe her in
Inked my heart and scarred my skin
And the needle drops again. . . .

When he opens his eyes, they find me. There's no one between us. No Holly and Jake. No cameras. No fans. No shouts or whistles. The words, the pain, and the emotion of his song have me stumbling toward the stage until I stand beneath him. He jumps off the stage.

"I'm sorry. So sorry," I say, reaching up and clasping my hands around his neck. Fighting back the tears that have been threatening to erupt, I say, "I never wanted to hurt you."

He shakes his head slightly and leans to my ear. "They'll be forever caught in the song, but I promise you those feelings are a faint memory." He softly kisses the skin under my ear. "Just always be waiting for me?"

And just like that, his love lifts the weight off my chest, because all that hurt is a memory for both of us. So in love with him, and finally completely aware of it, I could never be so self-centered again. Still clutching his neck, I lean back and meet his bright green gaze. "Forever."

Acknowledgments

I'd like to thank everyone who helped pull this book together. Thanks to Lisa for always reading my early drafts and offering unbiased suggestions. Thanks to Robin Cruise for her awesome editing ninja skills. Thanks to Dooley for putting up with my drive for visual perfection. And thanks to my agent, Jane Dystel, for not only selling this series, but also helping me every step of the way.

I'd also like to thank every reader who gave this story a chance. I'm honored that you would spend your time with my imagination. You all rock!

And finally, thanks to my husband and son for all their awesome support. None of this would have happened without it or them.

About the Author

J ean Haus is the author of the Luminescent Juliet Series, which revolves around a sexy, talented indie band in a small college town. She lives in Michigan with her husband and son, where she spends almost as much time teaching, cooking, and golfing as she does thinking about the tough but vulnerable rockers featured in her books. Visit Jean online at http://www.jeanhaus.com.